Praise for Dreami

"I love Phoebe—her foibles, honest truths, fun, and laughable antics! And this time, Phoebe's taking planes, trains, and automobiles—watch out world!"

—Cindy Martinusen, author of *The Salt Garden*

"Ever longed to shop at Harrods or indulge in high tea? Live vicariously through the faboo Phoebe Grant and her pals in this super-fun, romantic romp through England. Like me, you'll giggle a lot, sigh some, and experience a wild urge to brew some fragrant tea and rent some beautiful chick flick starring Hugh Grant and Emma Thompson!"

—Lorilee Craker, author of *We Should Do This More Often* and *When the Belly Button Pops, the Baby's Done*

"Phoebe rides again! With her usual humor and slightly-wrinkled style, our plucky heroine finds depth and delight in her relationships with her family, her friends, and her God."

—Gayle Roper, author of *Winter Winds* and *Autumn Dreams*

"A witty and charming tale that offers a forgotten truth—journeys can actually be enjoyed."

—Denise Hildreth, author of *Savannah from Savannah* and *Savannah Comes Undone*

dreaming in technicolor

dreaming in technicolor

[a phoebe grant novel]

laura jensen walker

WestBow
P R E S S
A Division of Thomas Nelson Publishers
Since 1798

visit us at www.westbowpress.com

Published in Nashville, Tennessee, by WestBow Press, a division of Thomas Nelson, Inc., in association with the literary agency of Alive Communications, Inc., 7680 Goddard Street, Suite 200, Colorado Springs, CO 80920.

WestBow Press novels may be purchased in bulk for educational, business, fund-raising, or sales promotional use. For information, please e-mail SpecialMarkets@ThomasNelson.com.

Except as indicated below, Scripture quotations in this book are from HOLY BIBLE, NEW INTERNATIONAL VERSION®. Copyright © 1973, 1978, 1984 by International Bible Society. Used by permission of Zondervan Publishing House. All rights reserved.

The Scripture quoted at the end of chapter 15 is from The New English Bible, © The Delegates of the Oxford University Press and The Syndics of the Cambridge University Press, 1961, 1970.

Scripture quoted during the York Minster scene in chapter 16 is from the New King James Version © copyright 1979, 1980, 1982 by Thomas Nelson, Inc., Publishers.

Publisher's Note: This novel is a work of fiction. Names, characters, places, and incidents are either products of the author's imagination or used fictitiously. All characters are fictional, and any similarity to people living or dead is purely coincidental.

Library of Congress Cataloging-in-Publication Data

Walker, Laura Jensen.
  Dreaming in technicolor : a Phoebe Grant novel / Laura Jensen Walker.
    p. cm.
  ISBN 0-8499-4524-0 (trade paper)
  1. Motion pictures—Appreciation—Fiction. 2. Obituaries—Authorship—Fiction.
3. Overweight women—Fiction. 4. Single women—Fiction. I. Title.
  PS3623.A3595D743 2005
  813'.54—dc22   2005004459

Printed in the United States of America
05 06 07 08 09 RRD 6 5 4 3 2 1

For Michael, the love of my life and my fellow Anglophile.
We'll always have England . . .

A lady's imagination is very rapid; it jumps from admiration to love, from love to matrimony, in a moment.

—Jane Austen,
Pride and Prejudice

chapter one

One Kiss Is Worth a Thousand Words

t he time had come, and we both knew it. We were ready.
I looked into his Clark Gable eyes as he drew me close and
saw the tender love in them, the deep fire of restrained passion.

I watched his lips—those beautiful, expressive lips—as they slowly
drew near.

I closed my eyes, felt his warm breath, knew the soft touch of his
lips on mine.

Time melted away in the eternity of that kiss. Our first kiss, long
awaited. I could almost hear music soar.

It was Bogie and Bacall, Scarlett and Rhett, Rick and Ilsa, Wesley
and Buttercup, Belle and her Beast. Of all the wonderful kisses since
the beginning of time, it was one of the best. It was not to be forgotten.

It was . . . it was definitely *not* happening.

I pulled back from my reverie and gazed across the table at my
date. And sighed.

Those lips. Those eyes. That mouth. Those gorgeous Gregory
Peck *Roman Holiday* lips—now closing in on an industrial-sized
cinnamon roll.

I sighed again. I know that old song says a kiss is still a kiss. But
when you're not being kissed at all, who cares what Sam the piano
player says?

"... thought we could hit Macy's first." Alex Spencer put down his roll and blew on his cappuccino with those wonderful, full lips before taking a sip and giving me a questioning look across the café table.

"Sounds good." I gulped my mocha, noticing as I did a trace of foam on his adorable mouth. *Is this man* ever *going to kiss me?*

Alex and I had been dating for three weeks now. Twenty-two days, actually, but who's counting? And things were going well. Quite well, in fact, considering our love-hate, mistaken-motives history. And the fact Alex was my new boss. And the whole kissing issue, of course— not that I'm obsessing about it or anything.

But they were going so well that in just a few minutes we were going to cross an important dating threshold: Alex was taking me shopping. In San Francisco. And since we'd never shopped together, I was a trifle nervous.

What if Alex turned out to be like most men, who loathe women's favorite sport?

That's why I'd already had a long talk with my shopping self and stressed that she behave with decorum and restraint. And she'd agreed to be on her best behavior. Unless we went into a shoe store. Then all bets were off.

Something you should probably know about me. I've had a love affair with shoes ever since I bought my first pair of Candies in high school. And although I'd had a spiritual epiphany of sorts a couple of months ago about scaling back and keeping things simple, that epiphany hadn't reached all the way down to my feet yet.

Or to my mouth. Or to my kiss-obsessed brain.

I was trying, though. I knew that the minute my lips locked with Alex's, there would be no scaling back. Also that my drooling might stain his leather bomber jacket, which, I might add, fit him extremely well and gave him a rakish, Brandoesque charm. So in an attempt to keep my smitten self in check, I resumed our favorite sport.

"Okay, Filmguy, what's the first Technicolor movie to win an Oscar?"

He shot me a smug grin as he set down his gooey cinnamon roll. "*Gone With the Wind,* in 1939. The same year of *The Wizard of Oz,* where they also made use of that innovative color change. But *Gone with the Wind* swept the Oscars, and the *Wizard* only won a couple."

"Brat." I stuck out my tongue at him. "Your turn."

"Right, then," he said with that competitive gleam in his eye that I knew and loved.

Whoops. Did I just say the L-word? No, no. I meant to say *like*. It's not the L-word yet. How could it be? We've only been dating a few weeks. Every single woman worth her romantic salt knows you can't say the L-word until he does.

Note to self: Do not even think the L-word. Otherwise, might blurt out unexpectedly at inopportune time.

Alex continued with our movie-addict game, seemingly unaware of my romantic inner turmoil. "Okay, Miss Movie Lover, which actress holds the record for the most Academy Award nominations?"

Now it was my turn for a smug smile. "For years, that honor was held by Miss Katharine Hepburn, with twelve nominations. Meryl Streep bypassed her a few years back. But the great Kate still holds the record for the most Best Actress Oscars—four."

"Didn't she win for *Guess Who's Coming to Dinner* with Spencer Tracy?"

I nodded but was thinking, *Spencer . . . the perfect segue.* Maybe now I could finally pin Alex down on his background.

Though not exactly the strong, silent type, my gorgeous date had proved remarkably reserved—evasive, even—in supplying personal information. And I had to admit I was curious.

I knew he was rich and successful—heir to the Spencer publishing dynasty, no less. He'd been a big corporate muckety-muck before deciding to downscale and become a small-town newspaperman—in my hometown of Barley, California, no less.

I also knew he'd been raised in England but wasn't really English. That bit of mystery had slipped out in conversation with my niece. But he'd never mentioned it again.

I absolutely knew he was a good Christian man—woohoo!—with

an athletic build, beautiful dark eyes with killer lashes, and delicious, kissable lips. He was one of the few people I'd ever met who knew more about movies than me. Beyond that . . . well, I just needed to know. And what was the point of being a reporter if I couldn't ask questions?

"Speaking of Spencer," I began innocently, spreading low-fat cream cheese on my bagel. "I've been wondering . . . what's your favorite color? And, uh, when's your birthday?" Then, quickly—"Oh, and what was your childhood like?"

His dark eyebrows lifted beneath his curly Jude Law hair. "That's three questions—none of them relating to movies."

"True. But I figure it's high time I learned a little more about *you*, Mr. Close to the Vest." I licked cream cheese from my fingers. "It's really not fair. You already know all about me—born and raised in Barley, joined the air force, got my journalism degree, worked in Cleveland and now California. But what about you, O corporate man of the world?"

Alex started to respond, but I interrupted him with a teasing smile. "Wait. Let me guess; you were born with a silver spoon in your mouth to a family of old money in New York. Or Connecticut— which would account for your upper-crust diction. And your grand-mother was English, which is why you spent time there growing up."

Or maybe it was your whole family, and they own half of the British—

Alex took another bite of cinnamon roll and wiped icing from his mouth.

Darn, I'd been hoping to take care of that for him. There can't be too many calories in one lick, right?

". . . was born in a blue-collar area of Pittsburgh, and the spoon was wooden, not silver. My mom cleaned houses, and my father was a steelworker—when he worked, that is."

I gaped at him. "But then how did you wind up rich and in England?" My inner Emily Post sighed. *You can dress her up, but you can't take her out.* "Sorry. I mean . . ."

He guffawed. "Don't apologize. That's one of the things I really like about you, Phoebe. You just say what you're thinking. I wish more people would."

Really like? I lingered over the first part of his sentence. With apologies to Sally Field, "really like" is just a step away from the Big L!

He went on, oblivious to my lovestruck trembling. "My father died when I was six. He was drunk and driving." A bitter note crept into his voice. "Of course he didn't have insurance, so that left Mom and me practically on the streets."

"I'm sorry, Alex." I reached over and touched his hand. "I had no idea."

No wonder we'd had an instant connection—beyond the whole movie thing, I mean. I'd lost my dad in high school.

Alex shrugged. "That was a lifetime ago—a lifetime I hardly remember. Mom became a live-in housekeeper to a wealthy English family, and when the son and heir came over for a visit, they fell in love." He smiled. "Quite the scandal, at first, but my stepfather is the kind of man who tends to get his way. Any rate, six months later they were married, and a year after that we moved to England. By that time, I was eleven and my parents had a baby." He slid me a sly grin. "I believe you know Cordelia."

My face flushed. "Don't remind me." When I first heard of Cordelia, I'd mistakenly assumed she was his girlfriend and had jumped to foolish conclusions.

But I was still confused. "If you had a different father, how come your last name's Spencer?"

"David Spencer was a far better father to me than my own dad had ever been." Alex's eyes darkened. "And a far better husband to my mother. He never once made me feel like an unwanted stepchild. So when he asked if I would like to become his son legally, there wasn't anything I wanted more. I've been a Spencer ever since."

Before I could go and get all mushy on him, he added with a grin, "And the Spencer publishing family has been swooping down and buying up struggling newspapers since I came into the fold. There's even talk they might start buying up entire towns now too."

"You're never going to let me forget that, are you?"

"Not in this lifetime, George Bailey."

Shortly after Alex moved to our Central California valley town as the new owner and publisher—and therefore, my boss—of the Barley *Bulletin*, I'd jumped to yet another foolish conclusion. The town was trying to save my beloved Bijou movie house, so we'd been selling theater seats in a desperate fundraising attempt. But even if we'd sold every seat in the house, it still wouldn't have been enough to save the cherished building from the wrecking ball. Then someone anonymously rode to the rescue with a huge donation, and I assumed it was Alex since he was the richest man in town. To me, that sounded way too much like mean old Mr. Potter from *It's a Wonderful Life*. I was sure Alex was going to take over the entire town and turn it into Potterville—uh, Spencerville. So I'd flown into full Jimmy Stewart righteous-indignation mode, accusing Alex of false philanthropic motives.

I'd had to eat some major crow when it turned out I was wrong. Unfortunately, I'm well acquainted with the taste of crow. Which is why I've been trying hard to reform.

No more jumping to conclusions. No more living in movie fantasies. No more longing meditations on certain newspaper publishers with amazing, kissable lips . . .

"Hey, are you going to eat that, or just play with it?" He pushed a packet of jelly my way and his voice took on a mock stern tone. "Eat, Phoebe, eat. You'll need your strength for our shopping marathon."

That's another thing I love about you—uh, I mean like, l-i-k-e, not love. You never say, "Are you sure you want to eat that?" like some guys I've known who have a thing for anorexic model types.

I lifted my bagel to my mouth but asked before taking a bite, "So, what was it like growing up in England?"

Alex released a homesick sigh. "It was a change, but I really liked it.

Part of it was finally living in a happy family. But we moved into this ancestral home in the country that looked like a castle, with horses and all this acreage to explore, so that was great. Then I went to boarding school in Oxford and—"

"Wow. Like Harry Potter?"

"Minus the wizards and dragons and creepy creatures hiding in the basement," he said dryly. "Just itchy uniforms, dreadful food, and ridiculous bedtimes. But my family also has an apartment in London, so it was always fun to go down to the city."

"Uh, how close is Oxford to London? Aren't they right next to each other?" Geography had never been my strong suit in school. Math either. But if they'd had a class in film, this movie lover would have made straight As.

"No, Oxford is a bit northwest of London—about an hour or so by train."

"Train? I've never been on a train." I gave a wistful sigh. "Is it as romantic as they show in films? All that swirling steam as they say good-bye, and she runs alongside the departing train as her sweetheart goes off to war. Except in *Doctor Zhivago*, when Omar Sharif was on the train and saw Lara through the window and tried to get her attention, but she never saw him and he died of a heart attack without her ever knowing. So sad. Although . . . come to think of it—*was* that a train? Might have been a streetcar."

"Wow. You didn't even take a breath." Alex shot me an admiring glance. "I never thought of riding the train as particularly romantic." He winked at me. "We'll have to take a train trip together one of these days."

Like on our honeymoon, maybe?

Down, happily-ever-after girl, down, my voice of reason commanded. *You've only been dating a little while. Rein in the romance. He hasn't even kissed you yet.*

And just why is *that exactly?* my familiar, neurotic self nagged. *Doesn't he find me attractive?*

7

My common-sense self stepped up to the romantic plate: *Of course he finds you attractive. Hasn't he told you so?*

But I glanced at Alex just to be sure. I was pretty sure he was giving me more than a "just friends" smile.

See, he's just exercising restraint like the strong, upright Christian man he is. Remember what it says in the Song of Solomon—"Do not awaken love before its time."

Yeah, my impatient self grumbled, *but just how much time is it going to take?*

"Phoebe? Still with me?"

Forever and ever, amen. I affected a nonchalance that belied my romantic fantasy. "Sorry. So, tell me more about England. Is the scenery really as gorgeous as it looks in all those Jane Austen movies?"

He smiled gently. "Well, not everywhere. We've got our share of urban blight, you know. But the countryside . . ." He got a faraway look in his eye. "You should see the Cotswolds, where my dad's estate is. Lush green hills dotted with sheep, villages with ancient churches and pretty stone cottages." Alex grinned. "And flowers *everywhere*. The English are quite proud of their gardens, and there are plenty of wild-flowers too."

"I wandered lonely as a cloud," I murmured, "that danced on high o'er vales and hills, When all at once I saw a crowd, a host of golden daffodils . . ."

He stared at me. "You know Wordsworth?"

"Not personally. But I studied him in English Lit." I didn't add that I'd first heard the poem on reruns of the *Rocky and Bullwinkle* show.

Alex continued to stare at me in amazement. "I didn't know you liked poetry."

"There's a lot you don't know about me," I said, tossing my hair. Or trying to. It's kind of difficult to execute a haughty flowing-tresses toss when you have a short, spiky cut. "I have hidden depths."

"I already know that." He gave me a flirtatious smile. "And I look forward to exploring more of them."

Note to self: Resist urge to climb over this table and kiss that adorable mouth and those to-die-for dimples this very second.

"But for now," he glanced at his watch, "we'd better go explore the stores before there's nothing left."

A few hours later, with several shopping bags between us but no shoe boxes—I'd salivated over some Jimmy Choos and Manolo Blahniks but had sacrificially passed them by in the spirit of the season and in deference to my reporter's salary—we made our way to the top of Neiman Marcus to have lunch in the rotunda.

Intent on the menu, I didn't notice the couple that had stopped at our table until a familiar voice interrupted me. "Excuse me, is this seat taken?"

I looked up to see my two best friends from Cleveland grinning at me. "Phil! Lins! What are you doing here?" I jumped up and hugged them both.

"We had a long holiday weekend, so we thought we'd come see what it is about California that could drag two of our Lone Rangers all the way out here," Phil said.

Alex and I had both been members of the No More Lone Rangers church singles group in Cleveland—back when I was a lowly obits writer for the Cleveland *Star* and he was the corporate type who cost me my job. Phil and Lindsey were still official Lone Rangers, but seriously dating ones.

"Wow, Alex, isn't this a great surprise?" I intercepted a grin between him and Lindsey as we sat down. "Wait a minute. You knew all about this, didn't you?"

Phil laughed. "Of course he did. How do you think we knew what restaurant to come to? Logic has never been your strong suit, Pheebs," he said affectionately.

"Never mind him," Lindsey said, shooting a dirty look at her boyfriend and patting my hand. "I totally get your chick logic."

"Of course you do, sweetie." Phil returned her dirty look with a mushy one. "And I wouldn't have it any other way."

Now it was her turn to return his gooey look.

"Okay, you guys, stop." I grabbed a sugar packet and shook it in front of them. "I'm about to have a sugar attack."

"Too bad," said Phil, grinning and leaning over to plant a big kiss on my best friend's waiting mouth.

All I could do was watch longingly . . . and pray that my kissless days would be over soon.

"Talk about eye candy," Lindsey said as we wandered around the fine jewelry department for some friend shopping time while the guys did their male-bonding thing.

I snorted. "Yeah. Expensive eye candy. Reminds me of Tiffany's. I couldn't afford anything there either."

Lins scrabbled around in her purse and held up her sterling silver key chain. "I could."

We burst out laughing as we remembered our grand adventure in New York not so many months before. She'd done her petite, blonde *Sweet Home Alabama* Reese Witherspoon impression to the upscale saleswoman while I'd tried unsuccessfully to be Audrey Hepburn from *Breakfast at Tiffany's.*

"May I help you?" A cool Grace Kelly blonde in a cobalt blue silk blouse and straight black skirt wafted subtle waves of Chanel No. 5 toward us from the counter.

"No thanks," we hooted, clinging to each other as the giggles overtook us again. I sucked in my cheeks in another attempt to be Audreyesque, but wound up looking more like Dory the blue fish from *Finding Nemo.*

We beat a quick retreat from Neiman Marcus to the misty streets of San Francisco, where we wandered around for a while like Humphrey Bogart in *The Maltese Falcon*—minus the trench coat and the *film noir* lighting. But it was John Wayne who stopped me in my pilgrim tracks.

"Hey, look! It's a movie store." I peered in the window past the life-size cardboard cutout of the Duke. "I'll bet I can find a Christmas present for Alex here."

And I did. A really cool *Casablanca* wall clock for his office. Since Alex and I had watched that beloved black-and-white film on our first date and were forever quoting to each other from the movie, it was perfect. I began humming "As Time Goes By," *Casablanca's* unforgettable signature song. Then I saw a paperweight bearing the line "I was misinformed" and snatched that up too.

Alex had used that same line from *Casablanca* in his early online correspondence with me, before we each knew who the other was. We didn't exchange names or addresses since, you never know, you could be writing to an ax murderer or something. To him, I was simply MovieLovr and he was my Filmguy. Who could've guessed we actually knew each other—that he was the corporate-raider troublemaker who had already cost me my job?

Well, anyone who's seen *You've Got Mail* and was paying attention could have guessed it. But I hadn't . . . and everything had still turned out great. Minus the kiss at the end, of course. But that was still to come.

Lindsey shot me a sly look as we left the movie store. "What do you think Alex will get you? Jewelry, maybe?"

"Oh, it's way too early for that." I sucked in my breath. "Isn't it?"

It doesn't have to be several carats, Lord. A simple but meaningful family heirloom works for me.

Note to self: Start practicing surprised look now so as to be ready by Christmas.

Near the end of an elegant candlelit dinner at an upscale Fisherman's Wharf restaurant that evening, a waiter set a silver-domed platter in front of me. "I didn't order anything else." I looked up at him in surprise.

Oh my! Be still, my heart. It's a ring, it's a ring!

Come off it, Pheebs. You know perfectly well it isn't. But I couldn't hear my practical self over the pounding in my chest.

"Permit me." The waiter removed the dome with a flourish. But instead of a jewelry box, the platter revealed a thick, creamy envelope with my name written on it in calligraphy.

Pretty flat ring, my practical self pointed out unhelpfully.

"What is it, Pheebs?" Lins got that feverish gift glint in her eyes. "Open it."

Oh my goodness. Shirley Temple took up residence in my head, totally quenching the voice of reason. *Could it be? A proposal . . . in writing?*

Not quite. Instead of "Phoebe, my beloved, I adore you and worship the ground you walk on. Will you marry me?" Alex had written, "At the end of the day you'll have seen your favorite musical." Tucked in behind the note were four tickets to a touring-company production of *Les Miserables.*

It's way too early for a proposal, my practical self reminded the disappointed me. *He needs to say the L-word first, remember. Focus on how wonderful and romantic this gift is instead.*

Alex had discovered that *Les Miz* was my favorite musical one day at the office. He'd been out to lunch, or so I thought. So I'd slipped on my headphones, shut my eyes, and lost myself in the musical I loved but had never seen on stage . . . until Alex's rich baritone jolted me back from Victor Hugo's Paris.

"Thought we'd make it a duet," he'd said, grinning at me when my eyes flew open. "Although 'Do You Hear the People Sing?' is best with a full revolutionary chorus."

He'd been right, of course. The chorus was stirring. Magnificent. When the lights came up after the show, Lins and I were both blubbering like babies. We heard a few sniffles from the guys too, but they insisted it was just the San Francisco fog.

We walked to Alex's car, debating the merits of each song and speculating on who should be cast in the movie version of the musical. Well, Alex and I debated and speculated. Phil and Lindsey just walked arm in arm and mooned over each other.

Realization dawned when we reached the distinctive claret-colored awning of the St. Francis Hotel. "Ah, now I know why you parked in the hotel garage." I smiled at my date. "It's so close to the theater."

"Actually, I parked here because we're spending the night."

I stopped short, causing Lindsey to bump into me. "Say what?"

Alex caught Phil's eye and winked. "I knew we'd be too tired to drive home this late, so I booked a couple of rooms—one for you and Lindsey and one for us."

"Oh," I said weakly. "Good idea." Another thought struck. "But I, um, don't have anything to—uh, a toothbrush or anything."

"Yes you do. Your mom packed an overnight bag, and I picked it up on my way to your house this morning. I had the valet take it to your room already."

Phil shot him an admiring glance. "Now I see how you got that big-time corporate title, buddy. You think of everything."

Alex lifted his shoulders in a modest shrug. "It's all in the planning."

Lins kicked off her shoes and lay down on one of the two queen-size beds, her feet dangling over the side. "Okay, dish. What's the latest with you and Alex?"

"Nothing." I began unpacking my overnight bag. "We're just enjoying each other's company. We have a lot of fun together."

She gave me a sharp look. "Yeah, right. Tell me another one. I know you too well, Pheebs. You're in serious like with that man."

"So what's not to like?" I said in my best Jewish mother voice as I pulled on my pajamas.

"True." Lins shifted on the bed. "How about working together? How's that?"

"So far, so good. He's a good boss and a really good writer. Not only that. He also appreciates my writing, which *I* appreciate." I grimaced. "Even when I'm only writing about stupid emus, cow-milking contests, or goat roping."

Lindsey wrinkled her nose. "I still can't believe that wussy, big-city you is getting so friendly with livestock."

"Comes with the small cow-town territory." I did not remind her that I'd actually grown up in that cow town. I just shrugged. "Not a lot of other writing options in Barley—other than my weekly review of whatever's showing down at the Bijou. Thankfully, there's the delicious perk of working side by side with Alex every day. Otherwise I'd have to slash my writing-career wrists."

"Enough about your wrists." Lindsey hugged her pillow to her. "Get to the good part. I want the whole romantic 411 on you and Alex! Have you guys kissed yet?"

"No. We're taking our time. Unlike some people I know."

She stuck her tongue out at me. "I'll say you're taking your time."

"Lins, we haven't even been dating a month yet. We're still at the getting-to-know-one-another stage. I mean, it was only today that I found out anything about his childhood."

"But don't you want to? Kiss Alex, I mean."

"Of course I *want* to. But it's not like I'm just going to jump him and grab him in a major lip-lock."

"Why not?"

"Hel-looow," I said, doing my best Billy Crystal while arching my eyebrows. "We *happen* to be trying to rise above the whole lusts of the flesh thing." An image of Alex's full lips flashed before me, effectively demolishing my superior stance and bringing me back to reality. I sighed. "Besides, I've done that in the past, as you well know, and it never works out. No, I'm going the old-fashioned route this time, waiting for *him* to take the initiative—which I believe he will take in the very near future, thank you very much." I gave my friend a searching look. "But what about you? You and

Phil were really doing some major face sucking today. Are you still keeping it pure?"

She nodded and grimaced. "But it's sure not easy. Especially as things get more serious."

"Serious? We're talking about the M-word here?"

"Hasn't crossed either of our lips, but we *are* dancing all around it. Her voice got all dreamy. "He's asked how many kids I want, what kind of house I like. Vacations—we both agree that wherever we go, we have to stay in at least a four-star hotel. No roughing it for this couple."

"I hear ya on that." I set my boots next to my suitcase.

Lindsey turned a speculative gaze to the low heels on my Kenneth Coles. "It's nice to see you've gotten over your short-men phobia."

I bristled. "Alex isn't short. He's more than an inch and three-quarters taller than me. Which is just perfect—I don't have to crane my neck to look up at him."

And kissing should be pretty easy too.

"I think this whole cultural thing about tall men being hotter is just way out of line!"

"Hey, down, girl. *You're* the one whose shopping list said at least six-foot-two."

"That's because big guys always made me feel smaller. But Alex doesn't like skinny women." I glanced in the mirror at my profile, sucking in my stomach. "He finds Jennifer Lopez and her curves a lot more appealing than any of those scrawny supermodel types." I lowered my head, sucked in my cheeks, and tried to look appropriately J.Lo sultry.

A soft knock at the door made me blow my cheeks back out to normal.

We looked at each other. Then at our watches. "The guys wouldn't be dropping by this late, would they?" Lins whispered.

I looked down at my oversized Winnie-the-Pooh slippers. "I certainly hope not."

"Room service," a muffled voice said.

"We didn't order anything," Lins yelled, peeking through the peephole.

"Courtesy of Mr. Spencer in Room 215."

Lindsey and I exchanged wide-eyed glances as she hurried to let the waiter in.

"Ooh, check out the gorgeous rose." Lindsey lifted the bud vase and held it up to the light once the waiter had left. "And that's not cut glass either, honey; that's crystal." She smacked her lips. "Let's see what the classy Mr. Spencer sent."

"Ooh." This time we both smacked our lips. Beneath the silver dome on a china plate drizzled with raspberry sauce sat the largest and densest piece of chocolate decadence cake I'd ever seen, topped with a generous dollop of whipped cream.

With two forks on the side.

In a sugar-fantasy fog I reached for one of the forks, but Lins stayed my hand. "Wait." She passed me a piece of folded creamy vellum paper from beneath the plate. I recognized Alex's familiar scrawl: "Since I deprived you of dessert, I thought you might like some now. Bon appetit."

"Oh Lins," I moaned as the first decadent bite hit my lips. "I just can't let this one get away."

chapter two

Fruitcakes

three days later, back in Barley, I sat in the *Bulletin* office, nursing a double mocha and pecking lamely at the keyboard. I was suffering from acute Lindsey withdrawal and finding it difficult to muster up the enthusiasm to write an advance about the upcoming Christmas craft festival at church.

Somehow, Mabel Wilson and her crocheted-doll toilet-paper covers didn't hold much appeal.

Then Gordon, my former potty-mouthed, chain-smoking boss, who'd cleaned up his act considerably since he'd begun wooing my mother, sprang to my rescue. He had just returned from visiting his brother in Phoenix and volunteered for the assignment.

"But you're supposed to be taking it nice and easy."

"If I take it any nice and easier, I'll be dead." Gordon leaned back in the ancient wooden swivel chair next to my desk until it squeaked in protest. Then he jumped up and began pacing, jerking his hands through his thinning hair. "I just got back from a week of doing nothing but sitting around playing cards and bingo. I knew it was time to leave when my sister-in-law said they needed a fourth for bridge because their usual player was in the hospital, getting her hip replaced." He gazed out the *Bulletin's* plate-glass window. "This retirement stuff isn't all it's cracked up to be. Makes a man feel da—um, downright useless."

Alex reappeared from the dusty back room. "Gordon. Great to see you. When'd you get back?"

"Last night." My former boss twisted the bottom button of his worn cardigan. "Uh, Alex, I was wondering—"

My new boss and boyfriend—*can I even call him that yet?*— interrupted him. "Good thing you stopped by. I was planning to ask a favor. We're pretty swamped with this special Christmas edition, and I'm not sure we'll be able to get to all the stories. Right, Phoebe?" He threw me a telling look behind Gordon's back.

Mouth full of mocha foam, I nodded.

Alex slung his arm around the former editor's shoulders. "Would you mind helping us out by writing a few articles? I'll pay you the going freelance rates, of course."

Gordon beamed. "No problem, son, no problem at all. Can't afford not to have the Christmas edition. It's a *Bulletin* tradition, and folks would sure miss it. You just give me those assignments."

Minutes later, Gordon bounded off with a newsman's zeal, the bell over the front door jangling behind him.

I shot a goopy look at my boyfriend, um, boss. *Could there be a more perfect man? Gorgeous, funny, and kind too. What more could a girl want?* That sixties song about going to the chapel swirled in my head, sticking on the ma-aa-arried part and playing over and over. "That was a very sweet thing to do."

"Sweet nothing." Alex grinned. "Good thing Gordon came back early; otherwise I'm not sure how you and I would have gotten the paper out."

The bell over the front door jangled again.

"Whenever a bell rings, an angel gets his wings." I smiled at Alex, knowing he'd get my reference to *It's a Wonderful Life.*

"Attaboy, Clarence." He chimed in with the Jimmy Stewart part.

"Who're you talkin' to?" The door slammed shut with a bang. "Name's Esther, not Clarence. Thought you knew that."

"Hi, Esther." I raised my voice a notch. "Nice to see you." I smiled to see the seventy-something former reporter sporting purple pants, a garish Hawaiian shirt, a thick lavender sweater, and a red wool beret.

Until a couple of months ago, I'd known Esther Blodgett as the hardworking, no-nonsense reporter for the Barley *Bulletin*—which just goes to show you can know a person all your life and never really know her. Esther had surprised us all by selling off a lot of land we didn't know she had, donating most of the proceeds to the Bijou— saving the theater in the process—and still retiring from the *Bulletin* with a nice little nest egg.

Since then, she'd spent much of her time traveling with one or more of her pals from the red-hatted, purple-clad ladies' club. She was trying to make up for lost time, cramming in as many trips as she could. This time she'd just returned from Hawaii.

Esther plunked down a perfect sand dollar and a couple of seashells on my desk. "Brought you all some souvenirs. They say if you put those shells up to your ear you can hear the sea, but you can't prove it by me. I can't hear a blamed thing."

"Thank you." I hugged her, hiding a grin. Esther couldn't hear most normal conversations, let alone a seashell.

"Now don't get all mushy on me." She wriggled out of my embrace and handed Alex a plastic Santa clad in a tropical shirt and shorts and riding a surfboard. "This here's Aloha Santa. He's a little reminder that even ol' Saint Nick needs a little vacation now and then. You remember that."

"Thanks, Esther. I'll remember."

"'Course it's December." She gave him a warning look. "Christmas is right around the corner. Hope you're prepared. Not good to wait 'til the last minute." She adjusted her beret. "Gotta go spread me some more holiday cheer. Don't work too hard."

"We won't," Alex and I chorused as she jangled out the door. Then he turned to me with a meaningful look.

No, not that kind of look. I only wish. On the job he was Mr. Professional.

So was Spencer Tracy in Desk Set, *but that didn't stop him from planting a big one on Katharine Hepburn.*

"You got flour on your nose, An Beebee." Lexie giggled.

"And you've got green sugar sprinkles on your chin," I said, leaning over and kissing the sweet spot off my adorable niece's face. "Mmm. Delicious. Why, I don't even need a cookie. I'll just have Lexie-girl for my sugar cutout instead." Swooping toward her, I made fake chomping Cookie Monster sounds.

Lexie squealed with delight and ran toward my sister-in-law, Karen. "Save me, Mommy. Save me." Karen reached down for her, but she veered off at the last second, careening straight into Alex's flour-covered knees and dissolving into giggles again.

"I think perhaps someone's had too much sugar," he said, hoisting my niece in his arms.

"Don't let her fool you," observed my mother with a grin. "She's like that most of the time." She glanced my way. "They all are."

"And you love it," I shot back, reaching for one of the cookies she'd just piled on a platter. She just smiled and swatted at my hand.

It was the first Saturday in December—traditional Christmas cookie-baking day in the Grant household. As a child, I'd loved the times when we gathered in our spacious kitchen to mix and cut out dough. In years that I'd been away from home, my brother's family had come over to Mom's to make the cookies. And this year, much to my delight, I was home to join in the fun. Even better, Mom had invited Alex to join us.

"You'd think you've never done this before," Ashley, my eldest niece, teased him as he wiggled the cutter to release a very lopsided Christmas star.

"Actually," he said to Ashley, "I never have."

Seven pairs of stricken eyes swiveled to him. "You've never baked Christmas cookies?" ten-year-old Elizabeth asked.

"Nope. My mom always did the baking by herself. Besides, they don't have Christmas cookies in England."

"Christmas without cookies?" Jacob and Lexie said in horrified unison. "But if you don't have cookies, what do you leave out for Santa on Christmas Eve?"

"I don't know. A mince pie, perhaps?"

Seven pairs of raised eyebrows met his.

"Mince pies are a British institution and are nothing if not compulsory at Christmas," Alex explained. "From the beginning of December onward, if you call in at any friend or family member's house, you will be offered tea, coffee, port, mulled wine, or some other beverage, but always a mince pie."

Elizabeth frowned. "What's it made of?"

My mother reached over to gather up scraps of dough. "Isn't it the same as our mincemeat?"

"Meat? In a pie?" Jacob licked a couple of chocolate sprinkles from his five-year-old fingers.

"Like chicken potpie, silly," Elizabeth said.

"There's actually no meat at all, but it does resemble a potpie, only smaller. It's filled with fruit preserves, cinnamon, nutmeg, and brandy." Alex released a wistful sigh. "But even more than that, what I really love is Christmas pudding."

"I like pudding too." Jacob beamed up at him. "Especially chocolate."

"What's Chwismas pudding?" Lexie frowned. "Is it 'stachio?"

"No. Sorry." Alex knelt down to her three-year-old level.

He's great with kids. He'll make a wonderful father . . .

"In England, *pudding* means dessert," Alex explained. "Christmas pudding is a fruitcake cooked in a large bowl and steamed for two or three hours, then turned upside down and served hot as the final course of Christmas dinner."

"Fruitcake?" I recoiled in horror. "You don't really like fruitcake, do you? Not that hard, dry thing that's heavy as a rock and has those icky red and green candied cherries and loads of nuts." I shuddered.

"You've obviously never had good fruitcake." He glanced at Mom. "No disrespect, Gloria."

"None taken." Mom grinned as she slapped more flour on her rolling pin. "I never make fruitcake, because no one in my family likes it."

I snorted. "There's no such thing as good fruitcake."

"Oh yes there is. When made right, it can be moist and rich." Alex kissed his fingertips like a television gourmet. "A subtle culinary triumph. Some people just don't know how to appreciate it."

"Oh, I appreciate it. The same way I appreciate a doorstop." He laughed as I made my exit through the dining room door.

I passed Karen in the hall on my way to the bathroom. "You and Alex sure make a cute couple," she whispered.

Uh-huh. So cute that he hasn't even kissed me yet.

But patience is a virtue, and I was willing to wait a little longer. After all, Christmas is coming up soon.

And if not then, there's always New Year's Eve.

I made it back to the kitchen just as a car door slammed and muffled feet bounded up the back steps. "Hey, is this Cookie Central? I've got the eggnog and some chocolate-chip cookie dough."

"Mary Jo!" Elizabeth hurtled out of her chair and hugged her plus-size, jeans-and-flannel-clad riding instructor, who also happened to be my best friend in Barley. "How's Pluto? Does he miss me?"

"Something terrible. Told me to say hello, in fact." She leaned her head back and whinnied, her thick, straight maple hair falling away from her square-jawed face.

"Hey Mom," I said, "I think our equine pal needs a few sugar cubes."

Mary Jo Roper stuck her tongue out at me and examined the plate of sugar-cookie cutouts the kids had decorated. "I'd settle for a frosted snowman." Under her breath she added with a chuckle, "Or any man, for that matter."

I choked back a laugh as she pulled a CD out of her backpack and held it up. "Gloria, mind if I put on some Christmas tunes?"

"Go right ahead, dear." My domestic-goddess mother removed a batch of cookies from the oven. "You know where the stereo is."

Soon a strange noise filtered in from the living room.

I raised incredulous eyebrows. "Correct me if I'm wrong, but is that Diana Ross and the Supremes singing 'White Christmas'?"

My Motown-loving friend grooved her Supreme-wannabe-self back to the table. "Sure is."

"Sorry, Mary Jo, but some things are sacred."

In seconds Bing Crosby's baritone filled the air.

"That's a little more like it." I looked around the table. "Don't you all agree?"

Everyone, including Alex, nodded, although a loyalties-divided Elizabeth scampered to her teacher's side and slipped her hand in hers. Karen smiled and patted Mary Jo's shoulder. "You learn pretty quick that this family is tradition-and-nostalgia bound when it comes to music."

"Should have guessed, especially with Phoebe's old-movie mania." She shrugged her shoulders and grinned. "No problem. I'll just listen to my *Motown Christmas* in my car on the way home."

I grinned back at her and shook my head. "I'm surprised you didn't bring your favorite Beatles Christmas album." Mary Jo's parents had raised her on their favorite music—R&B, gospel, and the Beatles. Instead of rebelling, she had become a fan, her car radio perpetually tuned to classic rock.

"I would have," she said, "except the Beatles Christmas albums— no carols, by the way, just funny songs with Christmas references— were only issued to members of the Official Beatles Fan Club in the sixties." Mary Jo tucked her hair behind her ears. "Just a little bit before my time. And it costs a fortune to get one now—I've checked on eBay."

She whipped out another CD from her backpack and grinned. "But I do have Paul's *Wonderful Christmastime . . .*"

We were putting the last batch of Mary Jo's chocolate-chip contribution in the oven when my weary brother arrived.

"Daddy!" Lexie flung herself at Jordy's legs.

"Hi, pumpkin. You been making cookies?" He scooped up his daughter and gave her a big kiss.

She nodded. "But we're done now. Let's go play."

"Not now, baby girl. Daddy's really, really tired."

Mom and Karen exchanged worried looks. Jordy had begun moonlighting as a carpenter nights and weekends to help make ends meet for his family. That work on top of his full-time teaching and coaching job was taking its toll.

"Honey, sit down and relax." Karen, carrying my newest niece and namesake, Gloria Phoebe, on her hip, planted a kiss on her weary husband's cheek. "I'll bring you a cup of coffee and some fresh-from-the-oven cookies."

Jordy sank gratefully into Mom's recliner and shut his eyes. "Sounds good."

Concerned, I shot up a silent prayer. *Lord, please help me win the Publisher's Clearing House sweepstakes so I can shower my family with money and Jordy won't have to work two jobs anymore—or any job at all, for that matter.*

A small smile tugged at my lips. *And after I take care of all of them, I can splurge on myself, too, and finally get a pair of Manolos.*

"Don't eat that, Bruce."

Sylvia Ann Woodring, her Dolly Parton curls bouncing against the fake white-fur collar of her red jumpsuit, playfully slapped her boyfriend's hand away from the plate of cookies I'd brought to our singles Sunday-school class.

Although for my mother's sake I attended earlier services at Holy Communion Lutheran Church—our Lutheran family's church for generations—I always scooted over to Barley Presbyterian afterward for Sunday school. Holy Communion didn't have anything resembling a singles group. And I craved the fellowship—though I couldn't quite get used to addressing fifty-something Sylvia Ann and Bruce Hubert as peers. Sylvia Ann was Barley's resident beautician, owner of The Bobby Pin. And Bruce had actually taught me in high school, though I knew him back then as Hubert the Horrible.

"Remember what the doctor said about your cholesterol," Sylvia Ann was warning her beau. "This looks loaded with butter and sugar. Have one of my low-fat, sugar-free oat-bran-raisin cookies instead." She batted her heavily mascaraed lashes. "I made them especially for you."

Jeff, our singles pastor, rapped his knuckles on the table. "Okay, everyone, time for praise and worship."

His copper-haired wife, Amy, strummed a few chords on her acoustic guitar, then launched into a beautiful guitar solo of "O Come, O Come, Emmanuel," followed by several contemporary praise songs.

As always, Mary Jo really got into the music. She swayed in her seat, eyes shut, hands raised, her Aretha Franklin–style voice shaking the rafters.

My voice shook a few things too. Dental fillings. Fingers on chalkboard. Great Danes two counties over. But I sang. I always sang.

Another reason that I came over to Barley Pres for Sunday school was that I enjoyed the livelier, more contemporary style. For years I'd been trying to break free from my staid Lutheran upbringing—we weren't called the frozen chosen for nothing—but old habits die hard. During my air-force days, when I was stationed in Biloxi, Mississippi, I'd attended a black Pentecostal church with my roommate, Shondra, and been shocked when she and all the other members of the congregation kept interrupting the pastor with "Go on, now!" and "Preach it, brother!" and a host of amens.

I was even more shocked when Shondra and everyone else—including the minister—started dancing in the aisles. I tried to join in, but have always been a little rhythm challenged, so wound up doing the female version of what Billy Crystal called the white man's overbite. And the whole raising the arms thing lost much of its praise-the-Lord impact due to worry over whether I'd remembered to shave my pits.

However, at the Presbyterian church I'd attended in Cleveland and now Barley, I'd discovered a great compromise: raising one discreet arm up, bent at the elbow.

After Sunday school, Pastor Jeff came up behind Amy and encircled her tiny waist with his hands. "Great job, honey."

Oh, to have a husband's arms round my waist like that. If he'd even be able to make it all the way around . . . I sucked in my stomach.

Sylvia sidled up to us with Bruce in tow and a knowing gleam in her eye. And dropped a bombshell: "So Jeff, Amy, I hear you two want to leave us."

"What?" Mary Jo and I chorused.

Jeff shot a look at his wife. "I'm just putting out feelers. We've been praying about my having my own church. God seems to be leading us in that direction, but right now we're just waiting on Him."

My face fell. But Mary Jo, who's less selfish and way more spiritually advanced than me, threw the couple a happy grin. "That would be great! You guys do a great job here, but I could really see the Lord using you in a larger ministry."

Note to self: Practice being more like spiritual giant Mary Jo, who can even wish the best to people about to desert us. The brat.

Sylvia turned to me with a bright smile. "Where's Alex today, Phoebe?"

Not to worry, Sylvia. He hasn't dumped me. But if he does, I'll alert the media—after I tell you, of course. Oops. Sorry, God. I know I just resolved to be more gracious and loving like Mary Jo.

"Oh, he's visiting a newspaper colleague in San Francisco." I bestowed a sweet smile in return for Sylvia's nosy one. "He hated to miss church, but his friend was only in California for one day. But he'll be back soon," I added. "Very soon."

Note to self: Buy mistletoe.

chapter three

Alone Again, Naturally

Question: What's worse than not having a boyfriend to kiss on New Year's Eve?

Answer: Having an actual boyfriend and still having no one to kiss.

This year, I'd thought that for once I wouldn't be a pathetic loser, all alone except for my double date with Ben and Jerry on the second most romantic holiday of the year. Alex and I had plans to attend the all-town party at the soon-to-be refurbished Bijou Theater. It was kind of a kickoff party for the renovations we'd raised money for. And I just knew it would be the night Alex finally kissed me.

It was the perfect time, after all. The perfect place—the site of our first real date. And I was ready. My lips and I were more than ready.

As it turned out, though, we would have to wait a little longer.

Two days before Christmas, Alex had received a call from overseas that his father had had a heart attack and had raced over to England to be with him. Thankfully, it had turned out to be only a mild attack. But this meant that instead of spending Christmas and New Year's with me, Alex (and his lips) had spent it with his family over in Merrie Olde England.

Leaving me here—still kissless—on New Year's Eve at the Bijou. It was enough to make a girl lose heart. Almost.

If it hadn't been for the Manolos, I don't know what I would have done . . .

I'd still managed to have a wonderful Christmas, even without the man I loved—*at least I think I love him*—at my side. It was, after all, my first holiday at home in three years. And I'd forgotten how fun it was to be around kids at Christmas. They got so excited opening their gifts.

But their excitement wasn't even in the same stratosphere as mine when I opened the present from Alex that he'd sneakily arranged for Gordon—who was rapidly become a fixture at our family gatherings—to put under the tree.

My jaw dropped as I lifted out the pair of black stiletto boots, and Shirley Temple returned. "Oh my goodness! Manolos!"

"Gesundheit," Jordy said.

I raised the soft leather to my face and inhaled. *Who needs sex? Or even a kiss, for that matter?* The *Casablanca* love song began to play in my head, then abruptly screeched to a halt. *All I got him was a clock and that paltry paperweight . . .*

"Wow, Aunt Phoebe, he must really like you," Ashley, my fashionista niece said. "Manolo Blahniks are *expensive.*"

"I know!"

Note to self: Begin planning wedding. After a gift like this, surely it won't be long now. Wonder if I can wear them under my wedding dress?

Mom looked at my boots and frowned. "How expensive?"

"At least five hundred dollars," Ashley blurted out before I had a chance to stop her. "Probably more."

My mother frowned again. "Doesn't seem a very appropriate gift from someone you've just started dating. A little too intimate, I'd say."

"Well, they *are* special. But remember, five hundred dollars to Alex is like twenty bucks to us. And it's not like he gave me lingerie or anything." I slid my feet into heaven. "They're even the right size! How'd he know?" I looked at my mother.

She shrugged. "I certainly didn't tell him."

My head swiveled to Karen and the girls, who were shaking their heads. "Not us."

"Don't look at me, Pheebert," Jordy said. "I have no clue about your sizes and wouldn't even attempt to guess." He grinned at his wife. "That's one thing I've learned over the years."

The mystery of the right-size Manolos was finally solved when Lindsey called later to wish me Merry Christmas and wasn't at all surprised by my gift. "I should have known it was you, Lins. Thanks, best friend." I flexed my boot-clad foot and preened. "The man really has great taste."

"We already knew that. He's dating you, isn't he?"

Oh, Lindsey, why are you there and I'm here?

And why, for goodness' sakes, is Alex Spencer way over yonder?

On the evening of Christmas day, after all the food was eaten, the eggnog drunk, the wrapping paper cleared away, and tired, happy kids put to bed, I'd gone home to my little garage apartment to e-mail Alex—and was thrilled to find an e-mail from him already waiting.

To: Movielovr
From: Filmguy791
   Happy Christmas, Phoebe, as we say over here. Hope you and your family had a wonderful time celebrating the birth of the King of kings. They released my father from hospital last night, so we kept things simple and had a nice quiet holiday at home—with the best Christmas pudding, I might add. Sorry you missed it. Know you'd have loved it.☺ Must run; more food and carol singing still to come. Give everyone my best. And God bless you every one.

                    Warmly, The Fruitcake Evangelist

I dissected his e-mail line by line. Polite, pleasant, and spiritual, with a touch of dry wit. High points for etiquette, but low points on the romantic love-meter scale. *He never said he missed me—although he did say he was sorry I missed the fruitcake . . .*

I looked over at my new boots, perched resplendently on my kitchen table. How could I even think that Alex Spencer was lacking in the romantic department? I reread the e-mail, this time between the lines.

I know! What he really meant was that he was sorry I wasn't there with him to share the holiday. Yes, that's it. He's just not very touchy-feely or comfortable expressing his feelings on paper, which is also why he said "warmly" rather than "love" in his closing.

I felt much better having figured that out. Now it was my turn.

Careful not to be too clingy or pushy. Be appropriately appreciative of his to-die-for gift, but also be witty and clever so that he'll miss you and hurry back to Barley.

> To: Filmguy791
> From: Movielovr
>
>   Merry, I mean, Happy Christmas to you too, Mr. Fruitcake Evangelist. So glad your father's back home and you were all able to spend the holiday together. Jacob loved his remote-control car, by the way, but not as much as I loved my gorgeous boots! Thank you. I've wanted a pair of Manolos forever. No fair, though. We said we'd exchange gifts when you got back. (Yours is still under my tree.) Any idea yet when you're returning? Please wish your family Happy Christmas—and don't save a piece of fruitcake for me.☺ God bless,
>   Your never-going-to-convert-to-fruitcake woman

I read it over carefully before sending, making sure I'd hit all the right notes. *Uh-oh. Does the "but not as much as I loved" sound like Jacob didn't love the remote-control car?* I arrowed up and changed the comma after "by the way" into a period, deleted the "but not as much as" and changed it to read "And I loved my gorgeous boots." Then I changed my closing line from *"Your"* to *"The"* and hit send.

First thing tomorrow I'll start thinking about a better gift for Alex. Something a little more meaningful.

Maybe I could write him a poem . . .

I began to compose love lines in my head, which soon led me down another track.

I wonder if he'll want to get married in England or in Barley?

On New Year's Eve, the whole town turned out for the Bijou celebration, happy to ring in the New Year in our beautifully decorated theater.

With my Alex—after the Manolos, I felt more than justified thinking of him that way—still in absentia across the pond, I'd been tempted to skip the party. But Mom and Gordon insisted I come since the fundraising drive had been my idea in the first place. Good thing, too. The mayor gave a speech and thanked me for my efforts, the theater manager gave me a three-month free popcorn pass, and the crowd applauded.

After all the hoopla died down, I scanned the lobby and noticed I was the only person in the room without a date. Everywhere I looked was like the Ark—with every creature paired off.

Except for old Mr. Soames, standing over by the lounges. But that didn't count. I mean, who's there to go out with after you're ninety?

I spoke too soon. A spry, blue-haired beauty in a red-velvet pantsuit studded with rhinestones made a beeline from the restroom to his eagerly proffered arm.

Note to self: In future, stay home and wash hair or insert bamboo shoots under fingernails rather than subject one's dateless self to pathetic public scrutiny.

Just then I caught sight of my old high-school boyfriend, Travis, and his new bride, Jenny, kissing and making goo-goo eyes at each other. Behind them I spotted Jordy and Karen and, next to them, Jeff and Amy dancing cheek to cheek.

Romance was definitely in the air.

Just not the air I breathed.

I glanced down at my Manolo-clad feet. *Think of the boots. Think of the boots and what they mean. Alex can't help it if he's stuck in England.*

Not wanting to be there when everyone started kissing at midnight—especially since Bruce Hubert had been sending me flirtatious looks all evening behind a purple-sequined Sylvia's back—I started edging to the exit. So intent was I on making a clean getaway, I didn't notice Mom and Gordon lurking nearby.

"Phoebe, where are you going?" My mother looked at her watch. "It's still forty-five minutes 'til midnight."

"I know, Mom, but I'm exhausted. And I have this awful headache . . ."

Liar.

"I think I'll just go home to bed."

"We'll take you, dear."

I saw an expression of dismay flit across Gordon's face as she started to collect her coat.

"No, you stay," I insisted. "My car's just over at the *Bulletin.* Think I'll just go home, take a nice hot bath, pop some aspirin, and go to bed." I kissed her cheek. "Happy New Year." I nodded and gave a wide smile to Gordon. "You too, boss." Then I leaned over and whispered in my mom's ear. "Don't do anything I wouldn't do."

"Phoebe!" She blushed and swatted at me.

"Happy New Year, everyone." I pasted on the most genuine smile I could and offered a happy wave good-night.

The minute I was outside and trudging toward my car, my perky demeanor drooped. "So much for ringing in the New Year with a boyfriend for a change."

And this year I don't even have any girlfriends to commiserate with. Lins was all the way in Cleveland, and Mary Jo was visiting her sister in Southern California.

It helped a little to slip into my trusty yellow Bug. We'd been through a lot together. But not even the cheerful rosebud in its little automotive bud vase could cheer me up significantly.

Times like these call for . . . chocolate.

Checking my glove-box stash, I found nothing but a wadded-up Snickers wrapper. I smoothed it out and licked it in hopes of discovering a fleck of chocolate or two, but no such luck. Tuning the radio to my favorite oldies station, I tried to lose myself in the music. Gilbert O'Sullivan's "Alone Again, Naturally" blared from the speakers.

I smacked the off button.

Once home in my apartment over Karen and Jordy's garage, I shed my boots and fancy velvet in favor of comfy flannel. Still in need of some chocolate sustenance, I grabbed the box of Little Debbie Nutty Bars I kept on hand for the kids and upended it on the counter. The last cellophane-wrapped two-pack tumbled out. Tearing it open with ravenous fingers, I wolfed it down. But it wasn't enough.

My *I Love Lucy* cookie jar beckoned from the end of the counter. I ripped Lucy's head off and peered inside. Empty.

What am I thinking? It's six days after Christmas. Of course there wouldn't be any holiday cookies left. Although . . . wait a minute, what's that? Looks like a few crumbs on the bottom.

I turned the cookie jar upside down, shook out the crumbs, and moistened my fingertip to lift the crumbs from the Formica.

Still didn't slake my chocolate thirst.

I rooted around in my single-girl cupboards: rice cakes, granola, tuna in water, fat-free chili, sugar-free Jell-O, macaroni and cheese, flour and other baking stuffs.

Baking stuffs? Light bulb! Maybe I still had some chocolate chips left over from my supplemental Christmas-cookie baking.

Ah, success.

I plopped down on the couch, just my half bag of chips and me, and hit the remote to watch the ball drop in Times Square.

Talk about more than pathetic. Next thing you know I'll be a crotchety old woman living alone with only her cats for company. Although it worked for Audrey Hepburn in Breakfast at Tiffany's . . .

Except, of course, she wasn't old. And could never, ever be considered crotchety. *And* she had the delicious George Peppard living in the apartment upstairs.

My kitten, Herman, purred and rubbed against my leg.

"Bad timing, boy."

Noticing a drop of milk on his whiskers, I suddenly remembered the ice cream in the freezer. I grabbed the Ben and Jerry's chocolate-chip cookie dough and started singing the mournful refrain "All by Myself."

How very Bridget Jones of you. Can you say cliché? Snap out of it! I told myself in Cher's no-nonsense *Moonstruck* voice. With a decisive snap, I replaced the lid of the ice cream carton and shoved it back into the recesses of the freezer.

Then my mother's recessive housecleaning genes kicked in, along with some "Man! I Feel Like a Woman" pride: I'm not some lonely, pathetic thirty-something single woman drowning her sorrows in ice cream. I'm a strong, intelligent woman with a cute apartment and plenty of friends, who doesn't need a man to make her complete. And besides, I do have a man. A wonderful man. He's just not here at the moment.

Popping in a little Avril Lavigne, I turned on my vacuum and ushered in the New Year wondering why things had to be so complicated.

My mom always cleaned to Barry Manilow or Elvis, but I preferred contemporary pop or some of my eighties favorites. A little "Uptown Girl" always got me in the mood. Then I'd segue into my *Flashdance* soundtrack and really go to town.

So with Avril and the vacuuming finished, I did just that.

Determined to start the new year right, I began cleaning my closet. First, I color coded all my shoes in the stackable shoe hive my brother, Jordy, had built for me. And for those that didn't fit and had to remain in boxes, I took photos of each pair with my cell phone, then printed them out and taped a photo to the outside of each box, so I'd know at a glance what nestled inside.

Next I tackled my underwear drawer. In basic training, we'd been taught to fold our panties into equal thirds, but over the years I'd gotten a little lax. After refolding them, I color coded them all too. Then I arranged my hanging clothes in an orderly fashion—beginning with blazers, working through blouses and dresses, and winding up with pants and jeans, all organized by color, hangers spaced two fingers apart (another basic training must-do). I surveyed my clothing rainbow with satisfaction.

Maybe things weren't so complicated after all. I could handle this little bend in the road with Alex. In fact, maybe this time apart was a good thing. Could give me time to work on myself a little, become a better person so I'd have more to bring to the relationship.

I could finally start going to the gym in Lodi, for instance. I pictured myself meeting Alex at the airport, all sleek and firm.

Get real, whispering-thighs woman.

And I'd been doing better with my money—cutting way back on the plastic—but I could do better with that. I really didn't need this much stuff.

That's better. Put that on the list. Resolved: I'm going to be even more careful with my money.

And I'd been meaning to get serious about spending more time in God's Word and having a quiet time every day. That was important. If I wanted our relationship to have a solid foundation, didn't I need a solid foundation myself?

The more I thought about it, the more I really liked the idea—a new devotional routine for the new year.

Note to self: Set alarm for six o'clock tomorrow morning in order to devote at least one full hour to prayer and scriptural meditation before getting ready for work.

But wait. It was *already* tomorrow, and I didn't have to go back to work until Monday.

Note to self: Make that Monday morning.

Satisfied with my resolutions and my clean apartment and my new, positive attitude, I finally took the DustBuster to my windowsill and curtains. Dust up, dust down. Dust up, dust down. I felt like the Karate Kid. Only noisier.

Through the din, I heard a ringing in my ears. I shook my head, but it didn't stop. I switched off the DustBuster and turned down Irene Cara belting out "What a Feeling."

It *was* a ringing. My phone. I snatched it up. "Alex?"

"Sorry to disappoint you. It's just me, your best friend. Happy New Year!"

"Lins!" I looked at the clock. Twelve fifty-eight. "It's three in the morning back there in Cleveland! What are you still doing up? Don't tell me the singles bash went this late."

"Nope. Well, actually, I don't know." She giggled. "We didn't go to the party."

"You didn't?" Phil and Lindsey were the consummate partygoers. And party planners. For the past three years running, without fail, they'd organized the annual No More Lone Rangers New Year's Eve singles party at church. Well, Phil and Lindsey and I had planned it, back before they were a couple. Before Alex.

Things change so fast . . .

"So what did you guys do instead?" I asked.

"Oh, nothing much. Went out to dinner, dancing, took a moonlit drive along the lake. Got engaged. Ate some ice cream . . ."

"Engaged?!" I screamed across the miles.

Lins shrieked right back. "I know. Can you believe it? Me and Phil?"

"What I can't believe is that I'm here and you're there so far away," I whined. "I need details. Give me the whole 411. And start at the beginning. How'd he propose? And where? Did he give you a ring? When's the wedding?"

"Slow down, Pheebs." Lindsey laughed. "We haven't set a date yet. You know I need at least a year to plan my dream wedding. And I promise I'll give you all the details, but before I do, let me officially ask you to be my maid of honor. You'd better, or else you're dead meat."

"Of course I'll be your maid of honor. I'd kill you if you asked anyone else." We blubbed happy-girl tears together for a minute. "Who's the best man?"

"Scotty, naturally. Even though Phil and Alex have become good friends, he wanted his baby brother to stand up for him," Lindsey said. "But not to worry, Alex will be a groomsman, so you'll still get to see him in a tux."

"Mmm. Can't wait for that."

"Speaking of wedding attire, Pheebs . . . I found this great shiny peach taffeta Southern-belle bridesmaid dress, complete with hoop skirt and scalloped white trim at the bottom, that will make you look like a giant Creamsicle."

"It's what I've always dreamed of."

We snorted together across the miles. "I promise you'll get a killer dress in a gorgeous color that makes you look absolutely fabulous, dahling," she said.

"Without upstaging the bride, of course."

"Given."

"So what *are* your colors going to be?" I adjusted the throw pillow beneath my head. "Still pink and cream?"

"Nah. After Trista and Ryan's wedding I got a little pinked out."

We'd both sat glued to the TV together when the first reality-show bachelorette married her hunky, poetry-spouting fireman in one of the most lavish weddings we'd ever seen—preceded by a couple of prime-time specials where the spotlight couple taste-tested several cake selections, sampled a variety of menus, and sought the perfect locale for the "celebrity wedding of the year" (or decade, as some ad pundits proclaimed). We'd drooled over the dresses, the decorations, the masses of pink flowers, and the to-die-for fifty-thousand-dollar diamond-encrusted shoes designed especially for the bride by Stuart Weitzman.

"Pink is no longer mah signature color." Lindsey parroted Julia

Roberts in *Steel Magnolias*. (After hanging out with me for a while, my friends are starting to spout movie lines like I do.) "Of course, it also depends on what time of year we choose, what the setting will be, whether it's a morning or evening wedding . . ."

I could just see her furrowing her brow across the miles.

"I'm thinking if it's evening I might go with silver and white and splashes of fuschia. Or maybe very sophisticated, black and white all the way, with just a hint of red? What do you think?"

"Either works for me. As long as you don't put me in orange or yellow, I'm happy." I bounded up from the couch, grabbed a bottled water from the fridge, and took a swig. "So, has Phillie agreed to sign the prenup?"

Lindsey and I had come up with our own version of the celebrity prenuptial agreement—except ours had nothing to do with money. Our prenup included, among other stipulations, that our husbands must never say yes when asked, "Does this make me look fat?"; that they must only have eyes for us, no matter how many hard-bodied *Baywatch* babes parade into view; and that they must lovingly say "yes, dear" when we presented them with our multipage honey-do lists.

"I haven't brought that up yet," Lindsey said. "Thought I'd better ease into it."

"Good plan. So you still haven't told me how he proposed. What are best friends for if not to live vicariously through?"

She expelled a romantic sigh. "Well, we had this wonderful dinner at that little French restaurant downtown . . ."

"What'd you eat? You know me—I need every gastronomic detail."

"For an appetizer we had baked brie with almonds, then for our main course I had coq au vin and Phil had rack of lamb. For dessert, delicious crème brûlée. Then we went dancing for a little while, did the whole midnight-kiss thing . . ." her voice trailed off.

"Save the kiss memories for later," my lonely, kissless self ordered. "I want the proposal. Setting and words, please."

Lindsey released another romantic sigh. "We drove along the lake, and he pulled into this quiet spot and wanted to get out. Well, you know what Cleveland weather is like in December. I wasn't about to get out of the car! But he pleaded, said it would only take a minute. By this time I had an inkling, so I agreed." She took a breath. "It was a gorgeous crisp night; the stars were out, and the lights were shimmering on the water. Phil led me over to this little bench—he put a blanket on it first." She sighed again. "Very chivalrous."

I sighed right along with her.

"He sat beside me, looked in my eyes, and told me he loved my goofiness, my relationship with God, the dimple in my left cheek when I laugh, the way I move my food around my plate in circles when I get nervous, even my shopaholic tendencies." She giggled. "Then he knelt down in the snow, pulled out this gorgeous vintage diamond-and-emerald ring, and proposed. Said he wanted to start the New Year with me as his fiancée and knowing that before the year was over, I'd be Mrs. Phil Hansen."

"Very *When Harry Met Sally*. Who knew Phillie was such a romantic?"

"I *know*!" Lindsey said in her Monica-from-*Friends* voice.

"You'll get married at First Pres, right?"

"Of course. We're going to ask Pastor John to marry us."

"How many bridesmaids are you going to have?" I stretched back out on the couch. "And who?"

"I don't know yet." She wailed, "Why'd you have to go and move all the way to California? I wanted to go through all this bride stuff with you—looking for a dress, checking out reception sites, choosing a D.J., deciding on favors—you know I don't want any Jordan almonds at my wedding." Lindsey sniffed. "It's not going to be as much fun with you there and me here."

I could just see her pout. "I know, Lins, but there's this wonderful invention called e-mail. Plus we both have picture phones, so you can send me photos of everything. And I'll make sure I come out the week before the wedding so I can do all those maid-of-honor things: throw you a shower, give you a bachelorette party, take you to the spa for a head-to-toe beauty treatment." I adopted a stern tone. "And make sure you get to the church on time, Ms. Always Late."

Her sigh of relief came through loud and clear. "Thanks, Pheebs. I knew I could count on you."

"Always. All for one and one for all, remember?" I chuckled. "I can't wait to call our third musketeer and congratulate him."

"I'm afraid you're going to have to," Lindsey said. "Wait, I mean. Phil's already home and is probably fast asleep by now. Poor guy . . . I think he was so keyed up with anticipation that it totally exhausted him. His eyes were really drooping when he drove me home."

"My, my. You already sound like a little wifey, taking care of her man. Just as long as you don't turn into a desperate housewife," I teased. "Okay, Mrs. Hansen-to-Be. I'll just e-mail your fiancé instead."

"Good plan." Lins changed course abruptly. "So what's up with Alex? I know he's still in England, but any idea when he's coming back to Barley?"

"Nope." I hurried to explain. "He's got so much to do, what with his dad and the family business and all. And I really admire the way he's helping out his father in his time of need . . ."

"Of course you do, but 'fess up, Pheebs. You still wish he'd hurry up and get his hot self back to town, right?"

"You know me too well."

"Best friends usually do." I heard her take a sip of her Sleepy Time tea. "So how's it going at work without him there?"

"Not as fun." I sighed again. "I mean, I love Gordon and everything—don't get me wrong. He's a great boss. But he's definitely not as nice to look at as Alex. Plus I miss our movie banter . . ."

"I'll bet you do. You must be going through withdrawal without anyone to play Silver Screen Trivial Pursuit with."

"I'm trying to teach my nieces, but they're even worse than you are. They think *all* black-and-white films are boring."

She laughed. "So, do what you did with me, Ms. Movie Nazi. Force feed them *Casablanca* until they cry uncle."

"Good idea." I looked at the clock. "Yikes! Do you know what time it is? You'd better get your beauty sleep. You don't want Phil to take back his proposal when he sees your bloodshot eyes in the morning." I stretched and sat up. "Love ya, Lins. And I'm so happy for you. Both of you. We'll talk soon."

She giggled. "You got that right. 'Night, Pheebs. Love you too."

I hung up and bawled my eyes out.

chapter four

A Grumpy New Year

i'm an awful best friend.

I should have been so happy for Lindsey and Phil. And I was, I really was.

Only . . .

I know You brought them together, God. But is it ever going to be my turn for the happily-ever-after? Or am I going to be single for the rest of my life?

Would that be so bad?

Yes!

"Oops. Sorry, God. Didn't mean it. I take it back."

Smart move, Pheebs—way to antagonize the Big Guy. That's all you need right now. Get Him mad at you and make sure you never get married.

Okay, I know that's bad theology, but it's hard to think straight when you're lonely and miserable—which was the way the new year was shaping up right now.

But January's a time when you're supposed to get a good start on being a better person, right? So I repeated the single woman's life-line Psalm: "Delight yourself in the Lord, and he will give you the desires of your heart." Then, wiping my eyes, I powered on my laptop—determined to forget my pity spree and do the good-friend thing.

43

To: Phansen
From: Movielovr

Hey Phillie, what are you doing sleeping? Lins just called me with the great news. I'm thrilled! Congratulations! Rejoicing across the miles with you. If I know Lindsey, your wedding's going to be amazing. You'd better take good care of my best friend, bucko. Remember, I know where you live.

Next I dropped a quick note to Alex.

To: Filmguy791
From: Movielovr

Happy New Year. Have I got some news for you, Filmguy. Guess who's getting married? Phil and Lindsey! She just called. Pretty exciting, huh? Although they haven't set a date or anything yet—she says she needs a year to plan. Hope your dad's feeling better every day and things are going well. All's fine here, but I'm longing to see you soon. I really miss you. —P.

Wait. Is that too pushy and clingy?

I reread the words again, then deleted "But I'm longing to see you" and instead wrote, "I'm looking forward to seeing you." I also deleted "really"—though I really did miss him.

I surfed the Net for a while, checking out a few bridal sites and losing myself in all the satin and lace. But not wanting the tears to start up again, I grabbed my Bible and decided to read the seventh chapter of Paul's first letter to the Corinthians: "It is good . . . not to marry . . . I would like you to be free from concern."

And that, of course, cheered me right up.

The next day, after church, I dropped by Esther's for a visit, thinking it would be nice to bond in singles solidarity with a fellow spinster—someone who'd been unmarried her whole life and seemed none the worse for it.

Handing her a tin of Christmas cookies from my mom's supply, I noticed all the postcards and souvenirs displayed around the room. "Esther, you've become quite the traveler."

"Yep, but I waited way too long to start, and now I'm too old to do everything I want." Esther turned her latest scrapbook toward me.

"Esther, you'll never be old."

"Cold?" She wrapped her sweater tighter about her and snuggled deeper into her wingback chair, glancing at my Manolos as she did. "You bet your uncomfortable-looking high heels I'm cold. That's what happens when you get old. Especially if you're skinny. Not enough flesh to keep a body warm." She shot me an approving glance as she pried the lid off the cookie tin. "You won't have that problem. You're a nice, healthy girl, Phoebe. Not skin and bones like most of these young girls today. You want one of these?"

"Sure," I said, deciding that if I already had the "healthy girl" look, I might as well keep it up. "So what is it you want to do?"

"Huh? Speak up. You'll never make it at the *Bulletin* if you're soft-spoken."

Ah, but do I really want *to make it at the* Bulletin? That was the question. And the answer, of course, had a lot to do with Alex.

I raised my voice. "You said you wished you'd started traveling earlier because now you can't do everything you want. Like what, for instance?"

Esther wolfed down one of Mom's Mexican wedding cookies. "Like climb the Dome in Florence, ski the Swiss Alps, and go to the top of the Eiffel Tower." She threw me a sharp look over her trifocals. "And don't you make the same mistake, young lady. Don't get so wrapped up in your job and your *relationships* that you lose the opportunity to see what the rest of this big, wide world has to offer."

"But I did that already, remember? I enlisted in the air force right after high school so I could leave Barley and see the world."

"And what exactly did you see?"

"Well . . . San Antonio, Texas; Biloxi, Mississippi; Dayton, Ohio. And Cleveland."

"Like I said." Esther snorted. "But have you ever been out of the good ol' U.S. of A.? The good Lord created the entire world, remember, not just America. I love my country, I truly do. And I'll fight anyone who says something bad against her. But we Americans have a tendency to get insulated in our little corner of the world and forget that our brothers and sisters live beyond our borders too."

She sighed. "I'm not tryin' to give you a hard time, Phoebe. Fact is, I'm talkin' to myself as well as you. Before September, I'd never left the States in my entire life." She plucked another cookie from the tin. "But even though I'm old, my hearing's goin', and I don't move as fast as I used to, I'm not going to shuffle off to some old folks home, watch paint dry, and reminisce about the good old days from my rocking chair." Esther grinned at me. "That's why I'm starting the New Year off right with a trip to Europe."

"*Europe?* When?"

She settled back in her chair, an expectant gleam in her eyes. "Me and Millie, one of my purple ladies, are leaving Tuesday for a three-week tour. These old bones may not be able to ski in the Alps anymore, but I can sure enjoy the view while I'm drinkin' hot chocolate and eatin' some Sacher torte inside a nice, warm chalet."

Her eyes danced behind the thick glasses. "I've wanted to do this all my life but kept puttin' it off for one reason or another—not enough money, too many obligations, and just plain old fear, I suppose. But no more. That's another thing gettin' old does for you. You become fearless. Or fearful, depending on your outlook."

"You've always been fearless, Esther."

"Hah, a lot you know. I just put on a good front. But that's the past, and from now on I'm livin' in the present." She straightened. "We'll start out in Austria and Germany, then head down to Italy, where even though I can't climb the Dome, I can still see the *David* and the Sistine Chapel. 'Course, I'll have to watch out for those Italian men—I've heard they're real pinchers." She gave me a sly wink. "But they'd better watch out. I'll pinch 'em right back."

I choked on a cookie. Then gulped my hot chocolate to wash down the crumbs.

After making sure she didn't need to do the Heimlich maneuver, Esther continued. "Going to the City of Lights too. Hemingway said Paris is a moveable feast, and I plan to eat with gusto."

"I'm jealous." I sighed. "Wish I could be part of your red-hat club and go along."

"No you don't." Esther snorted again. "Bunch of old women wearing funny clothes and silly hats. Besides, you gotta be at least fifty. You'd have more fun with someone your own age." She leaned forward eagerly. "We'll wind up our trip in London, where we'll see Buckingham Palace. And who knows? Maybe the Queen'll invite me in for a cup of tea." She chuckled. "I want to see the statue of Peter Pan in Kensington Gardens too. That was always one of my favorite stories." Saw the musical in San Francisco, too, a long time ago—not Mary Martin, but pretty good. Even liked that Disney version."

"I'd love to see the original stage play," I murmured, thinking of a showing of *Finding Neverland* I'd caught in Sacramento the week before. But Esther hadn't heard me.

"And of course, St. Paul's Cathedral is a must," she said softly. Her faded denim eyes took on a misty, faraway look. "There's something special there I need to see."

"What?"

"When they rebuilt part of the cathedral that was destroyed during the Blitz, they included a memorial to American soldiers," Esther said. "They have this book called the Roll of Honor with all the names of the U.S. military who died over there." She wiped her eyes.

"One of those names is of a boy I loved, Norman Howard. We were high-school sweethearts and wanted to get married before he shipped out, but my parents said I was too young. He was eighteen. I wasn't even seventeen yet. So we decided to wait until he came home." She gave me a sad smile. "Only he never came home."

"Esther, I never knew. You never said anything . . ."

"That's because it was a long time ago, a lifetime ago. But before I end this life, I want to see his name in that famous place and lay a rose at the altar for him." Esther sniffled, then gave herself a little shake. "Land sakes, I'm gettin' all weepy in my old age. Norman's gone to Glory and I'll see him again, but I ain't dead yet! This is an excitin' time, and I plan to enjoy every minute of my grand European adventure."

She shot me another sharp look. "You just make sure you don't wait as long. You should enjoy these things while you're still young and can move around freely. Besides, travelin' helps you learn more about yourself—discover who you really are and what kind of stuff you're made of. You hear what I'm sayin'?"

"I hear you." I didn't want to rain on her travel parade. "I think it's wonderful you're doing this, Esther, but why go now when it's so cold? Why not wait until spring?"

"It's called money, honey." She cackled. "I'm no Donald Trump. Besides, the good Lord's opened these doors, and I'm not about to refuse to walk through them. Besides, I've always wanted to see the Alps in the wintertime."

"The hills are alive . . ." I said softly, thinking of *The Sound of Music.*

Esther stared at me. "No, I'm not going to let Millie drive." She snorted again. "Woman's a slowpoke behind the wheel. No, sirree, we'll go by train or bus, and let someone else do the navigatin'."

I was working on my attitude. I really was.

But I was also beginning to suspect I was not only a terrible friend, but a spiritual loser.

For the fourth day in a row now, I'd reneged on my New Year's resolution. I'd failed to get up in time for my daily quiet time in the Word like all good Christian girls do.

Well, maybe not everyone. Lindsey, who is not a morning person either—although she forces herself on gym days—also struggles in this area. And when I lived in Cleveland, we'd commiserate about our shared spiritual failing over double nonfat mochas from Starbucks. But Lindsey, Cleveland, and Starbucks were a world away—well, at least several states and four time zones—and Lindsey was way too busy to buck me up now. I was on my own here.

Note to self: No matter what, will actually get up early tomorrow morning.

But when the buzzer sounded at the crack of dawn the next morning, I slapped down the snooze button and buried my head beneath my pillow.

Ten minutes later it rang again.

"Jus' nine more minutes." I hit the snooze button.

Nine minutes later I hit it again. And again. And again. By the time I finally got up, my devotional hour had shrunk to seven minutes. Yawning, I flipped my Bible open to Proverbs: "The sluggard's craving will be the death of him."

All right, God. I get the message. Time to get serious about this.

That night, I moved the alarm out of my bedroom. When it clattered like machine-gun fire against the tile kitchen counter the next morning, my long trek to slap it down effectively woke me up. I filled a mug with some French roast, grabbed my Bible, and curled up on the couch under a quilt, at long last ready to spend an hour with God. My newly acquired daily devotional pointed me to the fourth chapter of Philippians and one of my favorite verses: "Whatever is true, whatever is noble, whatever is right, whatever is pure, whatever is lovely, whatever is admirable—if anything is excellent or praiseworthy—think about such things."

I resolved to incorporate this ancient directive on a more regular basis into my daily life. Like when someone cut me off on the freeway. Or when the idiots at the fast-food drive-through gave me the wrong taco *again*. Or when Mom forgot and called me dumpling, the childhood nickname I abhorred.

Ten minutes after this profound spiritual resolution, however, I was fast asleep, Bible on my chest. (For what it's worth, I was *dreaming* about excellent and lovely things.) But when I woke up, I only had fifteen minutes to shower and get ready for work.

I'm a miserable, pathetic excuse for a Christian, I thought as I shampooed my hair and slapped in some gel so it could dry on its own. *Good Christians get up early every day of the week to have their quiet time. Mom does. Karen does. I'm positive that Mary Jo does. And so do all those faithful women who speak in stadiums around the country. Don't they?*

I toweled off and looked up. "But Lord, what if you're just not a morning person?"

"Amy, I have a confession to make." I shot a surreptitious glance around Books 'n' Brew, making sure no one was in earshot. I was talking to my associate pastor's wife, who did double duty behind the pastry counter of Barley's only bookstore.

"I don't think I'm a very good Christian." I bit my lip. "I'm finding it really hard—actually impossible—to have a quiet time in the mornings."

She handed me my mocha and muffin. "So who says you have to?"

I gasped at such sacrilege. From a pastor's wife, no less.

"Well, all these books say it's best to start your day with the Lord in study and meditation on His Word. That's what all the leaders of the faith and the WOGs do."

"Wogs?"

"Women of God. You know, those strong women with strong faith—Bible study leaders, pastors' wives, my mom, Mary Jo . . . even my sister-in-law, who has five kids!"

"Guess I'm not a WOG then." Amy gave me a gentle smile. "Phoebe, God's not going to mind if you don't spend an hour every morning in quiet time."

"I can't even spend ten minutes, though," I wailed. "I keep falling asleep."

"So pick a different time of day. Me—I kind of move it around. Sometimes I may have my quiet time at four in the afternoon, sometimes I have it midmorning, and sometimes I have it at home while dinner's cooking." She leaned over the counter with a mischievous glint in her eye. "And some days I don't even have a quiet time at all. Sometimes I take a bike ride and just revel in the Lord's creation and praise Him in a meadow."

"Sounds like a *Brother Sun, Sister Moon* kind of thing you've got going there." The seventies-era Zeffirelli movie about Saint Francis of Assisi had had a lasting spiritual impact on me—that and *Chariots of Fire*, with its missionary Scotsman with the great accent, who ran like the wind.

Amy looked confused for just a minute, then laughed. "Oh, yes—I remember that one. We saw it on video when Jeff was in seminary. Beautiful film in a hippie-dippy kind of way—and I loved the part near the end where the pope kneeled before Francis to show his humility. But seriously, Phoebe. Our relationship with God doesn't have to be rigid and tied to a set of rules. In fact, it shouldn't be. That's why they call it grace. I mean—watch out!"

I had stood up to get another napkin, stumbled over my purse, which I'd set near my feet, and spilled my coffee, barely missing my Manolos.

"Well," I said, "I've never had a lot of grace." We giggled together as we mopped up the mess. Then, setting my muffin and purse on a table out of the way of my klutzy feet, I began browsing the racks of books. Bookstores are my second favorite kind of place in the world—right after movie theaters. And though I'm a rabid cinemaphile—very rabid, my family says, pointing to my frothing mouth whenever I talk about movies—I can even think of ways that a bookstore is *better* than a theater.

The movie's over after a couple of hours. A bookstore doesn't have such constraints. You can lose yourself in a good book and not come up for *days*!

Scanning the glossy jackets of the hardcover best sellers, my eyes were caught by the hot-pink, in-your-face cover of the latest offering from one of the hip, sarcastic, contemporary female authors I enjoy. I picked it up and read the back cover. Intrigued, I opened to the first page and was instantly hooked. But checking the price tag, I groaned. Too steep for my small-town reporter budget.

Next came the classics. I'm determined to read at least three a year to become more of a Renaissance woman. Since I began this higher literary quest on my thirtieth birthday, I've read *A Tale of Two Cities* (Can you say long? But such great beginning and ending lines.), *Pride and Prejudice* (If I was Elizabeth Bennett, I'd have smacked Mr. Darcy.), *Wuthering Heights* (I wonder if Heathcliff might have been bipolar?), and *Oliver Twist* (Whenever I eat oatmeal, I always want to say in a forlorn English accent, "Please sir, I want some more.").

My fingers trailed across the paperback classics, trying to decide what to read next: *Anna Karenina, The Brothers Karamazov, Jane Eyre, Moby Dick,* or *War and Peace.* Since I hadn't read any of the great Russian ones yet, I picked up *War and Peace.*

And nearly sprained my wrist in the process.

Note to self: Remember not to read books that can hurt you. And work out more so as to be able to lift heavy, important literature tomes.

In a more romantic, English frame of mind, I finally selected *Jane Eyre.* Although I'd seen part of one of the movie versions when I was younger—with George C. Scott and Susannah York—I'd fallen asleep partway through and never found out how it ended.

As usual, I quickly bypassed most of the nonfiction titles. I've always preferred to lose myself in a story rather than submit myself to a barrage of facts or nosy advice. I have to confess, however, to having bought one or two—or fifty—of those Christian dating or how-to-be-content-in-your-Christian-singleness-while-not-succumbing-to-lust books. But now that Alex and I were together—I cast a reassuring look down at my Manolos—I didn't feel the need for the how-to-be-content-without-a-man scenarios. And since my particular man was in a whole different country for who knew how long, steering clear of lust wasn't exactly an issue.

I sighed and headed to the counter to pay Amy and order another mocha to go with my muffin. On my way, I passed by the animals section and noticed a book on emus. Ugh. Thanks to a recent assignment at a nearby farm, I now know more about those distant cousins to the ostrich than I ever wanted to.

That's the one downside to my job.

I thought of my salary. Okay, *one* of the downsides. The way things were going this week, most of my *life* was a downside.

When I majored in journalism, I never dreamed I'd be writing about emus, pigs, goat roping, and pigeon racing. (Yes, pigeons race. And if you really want to know more about that sport, although I can't imagine why you would, Google it.) Loving *His Girl Friday, Teacher's Pet,* and *All the President's Men,* I'd always fantasized about being an investigative reporter going after a big scoop.

What I got was a job writing obits. Then I'd graduated to covering livestock . . . and craft fairs . . . and restaurant openings. And I was fast learning that politics wasn't really my thing either—at least not the small-town variety. You try attending water boards, school boards, and cemetery district board meetings on a regular basis and tell me they're not boring with a capital *B*.

What I really longed to write were movie reviews and "lifestyle" columns. The movie reviews I was already doing, though on a limited basis, and they were my favorite part of my job.

Next to seeing Alex every day, of course.

Which was *so* not happening at the moment.

Back home, I powered up my laptop and checked my messages. Nothing from the man I loved. Heavy sigh.

But wait, what was this?

> To: Movielovr
> From: Etraveler
>   Hi, Phoebe, I'm writing from an Internet café in Munich. How's Barley? I'd say I missed you all, but I'd be lying. Having too much fun. Although Millie, my traveling buddy, is about to drive me up the wall. She's the slowest person I've ever met. Never knew it took so long for a body to get ready in the mornings. The time she spends on her hair and makeup is enough for me to have finished my break-fast and then some. But aside from that, my trip's been WONDERFUL. Don't know why I waited all these years. Had some schnitzel with mushrooms—called Jaeger schnitzel—that just melted in my mouth. The country is beautiful. So clean. Tomorrow we're off to Austria. I'll think of you when I'm eating my Sacher torte.
>   Auf Wiedersehen, Esther

I tried not to be jealous of my globetrotting, seventy-something friend, but it was difficult. Of course, everything seemed difficult these days. Something to do with the man I adore being so far away, and now Esther too, while I was still stuck in Barley. Oh, and let's not forget my best friend grabbing the happily-ever-after engagement ring either . . .

Envious, much?

Sorry, God. Guess I really need those quiet times to help me with such unchristian attitudes as envy and resentment and discontent.

But the quiet times were difficult too!

Thinking back on my conversation with Amy, I decided I'd try an after-dinner quiet time. I closed my laptop, pulled out my devotional and Bible, and curled up in my chair to read. But I just couldn't con-centrate. After fiddling around for fifteen minutes, I finally gave up and flipped open my computer again.

Hooray! Finally, a reply from Alex.

To: Movielovr
From: Filmguy791
    Hi, Barley girl. Sorry to be so long getting back to you—things have been impossibly hectic here. I already knew about Phil and Lindsey. Phil e-mailed me to tell me he was going to propose.

What? How come Phil didn't tell me? We've been friends longer.

    Now don't go and get all in a huff that he didn't confide in you. Phil knew there was no way you'd be able to keep it from Lindsey—she'd have heard it in your voice. So he decided the info had to be classified FMO—for men only.
    Dad's doing better. Thanks for asking. Our colleague George is a huge help at the office. Delia, too. Don't know what we'd do without them.
    I miss you too, Phoebe. I miss everyone there in Barley. Every time a bell rings here, I think: An angel just got his wings, and somebody just opened the door at the Barley Bulletin.
    Must run, though—lots going on. Talk later.

I signed off the Net with a smile on my face. *Whenever a bell rings here*—he really was thinking of me. For a few minutes I lost myself in a dream of the time when we'd finally be together again. *I'll meet him at the airport, and he'll run when he sees me, and I'll finally get my kiss . . .*
    But the next minute my smile slipped a little.
    He forgot to say when he's coming home.

Two weeks later, Alex still hadn't said.
    He e-mailed often, but mostly about work-related stuff, letting

Gordon and me know he still needed to stay and help his Dad out with the business and entrusting us to keep the *Bulletin* running smoothly in his absence. Over time, his personal e-mails to me grew less and less personal and more and more brief. He was always having to rush off to a meeting or family event or something.

But I understood. Or tried to. After all, Alex was a busy, important executive with a major newspaper empire to handle. He didn't need selfish, neurotic me hanging on his every e-mail. Right?

The trouble was, *Lindsey* was e-mailing me daily. Several times a day, in fact. And she was driving me crazy.

> To: Movielovr
> From: LinsRog
>   Hey maid of honor, what do you think would be better for the reception—a sit-down dinner or hors d'oeuvres?

I'd give her my two cents:

> To: LinsRog
> From: Movielovr
>   Depends on how many people you're planning to invite. Dinner can get pretty expensive per plate. So you've decided definitely on an evening wedding then?

But by then she'd have moved on to something else.

> To: Movielovr
> From: LinsRog
>   I'm thinking of going with magnets with our name and wedding date on them *and* bubbles for the wedding favors. They have these cute little bubble containers in the shape of two hearts. What do you think?

Before I'd even have a chance to respond to that, another e-mail would arrive:

To: Movielovr
From: LinsRog
  Definitely going with the bubbles. But I saw the coolest favor on this celebrity wedding special recently—cookies with a picture of the bride and groom on the frosting for each guest! (That way you could bite Phil's head off and not get in trouble.☺)

I'd like to bite your head off.
Bad maid of honor, bad, my best-friend self said.
I can't help it, my distressingly single, boyfriend-across-the-ocean self whined.

If Lindsey didn't e-mail, she'd call. About more wedding stuff. Often she'd call and e-mail the same day. Every conversation, every e-mail, every single word out of her mouth revolved around the wedding—which just served to highlight all the more dramatically how unengaged *I* was.

But the day my best friend took the wedding cake was when she told me she'd be doing the traditional bouquet toss.

I couldn't believe it. Whenever we'd attended weddings together—and we'd attended a *lot* of them, usually of couples who'd met at Lone Rangers—she and I had always escaped to the ladies' room when it came time for the ritual throwing of the bouquet. No way were we going to be a part of the pack of desperate, shoving single women all elbowing each other to participate in the passing of the floral bridal torch.

Now Lindsey had bought into it! It made no sense. The only thing I could figure was that she'd had a wedding lobotomy. I'd done my best to share in all her bridal excitement, but after several weeks of nonstop wedding discussions, I was a little weddinged out.

And tired of my job.

And missing Alex.

And envying Esther.

And still not doing so great with quiet times . . . at *any* time of day.

To be honest, January was not turning out to be my best month ever.

But then something happened that drove even my own misery out of my mind.

chapter five

Straight on 'til Morning

i 'd stopped by Mom's on my way home from work to show her a postcard Esther had sent me from Italy:

Hey Phoebe,

The Sistine Chapel is one of the most beautiful sights I've ever seen. You can't believe the colors! Glorious. Such reverence. Also saw the Pietà. Brought me to my arthritic knees. If man can create such glory, how can there not be a Creator who created man? I said that to one of the purple ladies who doesn't believe. Got her to thinking. Next stop, party time in the City of Lights! After that, London and you know what. Can't wait! (I'm going to make one of those stiff-upper-lipped English guards crack a smile if it's the last thing I do.)

Ciao from Esther, the old world traveler

I tapped the postcard on the kitchen counter and grinned. "Do you realize Esther's seen more in the past couple of weeks than either of us have seen in our entire lives?"

"I know. And at her age too. Puts us to shame, daughter."

There were times I was sure my Mom was part Amish. Or at least stuck in a fifties domestic time warp that her mom had placed her in. Not that she had ever done the Donna Reed thing with housedresses, heels, and pearls. Denim jumpers and hippie-type moccasins had been more her style—and for years, a long gray braid down the middle of her back.

That had changed about four months ago. After a very emotional letting-down-our-hair time that had brought us closer together, I'd talked her into updating her look and treated her to a makeover at Sylvia Ann's beauty shop, The Bobby Pin.

Now she looked more like Liz Taylor in those perfume ads. Except for the diamonds, of course. And the fact that she can cook circles around anyone in town. And her strange little Amish-like turns of phrase—like calling her only daughter "daughter."

Mom put the kettle on. "One thing's for sure, England will never be the same once Esther's through with it. If anyone can get one of those reserved English redcoats to smile, it's her."

"Hope she doesn't pinch him, though."

"What in the world are you talking about, daughter?"

We were still chuckling over my explanation when Gordon's car pulled into the driveway. Mom opened the back door for him, giggling. "Well this is a nice sur—"

She stopped short. Gordon's expression was bleak. "What is it? What's wrong?"

"It's Esther. She—she—" He gripped my mother's arm. "She's dead."

"What?" I felt the color drain from my face, and I jumped to my feet. "That can't be. I just got a postcard from her today."

"I'm sorry, Phoebe. Alex just called. Esther died last night in her sleep in London." He rubbed a shaky hand over his eyes.

Mom hugged him, but I stared in disbelief. "But how . . ."

Gordon wiped his eyes. "Her roommate, Millie, said Esther was usually the first one up in the morning, already showered and dressed and ready to go down to breakfast before she'd even gotten out of bed. But this morning when she woke up, Esther was still sleeping. But they'd gotten to bed late the night before, so Millie just figured Esther needed her sleep. She went ahead and took the first shower, but Esther was still in bed when she came out of the bathroom. Millie went to wake her and couldn't . . ."

Mom laid her hand gently on Gordon's arm, her eyes bright with tears. "How did Alex find out?"

"Esther had told Millie she was going to look him up while she was in town. She had his card in her purse, so Millie, who was naturally quite upset, gave the card to the hotel manager, who called Alex." Gordon wiped his eyes again. "And Alex called me. They think she had a stroke and just passed away peacefully in her sleep."

"Well, I'm glad she didn't suffer." Mom handed Gordon my postcard. "And that she was doing something she loved." She glanced at me. "Daughter, are you all right?"

I just shook my head. I could hear them both talking, but I still couldn't believe what they were saying.

Gordon fumbled in his pocket. "I got a postcard today too. From Paris." He handed the card to Mom and she read it aloud.

Bonjour former boss,

Hey, these Frenchies sure know how to kick up their heels! Ooh la la! Millie and I had a grand time checking out the Eiffel Tower and the Champs Élysées. The food's great. Eating lots of croissants and crepes. They have crepe stands the way we have hot-dog ones. Even tried snails! (They call it escargot.) I'm going to come home so fat and sassy you won't recognize me.

Au revoir, Esther

P.S. The Louvre is amazing, but I sure don't get what the big deal is about the Mona Lisa.

Gordon's downcast mouth curved into a fleeting smile. "That's Esther. Always calling it like she sees—saw it."

"She did that, all right." Mom gave him a small smile and patted his hand.

"But . . ." I still couldn't wrap my head around it. I looked at the calendar on the kitchen wall. "She was coming home in three days. I was looking forward to hearing about all her adventures."

Mom hugged me tight. "She's already home, honey."

I picked up my postcard again and stared at Esther's handwriting, imagining her writing the words.

"Something else Millie told Alex," said Gordon. "I can't quite figure it out, though. Seems the tour group had arrived in London last night, passing by Big Ben. As they drove past the illuminated clock, Esther murmured, 'Second star to the right and straight on 'til morning.'"

Mom looked puzzled, but I smiled through glistening eyes. "It's from *Peter Pan*. That's what Peter said when he flew Wendy off to Neverland. In the Disney movie, they flew right past Big Ben."

Alex took care of all the arrangements in London, and two days later, Millie flew home with Esther's body. Gordon wrote up a beautiful front-page obituary on his long-time friend and former employee, and the Bijou Theater board decided to mount a plaque in her honor. If not for Esther's financial rescue, after all, the theater would have been torn down.

There was a lovely service at the Methodist church where Esther had been a lifelong member—two pews on the right were filled with purple-clad ladies in red hats—and Gordon, who hadn't been all that at home in a church until recently, delivered the eulogy. He ended by saying, "Don't feel bad that Esther died so far from home. She was where she wanted to be—and having the time of her life. Besides"— he glanced at Mom—"as a dear friend reminded me, actually she *is* home." He coughed and blinked. "Second star to the right and straight on 'til morning. See you in the morning, Esther."

A week after the funeral, I'd just finished writing my latest movie preview for Wednesday's Black-and-White Night at the Bijou. They were showing one of Esther's favorites and mine, *Mrs. Miniver*, the poignant World War II story about the impact of the war on one English family and town. Greer Garson had won a well-deserved Academy Award in the title role.

Gordon was out on an interview, so I had the office to myself. Turning over the delicate snow globe from the Alps that Millie had delivered to me as a final gift from Esther, I cranked the key. The lilting strains of "Edelweiss" tinkled in the office air. As I watched the fake snow fall, I thought of Austria and all the places Esther had seen. Then I thought of Esther and her Norman and how they were now reunited—even though she never got a chance to visit his memorial.

Much better than thinking about the article I was supposed to be writing about Bobby Randolph's pet guinea pig.

The phone rang. "Phoebe Grant."

"Hey Pheebs, remember that woman with the spiky platinum hair who wrote a book in the nineties called *Stop the Insanity?* You don't happen to have a copy I could give my fiancé, do you?"

"Phillie, that book was about fitness and weight loss."

"I don't care," he grumbled. "I don't know how else to get through to her. Lindsey's in this weird wedding zone. That's all she thinks about *all* the time. And all she talks about. It's driving me crazy. What do I care what color the tablecloths are?"

"You have to understand." I smiled into the phone. "Most women dream of this day their whole lives. When we're little, we put pillowcase veils on our heads and Mom's high heels on our feet to walk across the backyard to our waiting groom—usually our brother—with grubby dandelions clutched in our hands." I turned the snow globe over again. "Besides, you know how Lins likes to plan parties and events. This is the biggest event of her life, and she wants it absolutely perfect."

"I know." He groaned. "But she's gone off the deep end. You've got to talk to her, get her to chill out. She's like Bridezilla or something. I'm telling you, at this point a Las Vegas wedding chapel is looking mighty appealing—with an Elvis impersonator to perform the ceremony."

"Don't even go there. I can't handle those muttonchop sideburns on a man." I sighed. "Okay, I'll try and talk to her, but I can't make any promises."

"Thanks, Pheebs. I owe ya. So how's the job going?" He chuckled. "Still writing about emus?"

"Today it's guinea pigs."

"That crocodile-hunter guy has nothing on you."

"Nothing except he lives in Australia, loves animals, and makes the big bucks. And I'm stuck in Barley, am so not an animal person, and I don't earn squat."

"I thought you had a cat."

"The kids gave me a kitten. And he's growing on me—although he prefers the big outdoors to my little apartment. But I'm still not likely to have my own show on Animal Planet anytime soon."

"Hey, I hear ya," said Phil, then cleared his throat. "So . . . how'd you like to ditch the small town, earn three times what the *Bulletin's* paying you, and never have to write about emus or rodents ever again?"

"And how'd you like to get a Jag for your birthday?" I toyed with the snow globe. "Ain't gonna happen, Phillie."

"What happened to the dreamer friend I know and love? Never say *ain't*, Pheebs. Aside from the obvious fact that it's bad grammar, that word shouldn't even be in your vocabulary." He paused. "I'm offering you a job."

"Say what?" I almost dropped the glass globe.

"You heard me. And I promise you, there are no animals involved." He snickered. "Although some of the guys can get pretty wild when they close a new deal. C'mon Pheebs, whaddya say? Come be the PR director of my company."

I stared at the phone. "But it's an investment firm." A *Gone with the Wind* scene flashed before my eyes. "I don't know nothin' 'bout no investment wheeling and dealing, Mr. Hansen." I shook my head.

"You know I'm no good with numbers—that's why Lins always had to help me balance my checkbook."

"Not a problem. We've got folks to take care of the numbers side of things. You just have to write it up and make it sound good to attract some high-end clients." Phil dangled the security carrot. "We provide a full benefits package, complete with dental, vision, 401K, and stock options." He zeroed in for the kill. "And remember, Pheebs; there are more restaurants and theaters in one downtown Cleveland block than in all of Barley." He paused. "And stores."

Visions of movie theaters and shoe stores filled my head.

To live and work once more in a city where I can see first-run movies, attend film festivals, have my choice of ethnic restaurants and stores. So many stores. Bliss.

Phil lobbed the friendship guilt grenade. "Please come home, Pheebs. I really need you. *Lins* needs you."

"But I already have a job."

He snorted. "A job you really don't like that doesn't pay anything."

He had a point there. *But my family's here. This is where I belong, isn't it? That's why I came back here in the first place. Besides, Alex will be back any day now, and things will really start moving with us then . . .*

I told Phil I'd consider his job offer—that whole friendship thing and all—although I really didn't think I'd accept. I mean, come on. Me? Writing about budgets and investments?

Nearly as bad as emus.

Sure, the money was good. Really good. But money isn't everything. I wouldn't want to leave Gordon in the lurch. Besides, no journalist worth her five-*W*s-and-an-*H* news training would ever consider becoming a public-relations flack.

After hanging up, remembering my promise to Phil, I called Lins.

"Did you say yes?"

"Huh?"

"To Phil's job offer." Lindsey bubbled over with excitement. "It will be just like before, Pheebs. Except of course for the rock on my finger." She giggled. "You can return to the city life you love so much and all the friends who love you *and* make great money in the process. How cool is that?"

"Well—"

She plowed ahead. "You only left Cleveland in the first place because you lost your job, right? But now you'll have an even better one—and still get to write!" Lins giggled again. "And as an added bonus, you'd be able to do the maid-of-honor thing up close and personal, which will help take some of the pressure off Phil."

Would you like a side of fries with that emotional blackmail?

"Speaking of Phil and pressure . . ." I gently tried to convince my best friend to cool it with the wedding obsession. But all my running interference for the groom did was get the bride mad at me.

Note to self: Kill Phil. Then call Dr. Phil.

After dinner that night, I climbed up to the top of my beautifully reorganized closet and pulled down all my No More Lone Ranger scrapbooks.

There were me and Lindsey dressed up in poodle skirts and bobby socks at the fifties sock hop we'd organized. And there we were in costume again—this time in hoop skirts doing a Southern belles skit at the singles retreat—and in soaking jeans and sweatshirts at the carwash fundraiser, dressed to the nines for opening night at the ballet, painting sets for the Christmas play, gabbing at Starbucks, working out at the gym . . .

The gym. Eew. How'd that photo ever see the light of day?

Lindsey of course looked cute as always, her petite little self in a sports bra and a pair of bike shorts, but my thighs in Spandex was not a sight I want the whole world to see. I wasn't too wild about seeing them myself.

Rip.

We sure did have a lot of fun together. And would again. Probably. I miss those days. Maybe I should give serious thought to Phil's job offer after all.

I turned the page and my heart clutched.

Alex. His first time at Lone Rangers.

I remembered everything about that night.

He wore black.

I wore red.

He ate Doritos.

I munched on pretzels.

I knew movie trivia and he matched me film for film, star for star. We played Trivial Pursuit together and wiped everyone else, including Phil, off the board.

That's when I knew we were destined to be together.

I sighed. How could I ever leave Barley and Alex?

Uh, Alex isn't exactly here right now, my bratty stop-and-face-reality self reminded me. *Hasn't been for a while.*

But I wasn't a *Gone with the Wind* devotee for nothing.

Ah won't think about that right now. Ah'll think about that tomorrow.

[chapter six]

The St. Valentine's Day Massacre

Valentine's Day found me moping around the office the same way I did every year on that stupid romantic holiday.

"If it were up to me, I'd banish this barbaric date from the calendar," I fumed to Gordon. "All it does is make single, dateless women everywhere feel like a bunch of junior-high-school wallflowers all over again. Even my beautiful niece Ashley is a basket case, wondering if this guy at school she has a crush on will give her a card. If he doesn't, she'll be crushed."

I was really on a roll now. "Did you know that these days boys are even having flowers delivered to their girlfriends at school? Right to the classroom! Guess how that makes the rest of the girls feel? Can you say Loser with a capital *L*?"

Gordon was looking around for an escape route.

But I was just getting started.

"It becomes this big competition: *My* boyfriend-slash-sweetheart-slash-fiancé-slash-husband loves me more than *yours* . . . Look what he sent." I ran my hand through my hair and scowled. "When I worked at the *Star,* there were always a few women who got huge bouquets of roses, balloons, or boxes of Godiva chocolates—sometimes all three. Sometimes even jewelry! While the rest of us sat at our flowerless desks feeling like a bunch of losers."

I paced the floor. "A couple of us talked about sending each *other*

68

flowers—under false names, of course—just so we wouldn't look like unwanted, unlovable spinsters. How pathetic is that?"

"So did you?"

"Send the flowers? Nah. Couldn't afford it. Did you know that a dozen roses costs close to seventy-five bucks?"

Gordon blushed. "Actually, it's even a little more than that now."

Pausing in midrant to say "Awww" and bestow a brilliant smile on my boss for treating my mother right, I picked up right where I'd left off. "Valentine's Day is just another overhyped, overcommercialized holiday ploy created by florists and greeting-card manufacturers to earn big—"

The *Bulletin's* front door burst open to reveal an armful of daffodils above a T-shirt and jeans. "Phoebe Grant?" a muffled feminine voice said from beneath the sunny mass.

"You might as well just turn around and take that bouquet right back to the flower shop," Gordon instructed the florist delivery girl from Lodi, "or keep it yourself. Ms. Grant doesn't believe in this over-commercialized holiday."

The flowers inched down to reveal a perplexed pair of hazel eyes.

"Don't pay any attention to that crotchety old man," I said. "He thinks he's a comedian." I waved her over. "You can just bring those right over here. Thanks."

The delivery girl left with a backward bewildered glance.

A goofy grin spread across my face. And I couldn't help belting out the song that popped into my head—except it was *today* the sun had come out, not tomorrow.

Today was the first time a guy had ever sent me flowers on Valentine's Day. (My relationships always seemed to end at some point before February 14.) Unless you counted the single white rose my dad always used to give me as his "second-best girl" so I wouldn't feel left out when Mom got her bouquet of two dozen pink tulips. Dad had always said it was a cliché to send red roses to a sweetheart on Valentine's Day. Any man could do that. But his and Mom's love was so special; it called for a special flower. So every year he'd sent pink tulips instead.

And now, on this fourteenth of February, I got special flowers too. Daffodils.

Gordon's eyebrows knit into a frown as he gazed at my bouquet. "I thought roses were the flower of choice on Valentine's Day."

"Depends." I searched for the card, then glanced over and saw his eyebrows still knit together. "Gordon, Mom loves yellow roses. Don't worry." I grinned again, looking at my happy daffs. "Women love it when men send them flowers. It's an extravagant gesture that makes them feel special and appreciated."

Finally found the card. "Phoebe, hope this host of golden daffodils brightens a dismal February morning. Happy Valentine's Day. Fondly, Alex."

"Fondly?" And I was off again. "You men!" I shot daggers at Gordon. "So afraid to say the L-word. I don't think absence is making Alex's heart grow any fonder, to tell the truth. I think it's making it grow distant and forgetful."

Gordon peered over his bifocals. "And that's why he sent you flowers. Because he's feeling distant and forgetful." He cleared his throat. "Phoebe, I think it's time you took a vacation. Things are slow here. Why not take a little time off, get away from everything for a while?" He tapped his pen on the desk. "I hear they've got really cheap flights overseas right now."

My head snapped up. "What are you talking about?"

"I noticed in the *Chronicle* yesterday that they have some round-trip flights from San Francisco to London for just a couple hundred dollars."

"You think I should go see Alex?" I stared at him. "I'd love to, but I thought men hated it when women chased after them."

"Who said anything about chasing?" Gordon slid me an innocent look. "Haven't you always wanted to go to Europe? Seems like I remember someone way back in their high-school days who was deter-

70

mined to see the world—so much so in fact, that she up and joined the air force right after graduation."

"Yeah. And the farthest I got was Cleveland."

"Well, here's your chance to change that. You've got a passport, haven't you?"

"Uh-huh. A blank one that never gets used."

"So put it to use. Give it a workout. Like our friend Esther did." He gave me a gentle smile. "Life's short, you know."

"But what about the paper? With Alex gone, and now me . . ."

Gordon scratched the nicotine patch on his upper arm. "Esther and I ran the *Bulletin* by ourselves for thirty years without any problems. I think I can manage for a few weeks without you." He squinted at me over his bifocals. "Besides, young Ryan Moore wants to get some newspaper experience before he goes off to college, so I thought we could do a little internship like you did back in high school."

He gazed thoughtfully out the front plate-glass window. "Don't you tell your mama I said this, but sometimes you've just got to go after what you want. If you don't, you might lose your chance. Or someone else might get there before you do."

All right. Now I understood. Gordon had been sweet on my mother for years. She first caught his eye her senior year in high school. But he was nearly ten years older, and she was too young, so he'd bided his time and waited. Unfortunately, he had waited just a little too long. My father had come to town the summer after Mom graduated from high school. And once they met, no one else had stood a chance.

Do I want to wait around and take the chance of someone else swooping in and stealing Alex from me?

"What's that Latin saying—*carpe diem?*" Gordon was saying. "Well, I think you need to carpe your diem over to England posthaste, young lady. And if you have time, maybe you can even squeeze in a quick trip to Paris while you're there. They've got that Chunnel now; you can go right under the English Channel." He sighed and leaned

71

back in his chair. "But if you go to Paris, you need to make sure and have a drink in Harry's Bar for me. That was one of Hemingway's favorite haunts."

Ernest Hemingway was one of Gordon's favorite authors. I remembered Esther mentioning Hemingway too, when she talked about her European adventure. And Hemingway wrote *To Have and Have Not*, which was made into the movie where Bogart and Bacall fell in love. And *For Whom the Bell Tolls*—that great scene where Gary Cooper gives Ingrid Bergman's character her first kiss . . .

Is this a sign, Lord? Telling me Alex is the one and you don't want me to lose him?

A Yodalike voice sounded in my head: *It's not all about Alex. The journey is what's important.* And Esther's words replayed in my head like an old summer rerun: "Don't wait as long as I did. Enjoy these things while you're still young."

"Gordon, do you still have yesterday's *Chron*?"

Sure enough. There it was in black and white: supercheap airfares to London. Cheaper than flying to Cleveland, as a matter of fact. Definitely affordable. "But what about hotels? I hear London's pretty expensive."

"He—I mean, heck, you could just stay with Alex," Gordon said. "Then it would be free. I'll bet he has plenty of room."

I raised my chaste good-girl eyebrows at him. "Uh, I think it'd be better to just find an inexpensive hotel. Besides, if I go—and that's a big if—I want to surprise him."

"Well, you're a journalist. You know how to research." He gestured to my computer. "I'll bet if you go online you could find some reasonable places to stay."

"True." I snapped my fingers. "And if I have someone go *with* me, that would cut the lodging cost in half." I beamed. "Lindsey and I can finally do our European grand tour like we've always wanted! At least to London. Maybe Paris too." A satin-and-lace thought intruded. "I wonder if I can get her to forget about the wedding for a while and come along?"

72

"Don't know unless you ask. So call her already."

Bouncing off the four walls I was soon to leave behind, I punched in my best friend's work number, glad she'd gotten over being mad at me.

"Lindsey Rogers," she chirped in her professional but perky human resources voice.

"Hey, Lins, have I got a deal for you. How'd you like to—"

"Oh Pheebs, I'm so glad you called," she interrupted. "I was just looking at the latest *Bride's* magazine, and they have all these great bridesmaid dresses, but I'm having a really hard time deciding between the floor-length navy or the tea-length silver."

"I thought you were going with classic black?"

"I was, but now I'm wondering if that might be too austere. My mother, of course, thinks so; she wants me to go with all these boring pastels . . ."

"Hold that pastel thought. And hold on to your veil too, while you're at it. I have something exciting to tell you." I grinned into the phone. "Are you sitting down?"

"Yep. Usually do at work. So what's up?" She gave an excited gasp. "Please tell me you've decided to accept Phil's job offer and you're moving back home soon!"

"Uh, well, I'm still praying about that, but that's not why I called, Lins. You see—"

"Oh. Well then, please, please tell me you found the perfect wedding headpiece in San Francisco. I can't find diddly here."

Down, wedding girl, down.

"Even better. How would you like to be Thelma to my Louise— without the guns of course." I paused for effect. "Only go to *London*. And maybe even *Paris* with me?"

"What? What are you talking about?" Lindsey giggled. "Did you win the lottery or something?"

"I think you actually have to buy a lottery ticket to do that."

A muffled snort sounded across the miles. "So when were you thinking of doing this Thelma-and-Louise trip?"

"I'm not exactly sure yet, but it would probably have to be within the next few weeks to take advantage of this great airfare deal that's going on right now."

Lindsey gave an incredulous laugh. "You've got to be kidding. There's no way I could go anywhere right now. I have too much to do to prepare for the wedding."

"But that's not 'til late September." I counted on my fingers. "Seven months."

"I know. But there's a million and one details to take care of. You have no *idea*."

"Actually, I do." *I've only been hearing about every one of them non-stop for the past month and a half already.*

"Lins, we've always talked about how we want to go to Europe together. Here's our chance." Another idea struck. "It could be our last hurrah before you get hitched. Sort of an early bachelorette party! What do you say? Bet you'd be the only bride on your Cleveland block who shops for wedding favors and bridesmaid gifts in London."

She sighed. "I'm sorry, Pheebs. Much as I'd love to, I just can't. I have way too much to do. Plus we're using all our vacation time *and* money for the wedding and honeymoon. My parents are paying for a lot, but I am thirty, after all. Since I've been living on my own for ages, I can't expect them to cough it all up—especially since Phil and I both have good jobs. Besides . . ." She lowered her voice. "You know me. I've always been a champagne girl, and I'm not about to settle for a beer budget at my wedding. I'm only getting married once, and I want to pull out all the stops."

You're definitely doing that. I slumped in my chair. "Okay. Sure. I understand. Maybe another time."

Yeah, right. Like after she's married? You can kiss your girl time good-bye then. Note to self: Remember not to become so wedding obsessed when I get engaged—if it ever happens—that I alienate best friends and everyone else in my life.

In the background I could hear the ringing of another phone. "Sorry, Pheebs, I have to run. That's the wedding planner on my other line, and we have to talk about flowers. I'll talk to you soon, maid of honor! Love ya. 'Bye."

No problem. But next time why not just use a chainsaw to pop that balloon?

"Where's my best friend, and what have you done with her?" I muttered as I hung up. "It's like *Invasion of the Stepford Wedding Snatchers* or something . . ."

chapter seven

Chicks on the Road

"You're right," Gordon said, ignoring my glum face. "London's pretty expensive, but I've found a few places online that are a lot cheaper and 'just a twenty-minute train ride away' from town."

"Train?" My best-friend depression lifted at the magic word.

The smoke swirled about us, and the train whistle blew as we clung to one another, unwilling to say good-bye . . . Alex cupped my face between his strong yet gentle hands and kissed me tenderly. As the train pulled out of the station, my beloved ran in slow motion outside my compartment, his leather bomber jacket flapping in the breeze . . .

"Phoebe?"

"Sorry." I looked over Gordon's shoulder and read aloud. "Twenty minutes to the heart of London: Big Ben, Buckingham Palace, Westminster Abbey, and West End theaters. Wow! To see plays on London's Broadway. How cool is that?" I sighed. "But it won't be as much fun to go alone."

I sent up a quick prayer asking God if this was such a good idea. And if so, if it wasn't too much trouble, could he please maybe send me a traveling companion?

The bell over the front door jangled.

"Mary Jo!" I leapt out of my chair and enveloped my friend in a bone-crushing embrace. "You're an answer to prayer."

"What? The chocoholics prayer?" She disentangled herself from my suffocating clutch and held up a bag. "How'd you know I'd be bringing Valentine's truffle brownies from your mom? She stopped by to watch Elizabeth's lesson and asked me to drop them off." Mary Jo licked her lips. "Said I could have one too if I delivered them, so I stopped at Books 'n' Brew on the way and picked up some mochas to go along with them."

I waved off the chocolate. "Do you have a passport?"

Her eyebrows raised at my cavalier chocolate dismissal. "Yes. From when I went on a mission trip to Guatemala two years ago." She shot me a suspicious look. "Why?"

"How'd you like to go to *England*?"

Mary Jo looked at Gordon, and then glanced over at the mass of daffodils on my desk. "I think those flowers must have gone to your head or something. They from Alex?"

"No—I mean yes—look!" I thrust the newspaper at her. "They've got super low fares to London right now. Otherwise I couldn't afford it. Would you go with me? We'd have a blast!"

Her eyes slid from a beaming Gordon to me. "You're going over to see Alex, aren't you?"

"No." I met her penetrating gaze, but couldn't maintain it. "Okay, partly. But I'm also seizing the day. Carpe diem and all that. Remember *Dead Poets Society*?" She looked blank, so I added, glancing at Gordon, "I'm taking a page from Esther's book. She encouraged me to travel while I was still young and not to wait like she did. Besides," I added softly, "there's something I need to finish for her."

Gordon gave me a puzzled glance, but Mary Jo tilted her head. Was she actually considering?

"Well, if it's for Esther, that's a different—"

"Yippee!" I jumped up and down and moved to hug her again.

She held up her hand. "I haven't said yes yet. I'm not that crazy about flying."

"No problem. We'll just get you a couple of Xanax for the trip."

Gordon and Mary Jo both raised their eyebrows.

"What? I learned that from an old air-force friend who was afraid to fly."

Their eyebrows raised higher.

"Never mind. Here's what you do. Go to your doctor, tell him how anxious you are about flying and he'll prescribe you a limited number of pills just for the flights."

"You had me worried there for a minute, Pheebs. Thought there was this whole secret life you were keeping from us," Mary Jo teased. Then she frowned. "You do realize it's cold over there, don't you? Most people wouldn't go to England in the winter. They'd go to Hawaii or Florida. Somewhere warm."

"March isn't winter. It's spring. And we won't be outside all that much. We'll be inside cathedrals and theaters and museums and restaurants." I put my hands on my hips. "Besides, when was the last time you had a vacation?"

"Christmas—when I drove down to San Diego and saw my sister and her family."

"That doesn't count. I'm talking a single-girl vacation. You know, like *Thelma and Louise* . . ."

"Without the guns," Gordon parroted wryly.

". . . with fun, adventure, excitement, and . . ." I saved my best zinger for last, "lots of history."

Mary Jo had been a history minor in college.

Her eyes brightened. "I *have* always wanted to go to The British Museum. Did you know that's where the Rosetta Stone is? And I'd love to see some of the cathedrals, especially Westminster Abbey and St. Paul's."

"Don't forget Abbey Road."

She began to salivate. Beatles fan Mary Jo had all their music on CD and even a few original record albums displayed in her den. "Let's do it! Where do we start? Should we use the same tour company that Esther did?"

"Nah, that was pretty much geared for seniors. Besides, we don't want to get locked into someone else's schedule. Let's be adventurous and just do what we want, *when* we want."

You know who you really *want—*

All right, enough already, I told my nagging voice of moral reason. *Besides, he sent me flowers.*

Books 'n' Brew was empty when we arrived. Except for a huge bucket of wildflowers on the counter.

"Hel-lo. Anyone here?"

A red-faced Amy appeared from the back room, followed by our grinning Pastor Jeff wiping some lipstick off his mouth.

"Okay you two, get a room. You'd think you were newlyweds or something," I grinned. "But before you check in, can you recommend some good travel books . . . on *England*?" I could barely stand still from the excitement. "Mary Jo and I are going to London on vacation!"

The couple exchanged a look. "How cool!" Amy said. "When?"

"Probably within the next three to four weeks. That's why we're here. We want to do some research before booking our flight. The only thing we know is that we don't want to do a tour."

"Definitely not," Jeff agreed. "On a tour they just rush you from one tourist spot to another and you don't get to wander around and discover things on your own. What you girls need is one of these budget guidebooks that will take you off the beaten track." He pulled out a green-and-gold paperback and handed it to Mary Jo. "And make sure you don't limit your visit to London only. It's one of the great cities of the world, but England has some beautiful countryside too." He exchanged another look with his wife. "Um, Phoebe, does this trip have anything to do with Alex?"

Mary Jo shook her head as she flipped through the guidebook. "Already been down that road. And Phoebe's admitted she's looking forward to seeing him again, but basically we're doing this Thelma and

Louise carpe diem thing . . ." All of a sudden she gasped. "Check it out. The British Library has copies of original Beatles lyrics!"

Within the hour we booked our tickets and our hotel.

I decided to tell my family at Sunday afternoon dinner with the whole family gathered around, but I waited until dessert, when we were all enjoying Mom's pineapple upside-down cake.

Clearing my throat, I glanced across the table at Gordon, who gave me a slight nod. "Hey everyone, wanted to let you know I'll be going on a little vacation soon."

"That's great, dear." Mom passed Gordon another slice of cake. "Are you going back to Cleveland so you and Lindsey can work on wedding plans together?"

Incoming! Watch out. Friendship guilt, friendship guilt.

"No. She doesn't need me this soon. Actually, I'm going to . . ." I made the sound of a drum roll on the table with my hands, *"London! With Mary Jo. For two weeks."*

"What?" Ashley squealed.

"London—as in England?" Elizabeth asked.

"Yep." I smiled. "Gordon turned me on to some cheap flights he saw in the *Chron,* and Mary Jo and I jumped at the chance."

Everyone peppered me with questions while Mom gave Gordon a thoughtful look.

Later, after he had left and all the kids were watching a video, Mom looked at me across the dining room table, a worried frown puckering her forehead. "Men don't like to be chased, dear," she said gently.

"I'm not chasing. I'm seizing the opportunity to go to Europe, just like Esther did." I examined my nails. "Getting to see Alex is just an added bonus."

Careful. Breaking one of those Ten Commandments now.

I'm not lying, I assured my Sunday-school conscience. *I've always wanted to go to Europe. Besides, I need to complete Esther's unfinished mission.*

Interesting timing, though.

So I'm killing a few birds with one stone. Shut up, already.

Jordy shared Mom's concern. "Pheebert, if you want a little brotherly advice . . ." (My big brother had given me that nickname when we were little and I was enraptured with Bert and Ernie on *Sesame Street.* He was the *only* one allowed to call me that.)

"I don't." I gave him a warm smile. "But thanks for caring. Don't worry," I added. "I'm a big girl. I know what I'm doing."

In preparation for our English adventure, I tore through my closet, trying to put together a wardrobe that would befit the cosmopolitan world capital we would soon be visiting, yet also retain my own California-girl stamp of individuality.

Clearly I'd have to do a little shopping.

I invited Mary Jo to come along when I went to the Sacramento malls, but she said she had all the clothes she needed.

That's what I'm afraid of. Mary Jo is a fabulous person, great singer, good Christian, and an inspiration to all. But a clotheshorse she's not.

"Besides, Pheebs, can you really afford a shopping trip?" my frugal friend asked. "I thought one of your New Year's resolutions was to be more careful with finances . . ."

Yes, but you don't have to remind me of that now, thank you very much. Besides, that was before I knew I'd be going to England! Plastic was invented for such a time as this.

". . . and I don't think Alex would care whether you have new clothes or not," she continued, rubbing her dusty, scuffed boot on the back of her faded cords.

It was times like these that I really missed Lindsey.

More a froufrou, girly-type girl like me, she understood the importance of clothing, especially in the mating-dance ritual.

I ended up taking Ashley shopping with me instead. She might be fourteen—but *that* girl can shop!

Although I couldn't talk Mary Jo into shopping, she did consent to come over and watch all my English-setting DVDs as part of our pretrip preparations: *Sense and Sensibility, Emma, Persuasion, Howard's End, Shakespeare in Love, Notting Hill,* plus a couple of recent Shakespeare adaptations. And my latest acquisition, *Calendar Girls,* based on an actual group of middle-aged women in Yorkshire who posed nude for a fundraising calendar.

When the credits rolled after that one, Mary Jo set down her microwave popcorn and snorted. "I'm not taking off my clothes for any cause, no matter how noble it is."

"Me either. Not to worry, MJ."

I'd begun calling Mary Jo "MJ" lately. For one thing, it's shorter, which is what I told her. But it's also a little more hip and European sounding than Mary Jo—which I didn't tell her.

Mary Jo—I mean MJ—in turn made me watch *Becket, Anne of the Thousand Days, A Man for All Seasons,* and the more recent *Elizabeth,* with Cate Blanchett, so I'd have at least a vague historical awareness of this land of kings and queens we'd be visiting. Actually, I didn't mind. Those all turned out to be great films. But I was mystified when she started rereading a bunch of books by some English country vet-turned-author that she loved but I'd never heard of.

"Exactly who is this James Herriot guy?" I asked, picking up one of her well-worn paperbacks and thumbing through it.

MJ gave me an incredulous look. "Only the greatest writer of animal stories ever." She smiled a little shyly. "He's kind of my hero."

To educate me, she insisted I watch her DVD collection of the BBC series, *All Creatures Great and Small.* I found it charming . . . but a little too realistic. "Eew, what's he doing to that cow?"

"Checking the position of her calf. Isn't that cool?"

Remember. You'll be mostly in London. Theaters, galleries, shopping. No four-footed creatures.

I looked over at my shoe hive, where my Manolos ruled proudly. *Focus on the boots. Focus on the boots.*

I hadn't had a medical checkup in a while, so I'd decided it might be a good idea to have one before we headed over to Merrie Olde—although the real reason was to keep a nervous MJ company when she went in to get her Xanax prescription. Unfortunately, checkups invariably involve getting weighed. The bad news was . . . I'd gained five pounds over the holidays.

This called for drastic measures.

"That's only seventeen," Ashley said, holding my feet down in my apartment as I did sit-ups.

"Nope—nineteen." I wheezed. "I've been counting."

"Sorry, Aunt Phoebe. Only seventeen. I've been counting too."

Elizabeth agreed. "Yep. Me too. Only three more to go. C'mon, you can do it!"

What's that scripture again about children being a blessing from the Lord?

The next day I tried the sit-ups routine again while baby-sitting the kids, but Lexie and Jacob jumped on me every time I got on the floor.

So much for getting in shape.

Besides, sit-ups won't do much for thighs that whisper together when you walk . . .

I did manage to squeeze in a little more of a spiritual workout late that night though. Only seven minutes' worth, but who was keeping score? Besides, God spoke to me immediately in the words of Psalm 139: "If I rise on the wings of the dawn, if I settle on the far side of the sea, even there your hand will guide me, your right hand will hold me fast."

With this spiritual confirmation in place, I e-mailed Cordelia, Alex's twenty-three-year-old half sister, about our plans—asking her to keep mum. She thought the visit was a "smashing" idea. Even came up with a great way to surprise Alex.

Always knew I'd like that girl.

Mary Jo had been right; she wasn't a very good flier. She took one of her three physician-prescribed Xanax, clutched the armrest in a death grip, shut her eyes, and tried to listen to her copy of *Seabiscuit* on tape. And when we hit a little turbulence, she squeezed her eyes shut even tighter and began murmuring the Lord's Prayer.

Finally! Something I'm better at than Mary Jo. I don't believe it.

"It's okay, MJ." I patted her hand with my seasoned traveler one. "This is all normal. Don't worry. Why don't you try to get some sleep?"

I sat there praying for Mary Jo's fears to subside. Then, when I heard her breathing deeply, I picked up my *Jane Eyre*. For the next eight hours or so, when I wasn't reading about Jane and Mr. Rochester in the Gothic mansion on the Yorkshire moors or eating cardboard food or standing in line for the restroom—which involved removing my Manolos from the overhead compartment where I'd gingerly stowed them three hours into the flight and donning them for the walk down the aisle—I was flipping through the travel guide and highlighting must-see English monuments and points of interest, planning all the amazing things we'd do and see once we arrived.

Including Alex, of course.

I'd waited more than three months for that New Year's kiss, and soon my wait would be over. *Wonder if he'll cup my face tenderly between his hands the first time. Or will he go straight in for a serious Rhett Butler lip-lock?*

I took a long drink of my bottled water.

Or maybe it'll be a John Wayne Quiet Man one. I shivered with anticipation. What a glorious, definitely-not-quiet kiss that was—in full, gorgeous Technicolor. *Yes, I know it was set in Ireland, but England was right next door.*

Pushing my fantasies aside, I tried to focus on the in-flight movie instead. But after two burps, a couple of belches, and a few other bodily functions I refuse to go into—in what had been billed a romantic comedy—I yanked off my headset and watched our slow progress on the global positioning map in front of us. The tiny graphic plane on the TV screen showed we were now flying over Greenland.

Greenland. Iceland. That whole name thing is just wrong. They need to swap them. I mean, Iceland is the one that's all green and inhabited, and Greenland's basically ice and isolated. Right? At least that's what I remembered from geography—one of the few things I did remember. Whoever named them made a big mistake. Big.

But never mind. I'm on my way to England! Land of Shakespeare, scones, and Sense and Sensibility.

And Alex.

Now the little graphic plane showed us flying over the Atlantic Ocean.

On second thought, maybe I didn't want to watch. Instead, I leaned back, closed my eyes, and thought of England.

And Alex.

Going through customs at Heathrow, even casual, laid-back MJ got a little fluttery over the delicious accents all around us. I thought she was going to break into a little *Riverdance* when she heard a cluster of Irish nuns chattering away. And we both leaned closer when an older man in a kilt began to speak to his companion in a rich Scottish brogue.

"Shades of Sean Connery," my friend whispered as we towed our bags toward the Heathrow Underground station. "I like it here already."

"Oh my gosh, MJ. Look, there's Notting Hill Gate!" I pointed to the color-coded map of the London subway system on the station wall. "Wonder if Hugh Grant hangs around there much? And look, there's Piccadilly Circus and Westminster and . . . *Knightsbridge!*"

"What's at Knightsbridge?"

"Only the most famous and one of the most expensive department stores in the whole world." I sighed with longing. "Harrods." But my shopping lust was diverted by another stop on the map. "Charing Cross," I whispered. "I forgot about Charing Cross."

Mary Jo chuckled. "What's there? Another ritzy store?"

"No." My voice took on a dreamy tone. "There was this wonderful little film from the late eighties with Anthony Hopkins and Anne Bancroft, called *84 Charing Cross Road*. All about this feisty New York bibliophile—that's Anne Bancroft—who was searching for a hard-to-find book and discovered that a London bookstore at 84 Charing Cross Road had a copy. So she began writing to Anthony Hopkins, the British bookseller." I sighed. "They shared this wonderful twenty-year friendship across the miles, based on their mutual love of books. But they never met."

"Sounds like my kind of action-filled movie. Okay, Ms. Lost in Movieland, think we can exercise a little action ourselves and get this show on the road?"

I know the practical travel gurus say to bring only one small, rolling carry-on bag and a backpack, but this was my very first time in Europe and I was determined not to look like some ugly American. One small suitcase and a backpack simply hadn't cut it.

Especially since I was going to be seeing my Alex again soon.

I started having second thoughts, though, as we lugged all my bags down the labyrinthine tunnels and ramps to the Underground platform and then onto the car.

It was a good thing Mary Jo had followed the sage traveling advice. With her modest little roll-on in tow, she helped me lug my multiple bags into the nearest compartment. I sucked in my J.Lo derriere just in time as the heavy automatic doors sliced shut behind me. (Yes, I wanted to lose weight, but I knew there had to be a less painful way.)

Now I knew how sardines felt. Multicultural, indifferent sardines. No one spoke or looked around. Most people buried their noses in books or newspapers, while others gazed above our heads in rapt fascination at the ads or the tube map showing all the different lines.

And every time the train stopped and let people on and off, a cultured, disembodied English accent would intone over the speakers, "Mind the Gap."

Mary Jo, in her Wrangler jeans and sweatshirt, stared at me. "They do Gap commercials on the Underground? That store must be really popular here."

Two seats over from her, an acned teen with several piercings on his face sniggered. I noticed brief smiles from a couple of the more reserved passengers too, quickly hidden behind the ubiquitous newspaper.

Then I got it. *Mind the gap is like mind your step: don't fall when you get on or off.* I glanced down at my Manolos and their skinny stiletto heels and realized they could be a means to my destruction if I wasn't careful.

At our stop I disembarked gingerly.

Once outside in the open air again, we shifted our luggage and began walking. And walking. And walking.

I don't care what Nancy Sinatra says.
These boots are definitely not made for walking.

chapter eight

Mind the Culture Gap

Y ou girls are young an 'ealthy, so we've put you on the fourth
floor. All right, then?" The pasty-faced, dentally challenged
hotel desk clerk had to be at least sixty, but he handled the stairs with
the energy of someone much younger.

"Sounds great." I didn't care what floor I stayed on. I was in
England! And my beloved Alex was somewhere nearby. Under my
breath, I began humming "Get Me to the Church on Time."

By the third floor, though, I was singing a different tune.

Nigel, the clerk, had taken charge of my large rolling suitcase while
I followed behind with my smaller case and my cumbersome carryall,
which kept banging against the wall as we made our way up the narrow, crooked staircase.

Mary Jo was having her own difficulties. "What? The women don't
have hips over here?" she muttered behind me. "How do they make it
up these dinky steps? Haven't they ever heard of elevators?"

Nigel only heard her last comment. "We call 'em lifts here, luv, and
sorry this old 'otel ain't got one. Good exercise though." He turned
and shot her a lascivious, buck-toothed grin. "'Elp you keep your girl-
ish figger."

At the next landing I stopped, but he didn't. "Wait a minute. I
thought you said we were on the fourth floor?"

"That you are, luv. Just one more flight to go."

"I know I'm bad at math," I wheezed, "but even I can count to four—and we just passed the fourth floor."

"Over 'ere your first floor is our ground floor. The first floor is the next one up."

Behind me, I heard MJ groan.

Finally we made it to the top—exactly fifty-nine steps. I'd counted. *This had better be a room with a view.* My inner Maggie Smith clicked in, complete with waspish wit and dead-on, English accent.

Nigel opened the door with a flourish. "Right, then, 'ere you are. Anything you need, just ask. We sell bottled water at the front desk and the odd bit of Cadbury's now and then if Mavis ain't nicked 'em all. Lovely girl, our Mavis. Bit of a sweet tooth, though." He gave us a jaunty wave and bounded down the steps.

Slowly I surveyed the musty room. "Well, it's definitely not the Ritz. But then again, at these prices it wouldn't be."

Every movie I'd ever seen with stately English manor homes or Cotswold country cottages showed pretty chintz and lots of lovely floral fabric. And even though the fabrics didn't match—which I liked; too boring otherwise—they at least had a unifying color or floral scheme to tie them all together.

Nothing like that here.

The carpet looked like it might have once been a thick hunter green with red cabbage roses scattered throughout, but it had been trod upon so many times over the years that it had lost all its cushion and faded to more of a grungy pea-soup color.

But it was the bedspreads that really caught my eye. Once black with probably vivid tropical flowers—nary a rose in the bunch—they were now more of a dirty gray with pale peach birds of paradise.

And did I mention they were polyester? And stained?

"I think I'll sleep in my clothes tonight," I told my roommate.

"You're such a wuss." Mary Jo dropped her backpack on the bed nearest the door. "Think of it as camping." Her eyebrows beetled together. "Hey, check it out. The sink's in the bedroom. That's weird."

I glanced over at the chipped, dingy sink and cloudy mirror in one corner of the tiny room. "Wonder why?"

Mary Jo opened the bathroom door. "Um, there's no shower."

"Sure there is. My confirmation said 'en suite,' and that means shower in the room." I peered beyond her into the cramped bathroom. No wonder the sink was in the bedroom. There was no room for anything besides the toilet and the dingy blue bathtub. "There's the shower." I pointed. "See, it's one of those handheld thingies attached to the tub faucet."

My traveling companion eyed the narrow tub, then looked down at her not-so-narrow hips. "Great."

"It'll be fine. Don't worry. Besides, we won't be in our room much—just to sleep. We'll be busy sightseeing the rest of the time. And look, I'll bet there's a great view way up here." I hurried over to the ancient orange velour curtains and flung them open, coughing at the puffs of dust that filled the air.

And what a view it was. Oy. A lovely cityscape featuring the dirty rooftops of commercial buildings, enhanced by the encrusted grime on the window glass. But wait—what was that? I squinted at a majestic building off in the distance. Could it be Buckingham Palace maybe? Or the Tower of London?

My grumpiness disappeared in a New York minute. I looked at my watch. "It's only four twenty." I grabbed my purse and travel journal. "We can unpack later. Let's go exploring!"

We'd decided to play our whole trip by ear. No tours for us. I was a journalist, after all. My job depended upon my ability to explore brave new worlds, search out hard-to-find information, and go where no Barley girl had ever gone before.

"Oh my gosh, Mary Jo," I said. (I kept forgetting to call her MJ). "I think that's Buckingham Palace!"

And no, it wasn't what I'd seen through the window. That had turned out to be just another hotel, albeit a much grander and more expensive one than our meager lodgings.

But this—it certainly looked like the real thing.

We'd taken the tube to Victoria Station—a stop whose name I recognized from countless movies—and begun wandering through the city, passing by countless shops and pubs, restaurants, and yes, Starbucks. They were everywhere, just like in Cleveland. But then we'd turned a corner and found ourselves face-to-face with an imposing building surrounded by high iron fencing.

Could that really be where the queen lives? Right here in the middle of everything?

I'd always figured it would be off somewhere all by itself and totally inaccessible. The inaccessible part was right; the tall gates were locked, and I thought I saw guards in the distance, closer to the building. But in front of the main locked gate stood a majestic statue of Queen Victoria seated on the throne with a gold angel—we're talking major gold here—above her.

Amazing.

MJ looked up. "It must be the palace," she said. "The sign says Buckingham Palace Road." Unlike Lindsey, my Barley best friend isn't usually a squealer. But she looked across at the famous palace, then at me, and we both squealed in tandem, and then pulled out our cameras.

"Look. The flag's flying. That means the Queen's in." I shook my head. "To think that the sovereign of England is this close—maybe playing with her Corgis or having tea with her son." I gave MJ a telling look. "Or maybe even her hottie grandsons."

She sighed. "That William is sure yummy looking. Too bad he's so young."

We set out to explore the neighborhood, meandering through green parks and streets with such la-di-dah names as Grosvenor Place and Belgrave Square. Passing the beautiful white-fronted rows of upscale homes with striking doors in rich jewel colors—emerald green, ruby red, sapphire blue, and gleaming onyx, usually flanked by hanging baskets of flowers—I started to feel all Gwyneth Paltrow-ish—minus the thin thighs, rocker husband, and produce-named daughter.

I could live here. Easily. Behind a house with a blue door, like Hugh Grant in Notting Hill. Or at least commute between here and the States.

Note to self: Make sure to subtly weave this realization into conversation with Alex so he doesn't worry about my being homesick. That could be what's holding him back.

Suddenly I stopped dead in my tracks, all my Gwyneth Paltrow sophistication falling away to reveal my all-American tourist self. "Scarlett O'Hara lived here! We have to get a picture of this!"

"I thought she lived in a Southern mansion in Georgia somewhere."

"Very funny. No, I mean, the fabulous actress who played her." I stared at the round blue plaque on the white house front. "Do you know that every actress in Hollywood wanted that *Gone with the Wind* role—from Bette Davis to Katharine Hepburn?"

I'm a huge Scarlett O'Hara fan, having always admired her strength and tenacity. Until recently, in fact, when faced with a perplexing conundrum or sticky situation in my life, I used to ask myself, *What would Scarlett do?* I'd stopped doing that when I watched the movie with new eyes and realized Scarlett could be selfish and hurtful as well as plucky. But that didn't stop me from admiring the talented actress who brought her so vividly to life on the silver screen.

"Vivien Leigh also played Blanche DuBois in *A Streetcar Named Desire*." I turned to MJ. "Did you know she was married to Laurence Olivier? They had a turbulent marriage, though. She was bipolar or something."

She shook her head as we continued walking. "You really need to get a life."

"Says the woman who's addicted to horses and anything on four feet."

Feet . . .

Mine were really starting to ache. *Should have changed shoes back in the hotel room. I'll wear my Skechers tomorrow.*

". . . least I stick to the ones that are still alive."

Alive? I smacked my forehead. I was supposed to let both my mom and Cordelia know we'd arrived safely. I reached for the international phone card I'd bought back in the States, then we started looking for one of those adorable red phone booths.

And couldn't find one anywhere.

We couldn't find a phone of any sort. *Guess everyone's using cell phones here too.*

We had about decided we'd have to go back to our hotel and call when I spotted a glassed-in storefront with several touristy-looking people inside seated at computers. "That looks like one of those Internet cafés Esther was talking about. We can e-mail home and maybe even get in touch with Cordelia."

Luckily, when I logged on to the Internet, I was able to send an Instant Message to Alex's sister, who suggested meeting for dinner. She named a place near the Internet café and gave me directions, which I scribbled down in my new travel journal. Since I knew what she looked like from a family photo on Alex's desk at the *Bulletin*, I knew there'd be no problem recognizing her.

After that, I dashed off a quick "we're safe!" note to Mom, then wrote Lindsey.

To: LinsRog
From: Movielovr

 I did it! I'm here in England with Mary Jo, and it's everything they said it was and more. You'd love London! Talk about an exciting city. We just saw *Buckingham Palace!* Can you believe it? And we're about to have our very first English meal—fish and chips in a *pub,* no less. Tomorrow we might go to the Tower of London. (I'll think of you when we see the crown jewels, although I doubt I'll be able to bring you any back.) Any minute now I expect to see Hugh Grant or Colin Firth come riding up on a white horse.

Oops. Gotta fly. Miss you. Hope all's going well with
the wedding plans. And give Phillie a big hug for me.
—Love, P.

MJ, who doesn't share my e-mail addiction, was waiting outside for
me when I finished.

"Any luck?"

"We're meeting Cordelia for dinner at a pub called the Hangman's
Noose. She said it wasn't too far from here."

"That's good," she said. "I'm starving, and think I'm about walked
out too . . ."

She looked down at my elegant boots and shook her head. "I still
don't understand how you can walk a step in those things. Your feet
must be killing you."

I wasn't about to let her know she was right.

"I don't think we're in California anymore, Dorothy." Mary Jo
coughed through the cloud of smoke in the crowded pub. "Doesn't
the word *cancer* mean anything over here?"

"Guess not. But they must have smoke-free zones somewhere."

As it turned out, we were fifteen minutes early for our dinner date
with Cordelia. We made our way cautiously through the raucous haze
past a bar where several people sat smoking and downing beers while
cheering on their favorite soccer team. Mary Jo pointed to a small
table near the back that still had a good view of the front door, and I
headed in that direction, marveling at the ancient beams overhead
dotted with horse brasses. I should have been looking down. Halfway
to our table, I nearly tripped over a thick rolled-up rug in our path.

Only it wasn't a rug.

The large dog moved lazily away when I bumped into it, giving me
a fright.

"Haven't they heard of health codes?" I whispered to MJ.

A grizzled old-timer nearby caught my eye and grinned. "Yanks, eh?"

Mary Jo reached down and scratched behind the golden lab's ears. "Aren't you a good boy?" The dog rolled over and thumped his tail on the ancient floorboards, so she obliged him by scratching his stomach.

Eew. Wonder if he has fleas? Hope MJ washes her hands . . .

While we waited for Cordelia, we ordered a couple of packages of "crisps"—potato chips, actually—and two Cokes from a hot-looking young guy in jeans and a T-shirt. Well, he would have been hot except for that whole pale, anemic thing he had going on.

Haven't they heard of tanning booths over here?

Setting down our drinks, anemic guy leaned toward us. "So, where in the States do you two gorgeous girls come from?"

"California."

"With all the film stars? D'ya know Jennifer Aniston, then? Or Cameron Diaz?" His eyes took on a lusty gleam. "Or J.Lo?"

"No." Then MJ asked with a similar lusty gleam, "But do you happen to know Prince Wil—"

"Phoebe? Mary Jo?"

I looked up in surprise at the slim, dark-haired young woman in a conservative navy business suit, who'd materialized in front of us. *"Cordelia?"*

A smile creased her flawless Nicole Kidman complexion, and she extended her hand. "The same. Lovely to meet you at last."

"But I saw your pic—I was looking for a girl with fuchsia hair, multiple pierced ears, and funky clothes!"

She threw her head back—looking remarkably like her half brother when she did—and laughed, a rather hearty laugh for someone so petite and refined. "That was when I was at university. Now that I'm part of the family firm, I must look the part." She lifted her hair to reveal three diamond studs and a tiny silver hoop near the top of her ear. "But I still wear my funky bits on the weekend," she said with a sassy grin.

I just love English accents. Don't you? Especially the way they add emphasis to the final syllable with that lovely, musical lilt: Week*end.*

Mary Jo thrust her hand across the table. "Great to meet you, Cordelia."

"Actually, you can just call me Delia."

My Thelma traveling companion grinned and shot a wink my way. "And you can call me MJ. Now that I'm in London, Phoebe thinks I need to at least *sound* a little less hicksville." Her stomach grumbled at just that moment, surprising us all. MJ shrugged. "Guess my stomach just didn't get the message."

Delia laughed again, the pale waiter returned, and we ordered dinner. She was filling us in on all the details of the plan to surprise Alex when our fish and chips arrived, nestled alongside a pile of the brightest green peas we'd ever seen in our lives.

"That green is a color not to be found in nature," MJ said.

"Uh-huh. And since I don't eat peas, natural or un—want mine?" I shoved my plate her way.

Delia sent a curious look my way. "Why don't you like peas, Phoebe?"

"It's a whole texture thing." I scraped the little neon green BBs onto MJ's plate and shuddered. "I hate it when they squish in your mouth."

"We'll have to get you some mushy peas then." She signaled the waiter. "Excuse me?"

"Mushy. They're squashed together into a mass—sort of like mashed potatoes."

She gave the order, then leaned in to tell us the details of her plan. She and Alex and their family would be going to the theater tomorrow night, and we would surprise him there. MJ wasn't too sure that was a good idea—especially after all this time apart—but Delia thought it would be "brilliant." She reached in her bag and came up with two pairs of opera glasses, plus tickets for a production by The Reduced Shakespeare Company.

Then she noticed Mary Jo's face. "What's wrong?"

"Well, I don't mean to be rude since he's your greatest playwright and all . . ." Mary Jo squirmed. "I just think Shakespeare's so hard to understand, with all those *yon*s and *methink*s and stuff."

I stared at her. "But you love history, MJ! And you liked Kenneth Branagh's *Much Ado About Nothing* when we watched it."

She snorted. "I could *understand* that. Besides, that hunka burnin' love Denzel Washington was in it. And Michael Keaton, who was really funny."

"This will be too," Delia assured her. "I promise. It's hysterical."

At that moment my mushy peas arrived, looking very much like Gerber strained peas. Or little Gloria's diaper after she'd eaten them. Which was just one stimulus too many. The sight of those peas teamed with smoke and jet lag turned my face the same color as the roadkill vegetable in front of me. "Uh, Delia, if you don't mind, I think I'll pass on the peas altogether." I excused myself and fled to the loo.

And what an experience that was. Can you say toilet paper with the consistency of waxed paper? So far, England wasn't exactly living up to my old-world, upper-crust expectations. But I remembered what Esther had said and determined to be a little less wussy and critical and a lot more adventurous and accepting of different cultures.

Besides, it was only our first night.

When I returned to the table—devoid of the mushy peas, thank goodness—Mary Jo was saying to the waiter, "Could I have a glass of water please?"

Delia teased her. "MJ, it's not wa-derrr," she said, imitating Mary Jo's flat, nasal California accent. "It's wau-tuh. You want to sound like you have plums in your mouth."

"Plums in your mouth?"

"Yes. To speak posh, you need to sound like you're talking around a plum in your mouth." She pursed her lips to demonstrate.

We practiced our plummy accents. "Wau-tuh," "Right, then," "Ack-shwully . . ."

Delia grinned. "No chance of your being mistaken for the upper crust."

MJ poured ketchup on her chips. "Are you?"

"What?"

"Upper crust."

I spit out my Coke.

Delia laughed again. "By birth, not by preference." She made a face. "But the family is a bit, as you'll see when you meet them tomorrow night."

Monarchs swooped through my stomach. *How am I ever going to impress Alex's posh parents?*

Note to self: Be sure to brush up on diction and etiquette and wear best outfit. Including Manolos, of course. I flexed my Manolo-clad right foot, which was developing a blister.

Until then, switch to flats to give feet a rest.

". . . Mother's lovely—she's American, you know. And Dad's a dear, though he can be a bit intimidating—all that boarding school and landed gentry background." Delia rolled her eyes and then smiled. "But Mum balances him out nicely."

Hmm. Wonder if I'll have time to go to the library and read up on the Spencer heritage before meeting Alex's dad tomorrow night? If nothing else, maybe I can find another Internet café and Google them . . .

MJ yawned. "I don't know about you, Pheebs, but I don't think I can stay awake much longer."

"Oh, sorry! I've forgotten all about your jet lag." Delia was instantly contrite. "Let's get you back to your hotel."

She wanted to accompany us to our hotel to make sure we got there safely, but when we discovered she lived quite a ways in the opposite direction, we assured her that we could navigate the Underground without difficulty now.

Walking—well, limping—back to Victoria Station with MJ, something called my name—row upon row of Cadbury's chocolate bars in a little crowded shop that reminded me of a minimart without the gas pumps. We each grabbed one, but at the register something else caught my eye. "Look." I giggled. "Here's some Union Jack boxer shorts in a can. How cheesy is that? I just have to get this for my brother. And check out these great mini pub signs."

"This is only our first night here," my practical pal piped up. "Don't you think you should wait? We're bound to see lots more cool things. Don't blow all your money at the first store we go into. We'll have plenty of chances to buy stuff."

"Good thing I brought you along." I patted her arm. "You can be my voice of reason on this trip."

"In *all* things?" She quirked a knowing eyebrow at me.

I thought of Alex and how I couldn't wait to see him. And not just see . . .

"Well, maybe not all."

I was practically asleep on my (aching) feet by the time we made it back to our grungy hotel room. But we'd agreed to unpack before going to bed so our clothes wouldn't get too wrinkled, so I wrestled my bags onto the bed.

I winced as Mary Jo—definitely *not* MJ in this instance— removed items from her lone suitcase: a pair of screaming orange sweat pants, two turtlenecks, a plaid flannel shirt, one sweatshirt with horses galloping across the front, a nightshirt, a brown wool sweater, and her favorite pair of tan cord jeans—"in case we have to dress up a little."

The only thing she bought new for the trip was a pair of bright white Easy Spirit walking shoes, since "we'd be on our feet so much." I'd tried (but failed) to talk her into a more subtle, continental-looking black.

"You can take the girl out of the country, but you can't take the country out of the girl." I shook my head in affection.

"And never want to." Mary Jo grinned, pulling on her *Shrek* night-shirt—the only article of clothing I approved of.

Unpacking my delicates (folded in equal thirds, of course) and toiletries from my smaller case, I then unzipped the larger suitcase containing all my new clothes.

And shrieked.

MJ jumped. "What's wrong?"

"I've got the wrong suitcase," I said, slowly removing a pinstriped suit for what had to be a very large businessman.

My searching fingers flipped frantically through the suitcase for all the gorgeous clothes I'd put on plastic to give me that chic, cosmopolitan look I craved.

Instead, I found a couple of massive white shirts, some socks, a robe, and . . . a pair of the most humongous boxer shorts ever—black satin with red hearts.

chapter nine

Traveling Light

ew!" I jerked my hand away and slammed the suitcase shut. Then I looked down at the black sweater and jeans I'd been wearing for the past sixteen hours. "This is the only set of clothes I have."

MJ jumped in before I could let loose with another scream. "Calm down. Remember, you just said I would be your voice of reason on the trip. Listen to the voice."

I scowled, but decided to listen.

"It's elementary, dear Watson. Right now, somewhere in London, there's a very large businessman wondering where his suitcase is." She adjusted her imaginary deerstalker hat and began rummaging in the outer pockets of the wrong case. "He must have ID in here somewhere . . . ha! Here it is!" She held up a white business card.

Examining it, her Sherlock Holmes bravura slipped a notch. "What?"

"Looks like our businessman, a Mr. Klaus Schmidt, lives in Frankfurt. Germany."

I wailed.

But my voice-of-reason friend was not so easily put off. "We'll just call the airport and tell them what happened."

Mary Jo gave me an encouraging smile and checked her watch. "It's almost nine thirty, which means we've been in London nearly seven hours. Probably Mr. Schmidt has already called and turned in your suit-case." She looked around for the phone, then snapped her fingers. "That's right. I forgot. Nigel said there's a phone in the lobby for guests to use. Let's run down and call right now." She started to open the door.

"Um, I think you're forgetting something."

She shot me a puzzled look, and then followed the direction of my gaze. "Oops." After she pulled her clothes back on over her nightshirt, we headed downstairs.

Only problem was, I couldn't get a dial tone from the phone tucked away in an alcove beneath the stairs. Nothing. Nada. Zip. "What is it with phones in this city?"

"Maybe there's another one somewhere," Mary Jo said. "At the desk, probably." She returned moments later, shrugging her shoulders. "No luck. And no one at the desk either. Guess Nigel's called it a night."

"That's okay. I figured it out," I said, pointing to some slots at the top of the phone that we hadn't noticed. "You don't happen to have any coins, do you?"

She dug into her jeans pockets but came up empty. She looked askance up at the winding staircase.

"Don't worry, MJ. This is a hotel, after all, such as it is. Someone should be on duty twenty-four hours." I marched over to the chipped laminate counter and poked my head through the open window into the office. "Hello?"

Total silence.

"Never mind, Pheebs. I'll go back up." She grimaced. "Notice I didn't say 'run up.'"

Seven minutes later she returned, jingling change. We inserted the coins in the phone and dialed.

Still nothing.

At last we heard a sound behind the counter. I looked up to see a shock of burgundy hair above a plump, lined face. Stifling a yawn, burgundy-hair lowered her hand from her mouth, leaving a smear of chocolate on one of her chins.

This must be Mavis.

"Sorry. I was takin' a bit of a nap. Did you need somethin' then, luv?"

"Yes, please. Could you show us how to use the phone? We can't get it to work."

"You won't." She unwrapped a Caramello. "That phone's broken."

"Well, can we use yours then?" Mary Jo asked.

Mavis gave a regretful shake of her burgundy head. "Sorry, luv. Nigel keeps it locked up at night." She scowled. "'e don't want no one running up the bill."

"But what if there's an emergency?" I ran my fingers through my hair.

"Then I push this buzzer under the counter to wake 'im up and 'e makes the call." Her Bordeaux-penciled eyebrows lifted. "Is this an emergency, then?"

Yes. A fashion emergency.

"Not exactly." Mary Jo shot her a winning smile. "But it is important. My friend has the wrong luggage, and we need to call the airport."

Mavis jerked her head toward the exit. "Phone box down the corner."

Well, finally. For all the help it was.

The airline couldn't do anything over the phone. We'd have to schlep all the way back out to Heathrow tomorrow to turn in the large mystery man's suitcase and hopefully retrieve mine at the same time.

Racing to the red phone box without our coats, we'd gotten chilled, but by the time we reached our fifty-ninth stair, we'd more than warmed up. I know they say that women don't sweat, but "glisten"— but "they" would be wrong. Sticky sweat was now trickling down my back and underarms.

Peeling off my ripe sweater, I washed it out in the ancient sink and laid it on the radiator to dry overnight. I really needed a bath too, but I just didn't have the energy. Instead, I just did a fast face scrub and quick swipe under my arms before I donned my pajamas, which fortunately had been in the small bag. I slipped between the sheets just as Mary Jo began to snore lightly.

It could be worse, you know, I told myself. *You still have your Manolos—good thing you wore them on the plane. And you'll still be seeing the man of your dreams tomorrow night. At last . . .*

Images of Alex's surprised face . . . his arms open wide . . . and our subsequent, inevitable, unforgettable kiss played through my mind in a continual loop as I fell asleep.

Drying my sweater on the radiator had been a good idea, really— except that sometime during the night, the radiator turned off. So when I went to dress after showering—don't even get me started on the ineffectual shower—

Remember it's all part of the traveling adventure. It's all part of the adventure . . .

—my thick sweater, though no longer dripping wet, was still damp. Very damp.

"Good thing I didn't wash my jeans," I grumbled, grabbing my blow dryer and aiming it at my now-very-heavy black V-neck.

Mary Jo's stomach emitted its familiar loud rumble. "Pheebs, you're welcome to wear one of my shirts. I know I'm not the fashion plate you are, but it's just to breakfast and out to the airport, then you can change into your clothes."

She held up her two turtlenecks. "Take your pick." Then she grinned. "Unless of course you'd rather wear my sweatshirt?"

I took one look at the horses galloping across the front of her olive-drab sweatshirt and opted for the lesser of two evils.

Even though yellow always makes me look washed-out.

"Beans for breakfast?" Mary Jo looked askance at the full plate set before her. "I feel like I'm in a western. Only thing missing is the campfire and tin coffeepot."

"Remember; when in Rome . . ." But even I had to admit that our

traditional English breakfast of fried eggs, bacon, sausage, mushrooms, beans, toast, and fried tomato (or as they say, "to-mah-to") was
a bit daunting.

"What is this?" she hissed, poking at the round red blob on her
plate. "It looks like a blood clot."

"Shh. Remember *Fried Green Tomatoes*? This is just a grilled red
tomato cut in half rather than sliced thin." I pushed up the yellow
turtleneck's too-long sleeves and looked down at my overflowing
plate. *And they say Americans do everything big . . .*

The streaky bacon was a revelation—delicious and more like ham
or Canadian bacon. And the eggs and toast were equally as good. But
when I cut into my tomato, it bled all over the plate.

"Thanks, MJ."

I gulped my tea, which was perfection.

No one can make a cup of tea like the Brits. Steaming hot—no
little metal pitcher full of tepid water there—full-bodied, and rich.
With milk and sugar, of course.

MJ had allowed me to coax her away from her normal morning
coffee, but she balked at "milky" tea.

"I like my tea plain."

"C'mon. Have you ever tried it this way? When in England . . ."

She scowled and took a cautious sip. "Hmmm. This *is* pretty good."

When we rolled out of the dining room twenty minutes later, we
agreed that the next day we'd forego the full breakfast in favor of toast
and yogurt. And maybe a little fresh fruit.

Careful to mind the gap, we headed back to Heathrow to make the
suitcase swap. I pulled my leather jacket close to hide as much of the
baggy yellow turtleneck as possible, happy I wouldn't be wearing it
much longer.

An hour later, I wasn't as happy.

My suitcase was nowhere to be found. Today of all days, when I'd
at long last be seeing Alex.

My lip quivered, but before I managed to go into major meltdown mode, the baggage guy said hastily, "Don't worry, luv. Check back tomorrow. It'll most likely show up by then—maybe even later today." He handed me a piece of paper with a number to call.

"This was not how I planned to spend my first day in London," I whined to Mary Jo as we rode the Underground back into the city.

"I know. But stuff happens." She took a deep breath. "So let's go shopping and get you some clothes."

I stared at her. "You hate to shop."

She grimaced. "I know. But what's the alternative?"

The alternative was for history-buff Mary Jo to visit the British Museum while I shopped. We'd meet back up at the hotel in two hours and start our first official day of sightseeing together.

"Are you sure, Pheebs?" She tried not to look too excited.

"It will be a sacrifice. Missing all those Egyptian artifacts and old rocks and stuff in favor of racks and racks of brand-new clothes. But it's a sacrifice I'm willing to make for the good of our vacation."

An hour later, I stood in line at a Debenham's register with three pairs of pants, some cute T-shirts, a kicky little jean jacket, two sweaters, a classic black turtleneck—that fit—and a gorgeous scarlet silk blouse.

Just wait 'til Alex sees me tonight in my smart trousers, silk blouse, leather jacket, and Manolos. It will be like when Rick first sees Ilsa. He'll only have eyes for me . . . The "As Times Goes By" melody began to play in my head.

A clipped English voice snapped me from my *Casablanca* fantasy. "Sorry. Your card has been declined."

"Excuse me?"

She repeated, "Your card has been declined."

The blood rushed to my face. Behind me in line, someone tapped her foot.

"Sorry." Cheeks flaming, I fumbled in my wallet. "I gave you the wrong card." I yanked out my Visa and handed it to the salesclerk with an apologetic smile. Then I pretended an absorbed interest in a scarf display off to one side.

"This one's been rejected too."

"Do you take ATM?" *Please God.*

"Of course."

I punched in my pin number and studied my French manicure. "Declined" flashed across the pin pad. I hit clear and tried again, flashing another apologetic smile to the women lined up behind me. "Sorry, I think I typed in the wrong number. Won't be a minute."

"Declined" flashed again.

"Perhaps you'd prefer to pay cash?" the clipped voice said.

Cash? I did some quick mental calculations. MJ and I had withdrawn forty pounds apiece from the airport ATM. With dinner, the tube, candy, the Internet café . . . I may be hopeless at math, but even I could figure out that the twenty-odd pounds remaining wasn't enough.

"Uh, no, that's okay." I slunk out of the store.

What is wrong with my ATM? It worked fine last night. I know my balance was getting low, but my paycheck was deposited today.

Or was it?

A sick feeling washed over me. Before I'd left on vacation, I'd finally gotten around to closing out my Cleveland checking account and opening a new account in nearby Lodi. And I'd filled out the paperwork to have my *Bulletin* paycheck deposited directly into my new bank. I'd planned to drop off the paperwork at the bank before I left. But in the rush of the trip, I now realized, I'd forgotten to do it. In my mind's eye I could see the bank envelope still on the right-hand corner of my desk at work.

Idiot. Stupid, irresponsible idiot.

Feeling lightheaded, I ducked into a Wimpy's restroom and checked my money belt, hidden beneath Mary Jo's turtleneck: twenty-seven pounds and some change.

I asked the pockmarked teen behind the counter for directions to the nearest Internet café, where I shot off an urgent appeal to Gordon

to rush my paperwork to the bank—"without telling Mom, please."
*Wouldn't want to worry her. She already thinks I'm scatterbrained, always
going around with my head in the clouds and—*

So did Mary Jo.

MJ! What am I going to tell her?

Tell her the truth, my reasonable self urged. *You goofed up. She's your
friend. She'll understand. Goes with the whole spiritual-giant territory . . .*

Nope. Too humiliating, my embarrassed spiritual-loser self argued. I
won't say anything. Won't need to. By tomorrow, Lord willing, my
cash-flow problems should be solved.

Just need to make it through today.

But at this point, Phil's big-bucks job offer was looking awfully
tempting. If I took it, I wouldn't be living paycheck to paycheck and
finding myself in this kind of predicament.

Once I had paid for my Internet time, I was down to less than
twenty-five pounds. And still with nothing to wear tonight. No way
was I going to meet Alex in Mary Jo's baggy yellow turtleneck. Not
after all this time.

I gazing longingly in dazzling store window after store window.
And as I continued to wander in an abject daze, all of a sudden a
smaller, much-less-dazzling window hove into view.

A charity shop?

I peered inside the thrift store window and saw racks of clothing.
Not exactly my normal shopping territory, but it would have to do.

Before MJ and I set off sightseeing, we put our heads together and
agreed to forego the bunch of men in white wigs in Parliament and
visit Westminster Abbey instead.

I'd seen the Abbey before on TV—who could forget Princess
Diana's funeral, with the heartrending white envelope on the royal
casket that simply said "Mummy"? But television couldn't prepare me
for the wonder and majesty of the real thing.

The gorgeous stained glass absolutely took my breath away, but it was the floor that really captured my interest. "Check out all these dead people we're walking on, MJ." A former obit writer, I was fascinated by the wealth of material at my Manolo-shod feet. We walked over and around—with me being especially careful in my skinny heels—the graves of such notables as Oliver Cromwell, Charles Darwin, and David Livingstone of Stanley and Livingstone fame.

Then we made our way to Poet's Corner, where I was brought up short to see all the great writers memorialized there: Charles Dickens, T. S. Eliot, Lewis Carroll, Jane Austen, and the Brontë sisters. Even Wordsworth, my daffodil poet!

"I'll bet none of them wrote about emus or investment portfolios," I whispered to MJ, who was walking around in a daze. "Such exalted company—makes me want to rush right back to our hotel room and start working on the great American novel."

Or at least one little story, which could later be the basis for the great American novel.

Mary Jo fidgeted. "Can you hold that thought for a while, Ms. Novelist Wannabe? I really need to find a bathroom."

"You mean loo."

"Loo, schmoo. I don't care what they call it as long as they have one."

They didn't. We searched and searched and finally asked a guide, who informed us, "The Abbey is an ancient building, so there are no public lavatories inside."

She did, however, direct us to a public lavatory across the street where MJ could take care of business. We emerged from the loo ready to resume our sightseeing—except now it was pouring down rain, and neither one of us had brought an umbrella.

There was no help for it; we would have to hail one of the cool black London taxis that look like a holdover from some thirties black-and-white movie. With any luck, we'd get a driver who looked like Cary Grant or Peter O'Toole. Or maybe Clive Owen.

What we got was Simon Cowell with a cockney accent. And without the wit.

Once the acerbic cabbie dropped us off at Trafalgar Square, I dragged Mary Jo to the National Gallery, where I feasted on Renoirs, Monets, and Van Goghs. But my fidgeting friend wanted to feast on something that would stick to her physical ribs a bit more—and my feet were beginning to throb again. So after an hour, I sighed. "All right, you Philistine, let's go get some lunch." One of the gallery guards recommended the nearby café in the Crypt below a church called St. Martin's in the Field.

"Lunch in a crypt?" MJ said. "That's a bit macabre."

"I see dead people," I parroted Haley Joel Osment.

But tonight at long last I'm going to see one of my favorite live ones.

I tore into my sandwich with lip-smacking relish.

MJ looked at me in surprise that evening as we got dressed for the big surprise. I kept my same pair of black jeans on but also donned a red Christian Dior sweater. "Is that all you bought on your shopping spree today? I figured you'd buy out the store."

"Nope." I tossed my head. "I'm going with the less-is-more approach while I'm here."

Her eyebrows knit together. Then her face cleared, and she gave me a searching look. "Phoebe, do you need money?"

"No!" I answered a little too quickly.

Lord, please forgive me for that little white one and the one I'm about to tell now. "Actually, I was remembering how awful it was getting all my luggage on the train when we first arrived. If I go and buy a bunch more clothes now and then the airport finds my bag, where in the world would I put them?" I shuddered. "The last thing I want to do is add another suitcase to the mix."

She looked at me in delighted amazement. "Wow. I think you're getting logical in your old age, Pheebs."

We settled into our seats, and I pulled my leather jacket closer to conceal the small rip at the bottom of my beautiful new thrift-store sweater. I picked up the opera glasses Cordelia had given us, eager to catch a surreptitious glimpse of my Alex. Delia had told me where they'd be sitting—in their family box on the other side of the theater—so there'd be no chance of our running into him until after the play.

Where is he? I can't find him! My heart clenched, then relaxed. "There he is," I whispered to Mary Jo. "Adorable as ever—he's gotten a haircut, though. And those must be his parents behind him, and there's Delia sitting next to her dad. But wait—who's that?" I gripped the glasses tighter. "*She* wasn't in the family portrait."

"Who?" MJ picked up her pair of opera glasses.

"The gorgeous blonde who keeps clutching his arm." At that moment, said gorgeous blonde whispered something in his ear and Alex threw back his head and laughed.

I lowered my glasses, feeling sick. "He did that with me too."

"Does he have another sister?"

"No, just Delia."

"Well maybe it's a cousin or something. Don't jump to conclusions, Pheebs."

My stomach unclenched, and my face brightened. *Note to self: Relax. Breathe. And listen to wise friend. Remember, back in Barley you assumed Cordelia was Alex's girlfriend. So rein in the neuroses already.*

When the curtain began to fall, I whispered to Mary Jo, "Okay, let's book it. We don't want to miss them." Hurrying to the other side of the theater, we affected a casual stance on the far side of the curtain outside their box.

Delia appeared first and gave us a big wink, followed by her parents, who didn't notice us, and finally Alex and . . . that woman. Seeing the too-gorgeous and way-too-skinny blonde with her arm linked through Alex's made me hesitate and wonder if I was doing the right thing.

But it was too late now.

I nodded to Mary Jo, who began to hum "As Time Goes By." Then I took a deep breath and said in my best Bogie voice, "Of all the theaters, in all the towns, in all the world, you walked into mine . . ."

[chapter ten]

Surprise Attack

alex dropped the blonde's arm and spun around, his gorgeous, kissable mouth hanging open.

"Care to buy a vowel?" I teased.

"Phoebe! Mary Jo! What are you *doing* here?"

Coming to see you, you big goof. So why aren't we in a lip-lock yet?

Down, passion girl. My cold-shower voice of reason held me in check. *You don't want your first kiss to be in front of his parents, do you?*

Well, maybe not . . . But he could at least run up and take me in his arms.

"Surprised?"

"Surprised? I'm gobsmacked!"

"Gob what?" Mary Jo moved in to give Alex a friendly hug.

He returned her hug and laughed. "Sorry. There goes my English. Gobsmacked—stunned." Then he turned to me and gave me a hug as well.

Just a hug? And second in line? This is so not what I had in mind.

Remember about jumping to conclusions . . .

". . . to see you," Alex was saying. A line creased his forehead. "H-how, when did you get here? Is everything all right?"

You tell me. Why are you acting so strange and stiff?

"Everything's fine." I gave him a bright smile. "We just found some great airfares and decided to take advantage of them. Gordon's idea, actually. We got in yesterday."

Alex chuckled. "How is old Gordon? And everyone else in Barley?"

The mystery blonde gave me a speculative look that lingered on my sweater. I pulled my jacket tighter. She was even more gorgeous up close and personal, with cascading Jessica Simpson hair but a much-smarter-than-Jessica look on her heart-shaped face. And she was teeny-tiny to boot—

No whispering thighs on that woman.

—and she barely came up to Alex's chin, while my Manolos gave me a bird's-eye view of the top of his curly head.

Next to her, I felt like Pinocchio. Only instead of my nose growing, it was my thighs that were getting larger by the second.

"Alex?" a deep voice intoned. "Are you going to introduce us?"

He whirled around. "Oh. Sorry. Dad, Mum, these are my friends Phoebe and Mary Jo from Barley. You've heard me speak of them." He turned back to us. "Phoebe, Mary Jo, these are my parents, David and Grace Spencer. And this is my sister, Corde—" He stopped short when he saw her grinning face. "You little minx. Why do I have the feeling you've already met?"

Delia fluttered her eyelashes at him as she hugged first me, then Mary Jo. "Someone had to help with the surprise on this end, brother dear."

"Well, you certainly surprised me." Alex finished up the introductions by gesturing to the gorgeous blonde. "And this is George— Georgina—Fairchild, Dad's right arm and mine."

My mouth dropped open. "*This* is George?"

Open mouth; insert big, ungainly foot.

I shook her tiny proffered hand and was instantly back in junior high again, the wallflower at the school dance. I felt like a wide-hipped, thunder-thighed Amazon next to this doll-like vision.

"Let me guess. Dear Alex never said I was a woman, right?" She gave him a playful punch on the arm. "Thank you very much indeed."

"Go on, George. Give him what for," Alex's father said, bestowing a fond smile on the two of them. He turned to me, still smiling. "George is practically one of us. Our families have been friends and neighbors for years. And these two were at university together."

Well, isn't that special? The old *Saturday Night Live* church lady took up residence in my head.

"Was journalism your major as well?" I asked George politely.

"Oh, good Lord, no." She laughed—not a rich, full-bodied guffaw like mine, but one of those lovely, petite, musical laughs that sounded like expensive crystal clinking together.

Crystal I'd like to break.

"There's no money in journalism unless you're part of the Spencer dynasty," she added, giving Alex a playful poke in the side this time. "I studied law."

My smile stuck to my lips. And I longed to give her a not-so-playful poke.

Now I knew how Kate Winslet felt in *Sense and Sensibility* when she entered the glittering society party and saw the man she adored standing beside a wealthy, glittering debutante-type.

"What was your concentration, Phoebe?" Gorgeous George asked me.

"Journalism."

Her tiny hand flew to her mouth. "Oh, sorry! I've gone and put my foot into it, haven't I?" But her contrition didn't quite reach her eyes. "No offense meant. Really."

"None taken." I meant to give her a subtle but dismissive once-over, with a cool glance from head to toe. But that intention fell apart when I glanced down at her little feet. And died.

She was wearing the same Manolos as I was—the very model Alex had given to me as a Christmas present. Only on her they looked dainty and demure. I haven't been dainty or demure since I came out of the womb.

"Great boots." I croaked past the lump in my throat.

"Thank you," she said, trying not to preen. "I just love my Manolos."

"Me too."

Then George looked down and noticed that our feet were twins. Or quadruplets.

So did Alex, who flushed and tugged at his collar. "I thought they looked familiar."

"Well, they say imitation is the sincerest form of flattery." Alex's father clapped his hand on his son's shoulder and grinned.

His gracious, Anglicized mother saved the day. "Phoebe, it's so lovely to meet you," Grace said. "Alex has told us such wonderful things about you and your family. How long will you be here? You must come round for dinner. Or tea, perhaps?"

Alex cast her a grateful look. "Absolutely. Yes. Phoebe, Mary Jo, if you don't have plans for tomorrow night, let's all have dinner together."

"I'm afraid we have that dinner meeting with the board," George reminded him.

He frowned. "Blast. I'd forgotten."

"Oh, and your father and I are leaving for the country tomorrow afternoon, dear," his mother said with a chagrined look.

"Right. Of course. Don't know where my head is tonight. Sorry."

Poor man. He's totally flustered. I should have listened to Mary Jo and given him some warning.

"Oh, please—don't worry about it." With a monumental effort I adopted a nonchalant, free-spirited air. "We know this was spur of the moment, and we certainly don't expect you to rearrange your schedules for us. We're flexible. Right, MJ?"

"Right. We'll be in England a couple of weeks. We can always get together later."

His mother laid her soft, manicured hand on my arm and offered a welcoming look that included Mary Jo. "You must both come visit us in the country. We would love to get to know you better. Besides, you can't leave without seeing the Cotswolds. They're considered one of the most picturesque spots in all of England."

Her husband grunted. "Don't let a Yorkshireman hear you say that, my dear."

116

Mary Jo's face creased into a huge smile. "Hey! We're planning to visit both Yorkshire *and* the Cotswolds. I'm a big James Herriot fan," she added.

"Are you?" David Spencer gave her a meaningful nod. "I rather enjoy his horse stories myself."

Mary Jo followed his gaze down at her green sweatshirt with the horses scampering across the front. She'd added her orange turtleneck underneath to dress it up.

A flicker of disdain crossed Georgina's face as she took in Mary Jo's outfit. Then she turned her fashion attention to me. "That's a rather special top, Phoebe. Dior, isn't it?"

I nodded, pleased anew at my thrift-store find.

"My mother used to have one just like it." Her eyes narrowed as she fake-smiled. "It was her favorite, but she tore it riding one day, so we gave it to a charity shop. It was just a tiny tear near the bottom, and we figured some lucky woman handy with a needle wouldn't mind."

Alex cleared his throat. "Speaking of riding . . . Mary Jo has a stable in Barley and gives riding lessons."

"Well then, we'll have to arrange for a ride when you come out to the house." Alex's dad exchanged another fond when-are-you-going-to-become-my-daughter-in-law smile with his colleague. "Nothing like a nice, brisk morning ride in the country, eh, George?"

"It's one of the things I miss most when I'm in London," Georgina said, returning his smile. She turned to me with an innocent look. "Do you ride as well, Phoebe?"

As well as what? The kids on the plastic vending horse in front of the market?

Mary Jo started to snort, but turned the snort into a cough when she caught my eye.

"A little," I told George just as innocently.

Alex raised his eyebrows.

Delia jumped into the mix. "Just so you don't take them on one of those barbaric fox hunts, Dad."

Her father's face flushed. "Cordelia, riding to the hounds is an English institution."

"That doesn't make it any less cruel—the poor little defenseless fox against all those snapping beasts waiting to tear it apart."

"Defenseless fox indeed. Do you know the damage those creatures do to our chickens?"

"Well, then, set a humane trap." Delia's nostrils flared. "But don't make a festive sporting event out of it and say it's to protect the chickens."

"All right, you two—enough," Grace said gently. "This isn't the time nor the place to rehash that old family squabble." She turned to MJ and me. "You'll have to forgive my husband and daughter; they're always arguing about something."

She softened her rebuke with a fond look at both of them. "That's because they're both so much alike."

Delia smiled at her father, who returned it with a gruff one of his own. I noticed he was looking rather pale and remembered his heart attack just a few months ago.

Grace then changed the subject. "So what have you girls planned for tomorrow?"

I glanced at MJ and smiled. "We need to do a little shopping—Mary Jo's favorite sport. But we also want to go to St. Paul's and then maybe afternoon tea somewhere. I've heard the Ritz is fabulous."

Please let the money be in my account tomorrow.

"Yes, the Ritz is quite nice," Grace said, "but if you want the quintessential English afternoon-tea experience, you must go to Brown's. It's one of the oldest five-star hotels in London and has lots of lovely dark paneling and wonderful antiques. Agatha Christie used it as a model for her mystery *At Bertram's Hotel.*" She looked at her daughter. "What do you have on for tomorrow afternoon, Delia? Can you take them to tea?"

Delia pulled her planner from her purse. "Actually, I have meetings 'til around twoish, but we could meet there at three o'clock, if that's all right with you?"

"MJ?" I asked.

"Fine by me."

"Right. I'll make reservations then." Delia glanced apologetically at our outfits. "I'm afraid jeans and sweatshirts are frowned upon." She lifted her nose toward the ceiling and gave an exaggerated sniff. "All very posh and civilized, don't you know?"

"That's okay." I smiled. "We have no problem doing posh. Right, MJ?" *Just as long as my suitcase arrives.*

"Right."

Grace returned her attention to us. "Where are you girls staying?"

"King's Cross," we replied in unison.

George's perfectly arched eyebrows lifted, and she exchanged a telling look with Alex's father.

"King's Cross?" His mother frowned. "Are you sure that's safe, dear?"

"Oh, it's fine. No problem."

"How are you getting home?"

"Same way we came," MJ said. "The tube."

Alex looked at his watch. "Not this time of night, you're not. The last train left ten minutes ago."

I gulped, thinking of the cost. "Oh well, we'll just take a taxi then."

Grace glanced at her husband, who by now was looking very peaked. "Darling, shall we go? I'm getting a bit tired." She kissed Mary Jo, then me, on the cheek. "Lovely to meet you. I'm so sorry I won't be able to join you for tea tomorrow, but Delia will make sure you're taken care of." She reached in her purse. "Here's my card. Please do ring and let us know when you'll be in the Cotswolds, so we can have a longer visit."

"And go for that ride," David added, nodding his farewell as he linked his wife's arm in his.

Delia hugged us both. "See you tomorrow at three then. Just tell your taxi driver Brown's Hotel in Mayfair. He'll know right where it is."

Georgina gave us a brisk shake of her little claw, then stood waiting for Alex, who gave each of us another awkward hug—no kiss—before bidding us good-night.

This is just like in The Parent Trap *when that money-hungry, high-maintenance Joanna Barnes—also a skinny blonde—wormed her way into Brian Keith's life while daughter Hayley Mills was away at camp . . . and tried to shut out his real love, the voluptuous Maureen O'Hara . . .*

"Wonder why Alex never mentioned Gorgeous George was a woman," I said, unlocking our door.

"It just never came up," Mary Jo said, wheezing from the climb. "He's a guy. He's oblivious. Don't read anything more into it."

"Then why was she hanging all over him?" I yanked the door shut behind me. "Maybe she's why he's not hurrying home."

She sighed and sank onto her bed. "Alex hasn't hurried home because this *is* home for him. His dad had a heart attack, and he needs to be here to help out with the family business. You know he's not the kind of guy to dangle two women at once."

"You're right." I struggled out of my jacket, turning my back to Mary Jo so she wouldn't spot the sweater rip. "Although I'll bet George wouldn't mind being dangled. And his dad would certainly be thrilled if they got together." I bit my lip. "Did you notice how awkward Alex was at the theater? He didn't seem himself at all."

He didn't even notice that I'm growing my hair out!

"True." She frowned. "He wasn't his normal happy-go-lucky self. But then again, he's been worried about his dad—and we did surprise him. Maybe it's just that famous English reserve. When he comes back here it automatically slips into place, especially when he's around his father. He gets all stuffy and proper."

I sat down on my bed and took off my boots. The infamous boots. I didn't know if I ever wanted to wear them again now. Even though they were Manolos—probably the only pair I'd ever own . . .

I shrugged. I'd have to wear them again. They were the only footwear I had to my name here in England, and until my money came in, I couldn't afford to buy more. And they *were* Manolos, after all.

"Alex feels very beholden to his dad for all that he's done for him and his mom, and he doesn't want to disappoint him or let him down." I removed my socks. "But still, I'm not crazy about that George. Bit of a snob, don't you think?"

Mary Jo pulled down her covers. "Just a little." She grinned. "I noticed how impressed she was by my sweatshirt."

"You saw that? I thought I was the only one."

"I work with kids, remember? You learn to grow eyes in the back of your head."

"So what's your take on Alex, MJ? What do you think's going on with him? He sure didn't hug me very long. It was almost like we were total strangers." I took off my earrings. "Did I make a mistake coming here to surprise him? And is it just me, or does he seem to have cooled down in his feelings toward me? He sure didn't say much . . ."

"You know, I'm not too good at all this dissecting of every little thing guys say and do, Pheebs." She yawned. "Never have been. Too hard to figure out, and not sure it helps anyway or makes all that much difference in the long run."

"Are you *kidding*? This is a critical female need. How else can we let out our neuroses and figure out a plan?"

Lins, where are you when I need you?

"Why don't we just pray about it instead?" She yawned again and rubbed her eyes.

"Well, there's a novel idea." I sat cross-legged on the bed, suddenly aware that since getting to London I had completely reneged on my quiet-time resolution. "Go for it."

"Father, thank You for bringing us here safely to London," Mary Jo prayed. "And right now I lift up Alex to You. We don't know what's going on with him or what path You have for him, but we pray for Your wisdom and discernment. I pray too for Phoebe and that You would protect her"—she paused, and I could hear the smile in her voice—"neurotic heart and give her peace. And if this relationship is not Your will at this time, then please shut the—"

My eyes flew open. "Hey! I don't want Him to shut the doors. Don't pray for that! That's like praying for patience." All the admonitions I'd heard about being careful what you prayed for came rushing back to me. "Before you know it, you find yourself waiting in every single area of your life." I shook my head. "Tough way to learn patience."

"But effective."

There you go, being all wise and spiritually mature again. "Knock it off, will ya?" I smiled to show her I was teasing—sort of—and picked up my copy of *Jane Eyre*. "Heading for the tub now, MJ. I need a long, hot bath. Sweet dreams. Oh, and by the way—amen."

"Uh-huh." Mary Jo snored her good-night.

Unable to find any cleanser, I scrubbed the dingy tub with some bath salts I found on the grimy window ledge. I turned on the taps and dumped in a liberal amount of the muscle-relaxing Radox salts.

And while the tub filled, I had a little one-on-one with God.

"Hi, Lord. It's me, Phoebe. Uh, about Mary Jo's prayer . . . I'm really not at the point of wanting You to shut the door on Alex, so do You think You could maybe please just leave it open? Wide would be good. If it's Your will, of course. Thanks."

I lowered myself into the narrow, claustrophobic tub, my thighs wedging tightly up against the sides.

Definitely time to start exercising again.

In something other than stiletto-heeled boots.

[chapter eleven]

Not in Kansas Anymore

ise and shine Cinderella." I flung the covers off my jet-lagged roommate. "It's time for your posh makeover from your fairy godmother."

These days, the glass slipper appeared to be on the other foot. Back home, I was never a morning person, and Mary Jo was up at the crack of dawn to feed her horses and read her Bible. But here in England I was wide awake and eager to begin our day . . . only I couldn't get MJ out of bed.

"I'm on vacation," she grumbled. "And I don't want to be made over." She pulled the covers over her head. "I'm perfectly happy the way I am."

"Yes, I know. And that works great in casual California, MJ. But we're in England now and need to dress up a bit more." I donned my mostly dry and now rather itchy sweater. "Don't worry, I'm not going to do one of those extreme makeover things where they dye your hair, shoot you full of Botox, and bleach and straighten your teeth. This is just a little wardrobe adjustment."

She swung her legs over the side of the bed with reluctance. "Okay. But just for this fancy-schmancy tea thing today. When we're walking around checking out the sights, I'm wearing my comfy jeans." Her frugal eyes bored into mine. "And I'm not going to spend a lot of money on clothes I'll probably only wear once, either."

123

I'm counting on that.

Before waking MJ up, I'd run out and tried the phone and a nearby ATM, but my cash hadn't shown up yet. Nor had my suitcase.

"Not a problem, MJ. I know just the place."

After breakfast—canned grapefruit sections and a cold cereal called Weetabix—I herded Mary Jo to the same charity shop where I'd bought George's mother's discarded sweater. Once inside, I headed straight to the familiar rack of coats and jackets. "You can never go wrong with a blazer, MJ." Flipping through, I was delighted to find a nice navy jacket as well as a black wool one that I hoped would fit my friend's bulkier frame. I also spotted a nice gray tweed I wanted to try on, especially since it was less than ten pounds.

She kept gravitating toward sweaters and "cute" tops with animals on them, and I kept pulling her away.

"We're going for classic and understated," I said, handing her a pair of black trousers. "Not cutesy. Every woman needs at least one pair of black pants. You can wear them anywhere—church, dinner, the theater—"

"A funeral," grumbled Mary Jo, who preferred bright rainbow hues and whose favorite color was orange.

"That too."

We left with two blazers—the black wool for MJ and the gray tweed for me. No pants though; the nice-looking ones were too tight.

Our next stop was Marks & Spencer, which I'd learned yesterday was having a sale. Immediately we found Mary Jo a pair of slimming black trousers that fit—and were half-off.

Much to my regret, a similar pair in my size weren't on sale.

I scratched my shoulder blade, where my uncomfortable, still-damp sweater was itching, hoping to find another charity shop before teatime. "MJ?" I turned around looking for my friend, who had disappeared.

"Here I am, Pheebs. So what's next?" She shivered. "I'm not used to this cold weather. Why don't we go look at sweaters—I mean jumpers?"

I stared at my newly compliant friend in surprise and nodded.

She settled on a fuchsia pullover, also on sale, that gave her the color she craved. And as we passed by the shoe department, a pair of hot pink stilettos called to me. "MJ, these would go perfectly with your new outfit!" I held them up against her sweater. "See how they *almost* match without looking too much like a canned outfit?"

Mary Jo looked at the spiky heel and snorted. "I don't care how well they almost match. You'll never catch me in a pair of heels that high. Or that skinny. I'd fall flat on my face. And there I put my foot down."

Which she did, ten minutes later—right into a pair of soft black leather, low-heeled boots.

Mary Jo walked by the mirror, admiring the fit. "Now, good boots I'm willing to spend money on."

Her eyes caught mine in the mirror. "Okay. Your turn."

"Uh, I didn't see anything that was really me."

"I did." She linked her arm through mine. "Come on. My turn to choose for you." Mary Jo steered me back to the sweaters. "I know how much you like yellow, so how about this yellow-and-purple-checked turtleneck?"

I tried not to shudder. Then I noticed her smirk. "Cute. Very cute. Okay, shall we go now?"

She plucked at my damp, itchy sweater. "You need something besides that to wear. You're going to get sick." She grew serious. "Phoebe, you've been a wonderful friend, inviting me along on this trip and everything, so I'd like to give you a gift as a thank-you." She extended a shopping bag my way. I hadn't even noticed she was carrying it.

"MJ, you didn't have to do that."

"I know I didn't have to. I *wanted* to. Open it."

Inside was a black turtleneck and the pair of black trousers I'd tried on earlier; along with a matching pair in a delicious soft gray.

I stared at her.

"I thought those might go with that gray tweed jacket you just got." Mary Jo shot me an anxious look. "Do they? I'm no fashion maven like you."

"They're perfect, MJ, but I can't let you buy me clo—"

"Just say thank you and shut up." She grinned.

"Thank you."

She looked down at my Manolos. "And now we're going to get you some more comfortable shoes for trudging all around this city."

And at that I couldn't keep quiet any longer. I had to 'fess up to my mistake. But Mary Jo had already guessed. And it didn't matter.

Guess that's part of being a spiritual giant, huh, God? Not rubbing someone's nose in it?

"Uh, MJ. Now that you know . . . my little secret, I need to—"

She grinned again and pointed to my feet. "Are you ready to stop walking around on those torture machines?"

I straightened. After three days of walking around in heels, my feet were truly killing me, but I still had my pride. I was not going to tea with Alex's sister wearing sensible shoes. Or flat broke, for that matter.

"I'll think about it," I promised her. "But I need to ask . . . can you spot me for a flower and some tea?"

With still a few hours before we were due to meet Delia for tea, we decided to make our visit to St. Paul's Cathedral. Both of us had loved *Mary Poppins* as kids and were eager to go and feed the birds like the Banks children had done in the movie. And I, of course, had my little errand to run for Esther.

We softly sang the song from *Mary Poppins* ("Feed the birds . . . tuppence a bag") as we made our way to the cathedral, making sure we had change in our pockets, although neither one of us was exactly sure what a tuppence was.

Only when we got there, there wasn't a bird woman. No birds either. Not one. Anywhere we looked.

We wandered around the outside of the magnificent cathedral, whistling and calling, but to no avail. Finally we approached an elderly woman sitting on a nearby bench, who looked a little bit like the bird woman, except that her hair wasn't in a messy bun and she was reading a paperback with a hot-pink cover.

"Excuse me, ma'am," I said, "Can you please tell us where all the birds are?"

At the *ma'am* she looked up from her book. "Americans, right?"

We nodded.

"First time here?"

We nodded again.

"The birds are all gone. They made a frightful mess, quite dirty and smelly, so several years back the city bought out the licenses of all the feed sellers here and at Trafalgar Square and they cleared off." She took a sip from her water bottle. "Much cleaner now and more hygienic without all the nasty bird droppings."

"But not as romantic," I sighed.

The woman rolled her eyes. But when I asked, she did point out a flower vendor across the street.

"You still haven't told me what the flower is all about," whispered Mary Jo as we climbed the million steps up to the cathedral door, my Manolo-clad feet complaining all the time.

"In a minute," I told her, craning my neck as we stepped into the airy vestibule. "This was where Prince Charles and Diana were married," I whispered to Mary Jo. "I remember watching it on TV when I was a little girl." I sighed. "It was the perfect fairy-tale wedding."

It was MJ's turn to roll her eyes, but she had the grace not to mention the outcome of that perfect wedding. Instead, she was flipping through her guidebook. "It says here you can climb all the way up in the dome. Wanna do it?"

My blistered toes cried out at the very thought. "I think I'll let you do that on your own." I took the guidebook from her. "Does this thing say where the World War II memorial is?"

The gigantic nave of St. Paul's was strangely quiet, considering the tourists milling around inside. I clutched my rose all the way down the wide central aisle. A hush descended on my spirit as I entered the bright, open area under the dome, then made my way past the carved choir boxes and around the massive altar to a little chapel. This was the American Memorial Chapel, constructed by the British in gratitude to Americans who died in England during World War II. An American eagle graced the center stained-glass window, and beneath the high altar sat the Roll of Honor on a marble pedestal.

Under glass and inaccessible.

Just like Alex was last night. I don't understand what's going on with him, God. He seemed so different. And distant. What happened? Does he not feel the same anymore? Did he ever even care about me? Or was I just a small-town diversion?

Maybe he's just not that into you. The phrase from a popular self-help book flashed through my head, and I began to weep.

Seeing my tears, a guide approached. "Beg pardon, Miss; but were you looking for a particular name?"

Way to go, selfish one. Focus and remember why you're here. It's not all about you, you know. You're in church, for goodness' sake—and you've got something important to do. Get over yourself already.

"Miss?"

"Um, yes." I got hold of myself. "For a friend of mine."

"Follow me, please." He retrieved another copy of the book, available only by request, for visitors to be shown the names.

And there was Norman's. Under the *H*s. I laid the rose at the altar and thought of Esther, now reunited with her soldier boy.

Heavy sigh. Will I ever be able to say the same about me and Alex? *Stop that right now!*

"So have you completed your mission?" Mary Jo's voice sounded gently behind me.

"Esther wanted to do this when she was in England. And now it's done." We both stood there a long time, talking quietly about our friend and what she had made of her life.

When we finally exited the cathedral into the sunshine, we took a last look around for any stray birds. "Look! There's one. Quick, take a picture!" As MJ snapped, I sang, trying my best to sound like Julie Andrews.

The pigeon flew away.

"Now I know we're not in Kansas anymore," MJ whispered as we entered the muted elegance of the wood-paneled, antique-filled drawing room of Brown's Hotel, where an elegant upright piano tinkled classical music in the background.

"I know," I whispered back. "Any second now I expect to see Anthony Hopkins walk through the door with Emma Thompson on his heels, carrying a silver tea tray."

"Okay, don't tell me," said Mary Jo, who was getting used to my movie commentaries. *"Gosford Park,* right?"

I smiled. *"Remains of the Day.* Remember, the one about the butler and the housekeeper?"

"Sounds like *Gosford Park* to me."

"But without the murder mystery. Shh. She'll hear you."

It wasn't Emma, but an Emmaesque waitress clad in black and white who passed us bearing a silver teapot. And right behind her, in a corner, we spotted Delia comfortably ensconced on a plush Victorian settee, impeccably turned out in a crimson wool skirt, cream sweater, and gleaming leather boots. Not Manolos, mind you. But gorgeous.

We made our posh-clad way over to her.

"Ooh, MJ, don't you look smart?" she said. "Turn round. Let me see. Oh yes, very nice indeed." She glanced at me. "And you as well. Love the gray tweed." She motioned to the two tapestry armchairs across the delicate antique table from her. "Sit down and relax."

"Easier said than done." Mary Jo lowered herself gingerly into one of the chairs, hiking up her black trousers. "This isn't my normal cup of tea." But she let out her breath as she settled into the sturdy chair.

A different statuesque server dressed in crisp black and white appeared bearing a silver teapot and gold-rimmed china cups and saucers, which she set before us. "Milk and sugar?"

"Yes, please." I took a sip and shot Mary Jo a warning look as she started to crook her pinky.

Moments later, the server returned bearing a three-tiered silver tray filled with dainty sandwiches, scones, and little cakes and pastries—including something chocolate and delicious-looking on the very top.

"Now, this is the life." I leaned back in utter contentment, munching on a cucumber sandwich. "Forget New York. I think I could easily grow accustomed to this lifestyle. It's all so very civilized."

"Yes, quite." MJ raised her pinky discreetly. I stuck out my tongue at her . . . discreetly.

"Definitely a must-do at least once," Delia said. Leaning forward, she grinned and whispered over her teacup, "Although it's grown frightfully dear. It's all for the tourists now, you see. All of you wanting to have a proper English tea with all the bells and whistles."

"What?" Mary Jo stared at her over the top of her cup. "You mean you don't have tea like this every day?"

"Not even. Afternoon tea like this is now just an occasional thing. And then it's usually just a cuppa and some bikkies or a piece of cake or scone to take the edge off in the afternoon and carry us through to dinner." Delia gestured at the tea and all the accoutrements. "This whole posh do is just for special occasions—such as when we're trying to impress Americans."

"Is that butter or whipped cream?" MJ asked, pointing.

"It's clotted cream, actually."

Mary Jo scrunched up her nose.

"For your scone," Delia said. "Would you like me to show you the proper way to eat a scone?"

We both nodded.

"You cut it in half horizontally, then spread on the strawberry preserves, then top it off with the clotted cream. See? And if butter is also provided, you put that on first before the jam."

I looked at her hipless figure. "And you can stay that small with all this dairy?"

"Not if I ate like this every day. This is a treat for me too." She took a bite. "Mmm, lovely."

A few minutes later, hunger pangs sated, Mary Jo cut right to the chase. "So, Delia, what's the deal with this George chick? Is she hot for Alex or what?"

I choked on my scone.

Delia laughed. "That's what I love about you Americans. So direct. And yes, as a matter of fact, George is hot for Alex. Has been for years."

The delicious scone lost all its flavor. I set it down. "Have they ever, um, dated?"

"Years ago, I think, when they were both at university together." She sipped her tea. "But after he graduated, Alex went to America to expand the family business and has stayed there ever since. Until now, of course."

And now that he's back, she's got her little claws in him all over again. "So, what's she like?" I kept my voice casual. "George, I mean."

Delia made a face. "She's brilliant at business—I know that much. She studied that at Oxford, then went on to get her law degree."

"Just pound those nails in my coffin. Let's see: drop-dead gorgeous, tiny, and smart. What else?"

"Well, she's also very athletic." Delia grimaced. "Plays tennis, hikes, rides, and shoots—the quintessential English country gentlewoman." She sighed. "Her family and our family have been friends and neighbors forever, and Dad adores her. Sorry to say this, but I think he's hoping for an alliance."

"Just shoot me now and put me out of my misery." I grabbed a truffle.

"Oh, I'm against blood sports, I'm afraid." She gave a rueful smile. "But I do think there's reason for concern. My darling brother has always been a bit of a people pleaser. And right now with his concern for Dad, he wants to do everything he can to make him happy."

"Including spending time with Gorgeous George?" I scarfed down the truffle.

"Afraid so." Delia frowned. "Although to be honest, I don't really know how Alex feels about George these days. I mean, they've been mates for ages, but my big brother doesn't confide in me about his love life. Never has."

The corners of her mouth turned up. "Of course, I don't confide in him about mine either."

"Oh, do you have a boyfriend?" I leaned in.

"Not at the moment." She selected another scone. "Which is quite all right with me, mind you, as I'm very busy with my job. I'm still in that proving-myself stage to my father, even though I've been working at the company every summer since I was sixteen." Delia grimaced. "*And* full-time for the past year and a half."

"Doing what?" Mary Jo asked.

"All the financial bits and pieces," she said, growing animated— way too animated, if you ask me, for such a snooze of a subject. "Market analysis, trend forecasting, investment—"

Finally, when she slowed down, I looked at her. "And you're how old again?"

"Twenty-three. But I've been going to Dad's office since I was four." She smiled at the memory. "Even then, my favorite thing to play with was his calculator."

I'm nearly ten years older than she is, and I still don't know what I want to be when I grow up.

Delia kept on talking about spreadsheets and profit-and-loss reports, and I tried to feign an interest, but I couldn't help it. My eyes began to glaze over.

"Oh, sorry," she said, seeing my face. "I forgot you weren't the corporate type."

"Who says?" I squared my shoulders. "I'll have you know that just before I left, I received a job offer to be the public-relations director for a major Cleveland investment company."

MJ raised her eyebrows at me over her teacup.

"But let's get back to the fun stuff," I added, ignoring Mary Jo and winking at Delia. "Relationships. Wouldn't you like to meet someone and get married?"

"Of course. But not for a few years yet. Wouldn't want to get tied down too early, you know, and it's still *ages* before I'm thir—" Immediately she raised her hand to her mouth, her horrified eyes darting between Mary Jo and me. "Sorry."

We exchanged wry glances. "Yeah, I know I'm about ready to be out to pasture," Mary Jo said. "What about you, Pheebs?"

"Close, but not quite."

Delia's face flamed. "I'm so sorry. How rude—"

Mary Jo waved off her apology and returned to more pressing matters. "So, does George love movies?"

"Not the way Alex does. In that respect they're totally different."

I felt a glimmer of romantic hope. But I sucked down another truffle anyway.

"Right," Delia said, brushing some crumbs off her trousers. "So what about this hotel you're staying in then? What's it like?" She frowned. "King's Cross isn't the best area, you know. Are you all right staying there?"

Before either of us had a chance to answer, she added, "I'd invite you to stay in our flat, but it's a bit crowded these days with Alex and my parents all there. Besides," she shot a sly glance at me, "Mum and Dad will be heading back to the country, and I'm going back to my flat in Oxford. So after today it'll just be Alex, and we wouldn't want to give the appearance of evil and all that, right?"

Mary Jo stared at her. "You're a Christian?"

She smiled. "Yes, believe it or not. We do still have some here in England. Quite a few, as a matter of fact. We even have a few churches here and there."

It was Mary Jo's turn to blush. "I'm sorry. I'd just heard that even with all the historic churches, it's . . . well, pretty dead, spiritually."

"I'm just teasing you." Delia chuckled again. "I suppose from an American evangelical standpoint, it might seem that way. We're certainly not as outgoing as you—that whole British reserve and all. And our faith is definitely not as vocally or politically on display here the way it is in the States." She smiled in remembrance. "At university, Charlotte, one of my flat mates, said to me when we first met, 'All the Christians I've ever seen dress badly and have spots.'"

"Spautz?" I asked.

"Pimples."

Mary Jo snorted. "You Brits can make even a zit sound elegant."

"We try, darling. After all, we do have our upper-crust reputation to maintain." She set her cup down and leaned in conspiratorially. "Any rate, Charlotte went on in this whole Christians-are-daft tirade, saying, 'They all buy manor houses out in the country, turn them into communes, and do all sorts of strange cult things—singing and getting these glassy-eyed expressions and everything.'"

"What did you say to that?" I picked up my scone again.

"I just said I'd give her fair warning before I made a sacrifice in the lounge."

We laughed.

I drained my tea and tried to make my next question sound like an afterthought. "So, is George a Christian?"

"Good question." Delia frowned. "I think so. She's always gone to the local parish church at least, but I have a feeling she may be just going through the motions. Hard to say for certain. But back to your hotel—sorry, I have a tendency to get sidetracked sometimes." She sighed. "Mum's always on at me about it. So how is it, honestly?"

"Doesn't bother me, other than those fifty-nine steps," Mary Jo said, "but the stained bedspreads and dusty curtains rather offend Phoebe's aesthetic sensibilities."

Delia crinkled her nose. "They would mine as well. Right. Let's get that sorted out then." She punched a number into her cell and said while it was ringing, "There's a lovely little hotel we use for our business clients in central London. With our family discount, you can probably get a nice room for about the same price you're paying."

I protested. "We don't want you to go to any trouble."

"No trouble."

"Besides, we're still booked for tonight." I threw a helpless glance at Mary Jo.

"Yeah," MJ said. "We'd have to pay—"

Delia held up her hand for silence as she spoke into the phone.

Then Mary Jo and I exchanged amazed looks as we listened to Delia get us out of our cheesy hotel without penalties.

She flipped her phone shut and shot us a brisk smile. "Right. No worries. Shall we go then and collect your things?"

"How'd you do that?" I asked.

"Oh, I don't know," Delia replied with a beatific smile. "Perhaps a spot of divine intervention?"

chapter twelve

Notes from Abroad

sk your mom how my horses are doing," MJ said.

I scrolled through e-mail at another Internet cafe while she and Delia chatted away about horses and the other four-legged friends they had in common.

There were three messages from Lindsey, which I skimmed to make sure there was nothing urgent. But it was all trivial wedding-related stuff, so I just sent her a quick *Reader's Digest* update about what we'd seen and done in London thus far and said I hoped all the wedding plans were going along well.

I clicked open a message from my oldest niece, which turned out to be a message from my whole family as well:

> To: Movielovr
> From: AshGrant
>
>   Hi, Aunt Phoebe! Have you seen Prince William or Harry yet? What about the Queen? How's Alex? Are you in L-O-V-E yet? Wait a sec, Lexie just came in and wants to say hello.
>
>   hI Ant Phoebe, when r u coming HOME? I miss u. Can u come tomorrow? Then u could meet my turtle. His name is Jack. oK, bye. I love u.

Lexie insisted that I let her type, so we started that way, but then she got frustrated since it took so long. (Me too.☺) Anyway, I have to run. Elizabeth and Jacob say hi too. And Mom says to tell you that Baby Gloria is cooing and rolling over a lot now. (She's laughing too.☺) Dad didn't say anything 'cause he's never home, but I'll say it for him, for all of us: We love and miss you, but we're not jealous. Not so much. (That's a lie. I'm super jealous! Wish it were me.)

Love u lots! Ash

P.S. Hi, daughter, this is your mother. Ashley said she was writing you, so I wanted to add in my two cents. I hope you and Mary Jo are having a wonderful time and taking lots of pictures! And yes, we all miss you, but I'm thrilled you have this opportunity. How's Alex? And his father? Please give him and his family my regards and tell them they're in our prayers. All's well here, although your brother's working way too hard. I know you're busy, so I'll sign off now. Say hi to Mary Jo. I love you and pray God's blessings on you as you travel. Love, Mom.

P.S.S. This is Ashley again. I think this really cool guy in my English class likes me! Can't wait to tell you all about him, but I'd rather do it in person if you know what I mean. We all miss you and can't wait for you to come home! Luv ya lots! Ashley

I felt a little wistful as I read my niece's postscript. No, not home-sick exactly, but realizing she had never written me anything like that when I lived in Cleveland. And it was nice to feel I had my mom's blessing, that she saw the trip as an opportunity. That hadn't always been the case with us. Far from it. But we had a better relationship now. Something about living together for six weeks after she'd broken both her arms and bonding over chocolate and makeovers.

Going home to Barley really had been a good thing, even if my job was less than perfect. Even without Alex—though that was pushing it.

I pushed the button to respond to Ash's e-mail, but since the café charged by the hour, I kept my response brief.

> To: AshGrant
> From: Movielovr
>   Hi, everyone. Haven't seen William or Harry yet, but just finished having this la-di-dah tea at a posh hotel. I'll have to make you a proper tea when I get home.☺ And yes, we've ridden a double-deckah (that's how they pronounce it). Took lots of pictures from up top. We haven't been to a castle yet, but inside Westminster Abbey we saw cool statues of dead kings, queens, soldiers, and stuff. Saw Alex too and met his family—his dad looks good, altho a little tired. Mary Jo wants to know how her horses are. And you'll never guess: she bought some new clothes. She looks hot! Gotta run.
>   Love and miss you all, Aunt Phoebe

"Pheebs, check it out. They have an elevator! I mean lift. And we're only on the second—uh, first—floor." MJ grinned. "Already I'm a happy camper."

Inside the pristine lobby of our new hotel, an impeccably dressed older man who looked a lot like Alec Guinness welcomed us in his well-modulated British tones.

It took every bit of movie restraint I had to refrain from saying, "Help me, Obi-Wan. You're our only hope."

We rode the lift to the second floor and opened the door to our room with some trepidation.

Huge sigh of relief. It was tastefully furnished with two double beds (no stained bedspreads), a rich walnut antique armoire, the requisite sink (but this one a gleaming, white-pedestal confection), and a plush Oriental carpet. In the far corner, two cushy chintz chairs and a small table holding a tea tray, kettle, and basket of assorted tea biscuits and chocolate welcomed us. And on the antique nightstand between the two beds . . . a glorious bouquet of daffodils and purple irises.

I squealed with delight. "Daffodils—just like he sent me for Valentine's Day. Ha! Looks like I was worried about this Georgy Girl for nothing." I shot MJ a triumphant smile and reached for the card.

"Phoebe and Mary Jo," I read aloud, "hope this hotel makes your stay in London more pleasant. Lovely to meet you and hope to see you soon, Grace Spencer."

"Classy lady, his mom," Mary Jo said into the disappointed void.

Note to self: Practice adopting English reserve in place of jump-to-conclusions American exuberance.

While I stood there chiding myself, MJ checked out the bathroom and pumped her fist. "Yes! There's a walk-in shower!" She danced with glee. "First dibs."

While MJ took her shower, I unpacked my small suitcase, my carry-on, and my department-store shopping bags. *If my large suitcase doesn't show up soon, I'd have to buy a new one to put my new clothes in. That is, if my money ever comes through. Hope I hear from Gordon tomorrow . . .*

I sighed and turned on the small electric kettle to make tea. While it brewed, I pulled out my new journal, which I had bought especially for this. (I pulled out my devotional and skinny travel Bible, too, a little ashamed that I hadn't even cracked the covers since coming to England.)

There was something so comforting about a steaming hot cup of English tea, particularly with milk and sugar. And I was definitely in need of comfort. So I sipped my tea and munched on a chocolate biscuit as I began to journal all the things we'd seen and done on our trip thus far. Odd thing though; I found myself writing with an English accent.

> Alex's mother is lovely. I quite like her. And Delia's darling. His father seems bit of a stick, though one mustn't forget that he had a heart attack recently. One must make allowances. But what I can't quite make out is Alex. Rather distant and remote, I'd say. Although, to be fair, I've only seen him once. Seems he might have called, though . . .

Why hasn't he called, anyway? I mean, I know he's busy, but it just takes a minute to phone. Unless he's busy with a certain blonde . . .

I wasn't ready to face those possibilities. Instead, I asked MJ, who had just emerged from the bathroom, whether we should go out for dinner.

"Dinner? I'm still stuffed from that artery-clogging tea stuff. But I suppose we should get a little something before all the restaurants close. What do you have in mind?"

"I've actually been thinking we should have some curry. I read that Indian food is really popular here, and it's pretty cheap."

Mary Jo hesitated. "I don't know. I'm not exactly an ethnic-food person. I'm not all that culturally sophisticated like you are."

"C'mon, where's your pioneer spirit?"

"All the pioneers I'm familiar with ate steak." But at last she allowed me to talk her into it. We found a small, out-of-the-way Indian restaurant redolent with spices and ordered two small chicken curries—"your mildest, please."

But their mild was hotter than the spiciest Mexican food either of us had ever eaten. Eye-watering, mouth-searing hot. And the funny thing was, Mary Jo ended up really liking it. Whereas I gulped down glass after glass of water and vowed never to look another curry in the face.

"Hey, that was great," my pioneer friend said as I staggered from the restaurant, my eyes still streaming.

"So tell me, what's our next adventure?"

The next morning we were finishing breakfast in the antiques-filled dining room when a waitress approached. "Miss Grant? You have a phone call in the lobby."

My eyes widened at MJ. "Whoever could be calling?" I wiped my mouth and stood up. "Probably Delia, the darling. Or the airport calling about my things."

Mary Jo chuckled. "You do realize you're beginning to sound like that woman on the English TV show. The one that keeps putting on airs. Hyacinth something . . ."

"I do not sound like her," I huffed. "I merely have a good ear for the nuances of language."

"Right," she deadpanned. "Well, you'd better go see who the darling is that's on the phone."

I stuck out my tongue at her—nothing nuanced about that—then followed the waitress across the dining room and into the lobby. "Good morning. Phoebe Grant here," I trilled, then winced, realizing I *did* sound a little like Hyacinth Bucket. Or "boo-kay," as she was always telling people to pronounce it.

But the voice on the phone drove all thoughts of Hyacinth from my mind.

"Morning, Phoebe." Alex's long-lost voice was music to my ears.

I looked up at MJ, who'd followed me into the lobby with a quizzical expression on her face. "It's Alex," I mouthed, beaming. "He wants to know if we have plans for tonight."

He wants to see me, he wants to see me. Thank you, Lord. He wants to take me out! Um, I mean take us *out . . .*

Very nice, my conscience scolded. *Just leave your friend out in the cold in a foreign country so far away from home where she knows practically no one. And after she bought you that lovely bunch of clothes too.*

MJ shook her head. "Actually, if you don't mind, I'd really love to just stay in tonight."

My face fell.

She hurried to explain. "No, I mean just me. You guys go on." She grinned. "No offense, but I'd enjoy a little alone time. All I want to do tonight is stay in, order something to eat—pizza, hopefully—and watch a little TV."

I relayed this to Alex. "Really? You're kidding! That would be great. Uh-huh. I'd love it. Okay, see you then."

I hung up, eyes shining. "Alex has another dinner business meeting tonight, but afterwards we're going to see *Les Miz*! How romantic is that? He knows it's my favorite musical; he took me to see it in San Francisco, and I loved it. This will be almost like an anniversary or something."

My excitement faded as I looked at my friend. "Sure you don't want to go? I'd hate for you to miss *Les Miz* in London."

"You must have me confused with someone else. I don't care for musicals."

I stared at her. "But you sang 'Feed the Birds' with me and went to *Oklahoma* in Barley."

"That's different. I knew lots of people in *Oklahoma*—including you, Ms. Ado Annie. Wouldn't have missed that for the world." She chortled. "That flying girdle was one for the record books. And *Mary Poppins* is from my childhood. I also like *The Wizard of Oz*," she said dryly, "but after that I draw the musical line. I'm a Beatles/Motown girl. Remember?"

I remembered, although it was beyond me how *anyone* could pass up *Les Miz* in London. And I have to admit—I didn't argue with her. The prospect of an evening alone with Alex was way too tempting.

I pasted on a regretful look. "Well, if that's what you really want . . ."

Which didn't fool Mary Jo for a minute.

"It's what we both want, romance girl." She grinned. "Now, Louise. Are you all set for this morning's adventure?"

"Can't wait, Thelma." I linked arms with her and set off toward the elevator.

"We're off to see the Tower," I sang in my best Judy Garland voice. Only it came off sounding more like the happy scarecrow.

It was a great morning. Not even the aching of my still-stilettoed feet could diminish the excitement of seeing the Tower of London and the British Library. The prospect of seeing Alex that night didn't hurt either. I sailed through the morning on clouds of anticipation.

Back at the hotel, our gracious Alec Guinness host overheard me say I was going in search of an Internet café and offered to let me use their computer instead.

I could almost hear him say, "Use the force, Obi-Wan. Use the force."

Hoping and praying there'd be a message from Gordon with happy direct-deposit news, I breathed a sigh of relief when I logged on and saw his e-mail address.

To: Movielovr
From: GGreen

Dear Phoebe, Rest easy; your funds will be in your account by tomorrow. Sure hope this hasn't messed up your trip too much. Liked your e-mails though. Glad to hear you're having such a wonderful time in England. Pretty funny stuff about the food.

Hey, if you don't mind, I'd like to use some of your e-mails as a column for the Bulletin—sort of a 'dispatches from abroad.' (No, not 'a broad.' I don't want to get sued for sexual harassment.) You'd be in great company—Mark Twain did the same thing for the Sacramento *Union* more than a century ago. Think you could send me some England-through-your-eyes columns every couple of days? That way I can post them on our Web site and folks can have the chance to read them more than once a week.

Hate to make you work on your vacation, but you're a

fast writer, so it'd be a piece of cake. Needless to say, we'd pay the going rate. What do you say?

Give Alex my best and tell him all's fine here with the paper.

Gordon

P.S. Your mother sends her love.

Relieved to know my cash would start flowing again, I immediately fired off a reply:

To: GGreen
From: Movielovr

Hey, Gordon. I *love* the idea of writing a column. I've started keeping a travel journal, so it wouldn't be hard to come up with ideas. I'll try to put together something today or tomorrow.

By the way, thanks for taking care of my paycheck issue. And for keeping things going back on the home front.

Going to see *Les Miz* tonight with Alex! —P.

I sat there for a long minute before I began to type again. But when I started writing, the words just seemed to flow.

Gordon was right.

The column *was* a piece of cake.

NOTES FROM ABROAD

London is an exciting, fascinating city and I'm learning a lot over here in Merrie Olde. For instance, that you really *can't* judge a book by its cover.

Take the British Library. I'm a bibliophile from way back, so the words *British Library* alone conjured up this idyllic vision of an ancient stone building, perhaps with columns and portals, maybe a few gargoyles and some flying buttresses. Something classic and beautiful in an aged sort of way to house all the sacred texts and well-loved words from this venerable culture.

Instead, what greeted my dismayed and disappointed eyes was this hideous, contemporary [modern] and *orange* monstrosity. No columns, no portals, and no lovely, ancient gray stone. I hurried inside before the orange could leave a permanent bad taste in my mouth. But then the *inside* of the museum made me forget the outside in a London minute.

Talk about beauty. All those books—miles and miles of them. We saw a Gutenberg Bible, Handel's *Messiah,* an early folio of some of Shakespeare's handwritten plays, Virginia Woolf's *Mrs. Dalloway* scribblings, even original Beatles lyrics (which made my traveling companion swoon).

But this California girl is sure glad she didn't live back in Tudor times! Who knows? I might have lost my head to old Henry VIII. Not that I fancy him or anything. Definitely *not* my type. But that wouldn't have mattered. Back then, the king got whatever and whoever he wanted, *whenever* he wanted them. And what he wanted didn't seem to last very long. Especially wives.

So I don't think even those crown jewels in the Tower of London could tempt me to be a Tudor babe. Sure, they're drop-dead gorgeous, especially that giant Star of India diamond in the royal scepter. But I don't care how huge they are or how much they sparkle; diamonds are not this girl's best friend. I'd rather keep my head, thank you very much.

Think I'll just stick with the silver toe ring I bought for ten bucks at the mall.

Another interesting thing about the Tower. Legend has it that if the ravens were ever to leave, the monarchy would crumble. But not to worry. They keep the black birds' wings clipped to prevent that from happening. Sounds like they took a lesson from old Henry, huh?

I signed it with a flourish—"Cheerio! Your Overseas Correspondent," then shot it back to Gordon as an e-mail attachment. Then I sat at the computer for a long time, dreaming of possibilities.

I only left because Obi-Wan needed to use his computer.

My roomie looked up from her Bible when I burst through the door. "What's got you so excited? As if I didn't know . . ."

"Hey, this is something different!" Plopping down on the bed, I filled her in on my new column. "*So* much more fun to write about our Thelma-and-Louise travel adventures rather than emus and goat milking!"

"Way cool, Pheebs." She grinned. "Looks like our vacation was a God thing in more ways than one."

"I know!" I lay back and expelled a dreamy sigh. "The kind of writing I've been longing to do, *and* a date with Alex all in the same day? How much better can it get?"

It can only get better. I'll bet he's been longing for this too. Time alone together at last. I'll tell him about my column—he'll love that. Maybe he'll even want to publish it in some of the other Spencer papers. And after that we can go somewhere quiet, and . . .

Visions of that long-awaited first kiss carried me away. I hoped it would be all romantic and passionate. Like in *Room with a View*, when Julian Sand strode up to Helena Bonham Carter in that beautiful Italian field and swept her off her feet. But tonight it could happen on the way to a restaurant. Or on the street, oblivious to the pedestrians striding purposefully around us. Or even in our theater seats, with a glorious musical crescendo as a backdrop. Or outside the cab, just before Alex hands me in to go home.

The cab . . .

"Uh, Mary Jo, I really hate to ask again. But Gordon says my money will be in the bank tomorrow, and tonight . . ."

"I told you it's no problem," she said. "How much do you need?"

Riding in the cab to the theater, I sucked in my stomach—which was doing cartwheels on a par with any Olympic gymnast—and thought back to when Alex and I had seen the same musical with Phil and Lindsey in November and what a great time we'd all had.

But this time it would be just the two of us. Even better.

I hummed a little "On My Own," hoping I wouldn't be on mine for very much longer.

Perhaps we can summer in London and winter in California. No matter. As long as I'm with Alex, I'll be fine wherever I am.

Gorgeous George's blonde hair and lithesome body suddenly intruded on my happily-ever- after reverie.

Hey Georgy Girl, get out of my fantasy. There's no room for you.

Maybe not in yours, but what about Alex's? the perfect English catch retorted. *After all, I did go to Oxford, speak three languages, and play a mean game of tennis. And besides that, his father adores me. Can you make any of those claims?*

Game. Set. Match.

Do not listen to Georgy Girl, my rational self advised. *Focus on what you and Alex have.*

And just what exactly is that?

Remember; actions speak louder than words. Who's he taking out tonight?

True.

I leaned back against the seat and surrendered once more to dreams of kisses yet to come.

chapter thirteen

A Very Important Date

I was in a West End theater.

In London.

With Alex. Watching my favorite musical. Could life *be* any more perfect?

Certainly not the play. "Wow. This Eponine was even more amazing than the one we saw in San Francisco," I said as we left the theater. "In fact, all the actors were, although I thought the understudy playing Fantine was a bit weak. What about you?"

He gave me a distracted look. "Yes, it was quite good, wasn't it?"

"Alex, did you even *see* the play tonight?"

"Sorry. I have a lot on my mind." He glanced in the window of a pub we were passing. "I'm a bit thirsty. Fancy a drink?"

Inside, Alex took a sip of his mineral water with those gorgeous lips of his, then looked at me and said, "I've been wanting to talk to you about something."

At last! He's finally going to say the L-word! Maybe even the Big M. Surely not. Well, maybe . . .

Quieting down my preproposal jitters, I tried to look appropriately clueless and innocent and started mentally practicing the surprised but delighted look my face would show once he asked me to become his wife.

"Phoebe." His face flushed. "I don't know how to say this . . ."

Aw, look at that sweet man getting all awkward and tongue-tied. How cute is that?

Except . . . he doesn't look happy. Most men about to declare their love look happy.

That's when it hit me. There wasn't going to be any delicious first kiss. Or any kiss at all, except perhaps a brotherly peck on the check. Under cover of the tabletop, I began shredding my napkin into tiny pieces.

"Phoebe," Alex cleared his throat. "We had a wonderful time in Barley. I loved hanging out with you and your family, and I know there was something beginning between us. We had a connection, a spark, and we made a really great team working together at the paper. And"—he smiled—"in Trivial Pursuit, don't you think?"

"But?" I kept my voice light and forced a smile. "I know there's a *but.*"

He fiddled with one of the pressed-paper drink coasters. "But things have changed, what with my dad and everything. If we were back in California, that would be a different story. But I don't know when I'll be back. Or even *if* I'll be back. And, well . . ." Alex touched my arm. "I hope this doesn't impact our friendship."

Friendship? I've got plenty of friends already, thank you very much. What I want is . . . I flashed to Phil and Lins. The whole satin-and-lace, 'til-death-do-us part thing.

I struggled to maintain a stiff upper lip. "But what about the *Bulletin?*"

A trace of regret fluttered across Alex's face. "It was great running the *Bulletin,* and I enjoyed the opportunity to be writing again. You've got to understand, I really love Barley and everyone there . . ."

Everyone there? I don't want to just be part of "everyone" . . .

"But I need to stay here and help my father. He needs me." Alex took a deep breath. "That's why I want to transfer management of the *Bulletin* back to Gordon."

"What?" I stared at him dumbfounded.

He blew air out between his teeth. "It will still be a Spencer paper,

Phoebe—we'll handle all the business and financial stuff." Alex gave a wry smile. "I doubt Gordon will mind taking up the reins again. He's a great editor." His eyes bore into mine. "And you're a great reporter. I know I'll be leaving the paper in good hands."

Alex touched my arm again. "As for you and me, I wish we could be on the same continent, in the same town, actually—to see where our relationship goes. But we can't." He lifted his shoulders in a help-less shrug. "I need to stay here. And . . . well, you know that long-distance relationships never work."

"Sure they do. Remember in . . ." Frantic, I searched my mind for movies with successful long-distance relationships. "*Sleepless in Seattle!*" I bit my no-longer-stiff upper lip. "Although, they didn't actually meet until the end of the movie." I rushed on. "But you knew when you finally saw Tom and Meg together on top of the Empire State Building that she packed up and moved to Seattle to be with him and his son."

I saw that Alex was getting that scared commitment-phobe guy look in his eyes. Or maybe he was just scared of my wild-eyed rationalization . . .

Watch it, Pheebs. Remember to keep it light.

I cast around in my Technicolor memories for another long-distance relationship movie. Again, Tom Hanks's face swam to mind—how he kept the flame of his love burning bright for Helen Hunt even when he was cast away on that island for four years with just Wilson the vol-leyball for company. Of course, when he finally got rescued and made it back home, she'd married someone else and had a child . . .

This movie connection thing wasn't going too well.

"See what I mean?" Alex gave me a rueful smile. "It doesn't take much to see that the problems of two people don't amount to a hill of beans in this crazy world."

Don't you dare quote Casablanca *to me now. Besides, the quote is "three people"* . . .

He continued on, oblivious. "The good thing is that we didn't go out for that long and get our emotions all involved. That would make this so much harder."

Are you clueless? Or just plain stupid?

But I wasn't about to show him just how involved my emotions had gotten. I flashed him a bright smile, taking care not to look at the lips I'd hoped I would kiss tonight. "You're right." I stirred my drink with my straw. "So, how long have you and George been dating?"

"Say what?" His eyebrows lifted.

"Aren't you two involved?"

"No. Not at all. George is just a good friend and coworker."

That's what you think. I tried a new tack. "Are you happy here, Alex?"

He hesitated a fraction of a second before saying yes, then gave me a small smile. "I was happy in Barley too." He shrugged. "But this is what God has for me now. Sometimes we have to follow Him even when it isn't our dream. Even when it's not what feels right at the moment."

Right. Go ahead and get all spiritual now to appease your guilty conscience. That makes all this okay.

"True." I flashed him a stiff, plastic smile. "Besides, we'll always have Barley."

"That's my movie girl." He grinned. "I knew you'd understand."

And you don't, you great, obtuse idiot. The whole point is I'm not your girl!

I held it together when Alex hugged me good-night and gave me— yes, a brotherly kiss on the cheek.

I held it together when he put me in a cab and for the ride back to the hotel.

I held it together as I made my way through the lobby past Obi-Wan and up the stairs to our room.

Once inside the room, I completely lost it.

Mary Jo looked up in alarm at my tear-streaked face. "What happened?"

"Alex dumped me!" I wailed.

"I'm so sorry." My friend enveloped me in her sturdy arms and awkwardly patted me on the back. "I was afraid of this," she murmured.

"Wh-what?" I asked, extricating myself from her comforting hug to search for a tissue. I sank to my bed and blew my nose.

"Something just didn't feel right, ever since that first night at the theater," she said. "I know I told you not to jump to conclusions about George, but it was clear that things weren't the same between you and Alex as they were back in Barley."

"You could have told me!"

"I didn't know how. I'm sorry." She sent me a kind look. "Would you have listened, anyway?"

"Maybe." I sniffled.

"Really?" Mary Jo hesitated, then took her life in her hands. "Pheebs, sometimes you have this tendency to, well, create this whole dream world and then go live there. Maybe it's because of all the movies you watch." She gave me a gentle smile. "But could it be at all possible that maybe your relationship with Alex was more romantic fantasy than real?"

She held up her hand as I started to protest. "Yes, I know Alex was interested. That was obvious. Everyone in town could see that he liked you." She bit her lip. "But you hadn't really spent all that much time together. Right? Had you even dated a month before he left?"

"Yes." I bristled. "Christmas would have made it two months exactly."

"But Alex left before Christmas." Her voice softened. "You hadn't even kissed yet, right?"

I shook my head. "Not that I didn't *want* to." My mouth turned down in a pout. "And now I'll never know what it felt like." I sighed. "Here I was all excited about tonight, thinking that at last it was going to happen. But he just took me to the show to soften the blow."

I wailed again.

"Pheebs, you two have been apart longer than you were together." MJ kept barreling down the logic track. "His relationship with you that was just beginning got shoved to the back burner when his dad got sick. Then when he had to remain in England to run the company—well, the flame just died down." She sighed. "It's hard to maintain a long-distance relationship in the best of circumstances—"

A light bulb went off. "But that's just geography! If I were to stay here, who knows what might happen?"

"You can't force a relationship—"

"I wouldn't be forcing anything. What's wrong with just giving it a chance?"

She played the God card. "Have you considered that maybe God doesn't want this relationship to go any farther right now? He already knew that Alex would be staying to help his family." Mary Jo pushed her hair behind her ears. "I'm not saying it's forever, although I don't know that it won't be, either. But clearly, for now, the two of you aren't meant to be together. Alex has his own issues to deal with—"

"That's for sure." I let loose a bitter grunt.

"Was it?" MJ gave me another gentle look. "You've been wondering about Alex ever since we saw him that first night at the theater."

"True. But that's when I thought there might be something going on with Gorgeous George. Alex says there's not." I sighed again. "Maybe it's like in *Roman Holiday*. You could see that Gregory Peck and Audrey Hepburn fell for each other, but she was a princess and he was a reporter, and they had separate lives to lead." I managed a wistful smile. "At least they always had Rome. And Alex and I will always have Barley." I rolled my eyes as I repeated the *Casablanca* line I'd said to Alex. "Doesn't have quite the same ring to it, does it?

"Oh, Mary Jo," I wailed as I flopped across my bed. "I'm such a total reject in the romance department. I'm going to be alone for the rest of my life." *And I'm never going to get that passionate kiss.*

A flying pillow hit me in the head. "Hey, watch it!"

Mary Jo grinned. "You know what we need?"

"What?"

"A change of scenery." She bounced on her bed, eyes sparkling. "Let's go to the Cotswolds. And Yorkshire!"

"Yorkshire?"

"Yeah, you know." She gestured to my copy of *Jane Eyre* on the nightstand. "Brontë country, the moors and all that. And the hills and dales made famous by *my* favorite author, James Herriot." She clapped her hands. "C'mon Pheebs, what do you say?"

I didn't really feel like saying anything. Or doing anything. "But we still haven't seen all the items on your London list."

"All the ones that really mattered." She grabbed the travel guide and started thumbing through it. "Besides, they'll still be here when we return. We can come back to London a day or so before we fly home and see anything we might have missed." Mary Jo grew pensive. "To be honest, all the crowds and noise and stuff—it's starting to get to me. I'd really love a little fresh country air. What's that old poem? 'Away, away from men and towns. To the wild wood and the downs.'"

"Hey, I didn't know you knew Shelley."

"I don't know Shelley." Her eyebrows furrowed together. "Who's she?"

"*He*. Percy Bysshe Shelley. The poet who wrote those words?"

"Oh." MJ looked sheepish. "I didn't remember who said it, just recall hearing it in one of my college classes. And it's always stuck with me."

"I can see why it would, nature girl."

"Remember when we planned our trip? We said we'd be footloose and fancy free, able to go wherever we want, whenever we want. Whatever mood strikes us." She crossed her arms. "Well the country mood is striking *me*, so I say we go to the Cotswolds tomorrow."

I was beginning to catch the footloose spirit, but I wasn't quite up for the countryside yet. "Maybe we could go to Oxford first?" I asked meekly. "Delia recommended a great little bed-and-breakfast there."

"All right, all right. We go to *Oxford* tomorrow, then the Cotswolds. Then Yorkshire.

"Ma'am, yes ma'am!" I gave her my air-force salute. "Hey, have you ever considered becoming a boot-camp drill instructor? You could have a great second career going there."

She threw another pillow at me. Followed by a Cadbury's Dairy Milk.

The latter I inhaled. The former I punched before sticking under my head and turning it over a couple of times to find the cool spot. "We'll be just like those women in *Enchanted April* who couldn't wait to leave rainy London," I said, finally getting into the spirit. "Only instead of going to the Italian countryside, we're doing the English."

"Uh-huh," my sleepy roommate replied.

Once she fell asleep my brave face crumpled. *So why did I come all this way, God? I thought it was to get together with Alex . . .*

So much for pure motives.

I cried myself to sleep. But quietly.

"What's up with this whole 'gift of singleness' thing anyway?" I asked the next morning as we were packing to leave. "And how do I know if I even have it?"

Mary Jo started to answer, but I was on a frustrated roll after night-time dreams of Alex—which included that *kiss* and so much more on our happily-ever-after honeymoon—that I didn't give her a chance. "Do I have this special singleness gift if I'm not lusting or will never lust again? But even Jimmy Carter lusted in his heart."

She raised her eyebrows.

"I remember reading that when I did a paper on him in junior high. He said it in a *Playboy* interview or something when he was running for president." I shoved my socks into my small suitcase. "Of course, *he* was married and I'm not. So how can I have the gift if I'm still having lustful thoughts, even if they do include marriage wishes?"

I stuck out my chin. "Yes, I admit it. Even though things with Alex didn't work out, I'd still like to get married."

"Well, yeah, Pheebs. Who wouldn't? But wanting it doesn't mean it's going to happen. After all, you're nearly thirty-two. Truth is, you don't have much marriage shelf life left. That expiration date is fast approaching."

"Very funny, Ms. Has It All Together."

Mary Jo grinned as she folded her turtlenecks. "I so don't have it all together. But this is the way I see it: If you're single right now, then for now—today, this season of your life—you have the gift of singleness. Doesn't mean it will be forever; doesn't mean it won't. That's up to God. But how you handle it is up to you."

"Okay, Mother Teresa, I get the point." I carefully tucked my new clothes back into their shopping bags. "But please don't throw that scripture at me that married people do all the time—the one about trusting in the Lord with all your heart and He will give you the desires of your heart. Or if not, He'll take away the desire." I frowned. "That hasn't been my experience at all."

"Mine either."

"What?" I stared at my contented-single friend. "What are you saying?"

"I'm saying I struggle just like you." MJ sighed. "It's a constant process of turning things over to God. I can have days, weeks, even months of being okay with where I am as a single. Then something will happen—like maybe I come down with the flu and wish I had someone to take care of me. Or I'm watching the news and some awful tragedy happens that makes me wish there was someone I could curl up next to for comfort." She zipped her suitcase shut. "Or I want to move some furniture but I can't do it all alone and I wish I had some strong guy to help."

"So what do you do?" I stared again at my stalwart, I-am-woman-hear-me-roar friend. "How do you handle it?"

"I gnash my teeth, stomp my feet, and shake my fist at God. Then I call my friend from down the road—or just leave the furniture exactly where it is." Mary Jo grinned. "And when I'm sick, I ask someone to bring

me some chicken noodle soup. And as for the curling up with someone part"—her face split into a huge grin—"that's why I have Riley."

"Maybe I need to get a dog. Herman's more of a climber than a
cuddler." I gave Mary Jo a curious look. "So what about when you see
some tragedy on the news then?"

"I stop and pray for all those involved."

*And that's why she's a WOG and you're not, Pheebs. Get over yourself
already!*

"And as far as marriage goes," she added, "I'm so set in my ways at
this point in my life that if I got married we'd have to have a duplex.
Then he could have his space and I could have mine."

"With nighttime visiting hours of course."

"Of course." She expelled a resigned sigh. "Phoebe, I've been exactly
where you are right now; still go there sometimes. Do you know the
last time I had a date?"

*Date? Mary Jo? I've never seen her with anyone—at least not since
high school.*

I shook my head.

"Four—no wait, I think it may have been five—years ago."

"I'd slash my wrists," I blurted. My hand flew to my mouth. "Sorry.
That's just a really long time."

"I know. But there's not a lot of available men in Barley."

I gave her a curious look. "Why do you stay in Barley then?"

"Barley is my home," she said simply. "God hasn't called me anywhere else; except for this vacation to England. And that mission trip
to Guatemala."

"But your odds would be so much better in a bigger city."

"It's not about odds." She smiled. "And it's definitely not about
geography. I have girlfriends in both Sacramento and the Bay Area
who haven't dated in a long time either. One's our age, one's forty, and
another's forty-seven."

I winced. "And all this is supposed to make me feel better?"

"I'm just saying that it's not about location or statistics. It's about where you are with God and learning to be content in your circumstances." She gave me a gentle look tempered with a crooked smile. "Getting married isn't the only happily-ever-after, you know."

She frowned. "Those fairy tales we were raised on don't help. And unfortunately, a lot of churches tend to perpetuate them. I'm not talking about Barley Pres here. But do you ever notice how some churches gear everything toward couples and families? And whenever someone preaches on singleness, the message is always just 'Don't have sex!'"

"I hear ya on that." I grimaced. "Although I've also heard a few pastors lump all single women together and say the reason we're not married is that we chose to put off the highest calling of wife and motherhood to establish our selfish careers first."

Mary Jo shot me a wicked grin. "Hey, I know I've turned down plenty of proposals in favor of my selfish career. What about you?"

"More than I can count. Just too busy clawing my way up that good ol' corporate ladder, and those darn men dangling diamond rings got in my way." I tossed my head. "And now that I've reached the pinnacle of professional accomplishment, well it's just my own fault I don't have anyone to share it with. You know what they say: 'It's lonely at the top.'"

"It gets lonely sometimes wherever you are." Mary Jo shook her head. "Most single women I know are simply trying to pay the bills and make good use of the gifts God has given them. Sure, we struggle with the sex-and-romance thing . . ." She expelled a loud sigh. "Sue, my forty-year-old friend in the Bay Area, has even chosen not to watch romantic comedies anymore because it's just too difficult. She can be strong and walking with the Lord, fine with being single. Then she'll watch one of those love stories where a man and woman meet, have the requisite sparring and misunderstandings, and wind up happily ever after in two hours, and it sets her to longing all over again.

"That's why she started watching martial arts films," she finished.

I giggled. "But even *Crouching Tiger, Hidden Dragon* is a love story."

"I know. There's no escaping it. Romantic love is all around—always will be." She smiled. "But so is the love of God . . . and the friendships he puts in our lives."

"Preach it, sister. But be careful," I warned her. "You're veering into sappy territory here. Next thing you know, you'll be singing me the theme song from *Beaches*."

chapter fourteen

Oxford Dreaming

mary Jo ran her hands reverently across the ancient tabletop. "Just think. C. S. Lewis might have sat at this very table. Or Tolkien." She looked across at me, her eyes wide. "Maybe he even wrote some of *Lord of the Rings* here."

The Eagle and Child pub in Oxford is the one that the "Inklings" group—whose members included Lewis and Tolkien—used to frequent. Now *we* were frequenting it.

Delia had picked us up at the train station, insisting we stay with her instead of the B&B, since her roommate was away and there was space. She'd explained that she didn't actually *live* in her family's London flat, just stayed there like the rest of the family when she was in town for a few days. Most days, she commuted to work. But she'd arranged to stay in Oxford that entire weekend to show us around.

We'd dropped our bags at her flat, then she'd trundled us off to dinner at the famous pub. Now Delia and Mary Jo were engaged in a spirited discussion of Lewis's theological works while I sat there mute, pretending an absorbed interest in my surroundings.

Note to self: Start reading deeper Christian books so as to be able to converse intelligently with spiritual-giant friends.

Do The Chronicles of Narnia qualify?

Might as well face it, Pheebs. You're never going to be a spiritual giant. You're not even a spiritual tall person.

During a lull in the conversation, I piped up. "Didn't you just love *Shadowlands*? Although Debra Winger wouldn't have been my first choice to play Joy. But Anthony Hopkins sure made a great C. S. Lewis." I sighed. "Of course, that man could read the telephone book and I'd watch."

MJ took a bite of her chicken-and-mushroom pie. "Phoebe's our resident movie expert. She knows every movie ever made. And then some."

"I know." Delia smiled. "Just like Alex." She put her hand over her mouth. "Sorry. I've gone and put my foot into it, haven't I?"

"No." I gave her an oh-well smile and tilted my head. "Obviously, it just wasn't meant to be."

"Or my brother's just daft. At least where our father's concerned. Alex never looks beyond what Dad wants to what he wants." Delia took another sip of her drink and muttered. "It's not as if he's the only member of the family who could run the company." She gave herself a little shake, then offered me a warm smile. "I think you two would make a great pair, even if my brother is being a great idiot."

"It's all right. Really. Alex and I didn't have any kind of . . . understanding," I said, echoing Emma Thompson's *Sense and Sensibility* line. "We'd only been dating a little while before he came back here." I shrugged my shoulders. "No harm, no foul. And he's right, you know. Long-distance relationships never work." I slid Delia a weak grin. "But please do me a favor and don't tell me if he ever starts dating George."

One of the many benefits of staying with Delia—other than the obvious financial one—was that I didn't need to scout out an Internet café to send my e-mail. While MJ and Delia watched *The Office* on BBC, I checked my messages and double-clicked on one from my sister-in-law.

To: Movielovr
From: Kgrants7

   Hey Ms. Continental, how's everything? Hope you're having the time of your life. Don't worry about the little people you left behind—especially those of us who majored in English and drama and would give their first-born child (not to worry; Ash understands☺) to be in the land of Shakespeare and Sir Laurence Olivier. But I'm not bitter. Not at all. Hah! You'd better at least bring me back a sweatshirt from Oxford, that noble ancient seat of learning. If you go, of course. The kids are doing great, other than Ashley having some boy trouble, but they all miss you. And Jordy's working way too hard, but I can't get him to slow down. A little thing called bills and seven mouths to feed. I'm thinking of becoming an Avon lady or Mary Kay rep to help out. (Can you imagine me in a pink convertible?☺)

                                        Love, Karen

An e-mail from Lindsey with the subject line, "Looking for Lost Best Friend" wasn't quite as chipper.

To: Movielovr
From: LinsRog

   Hear ye. Hear ye. Looking for lost best friend whom I haven't heard from in a while, other than a couple of impersonal e-mails that went out to a mass-mailing list. She abandoned me to go hobnob with the Queen and hasn't been seen or heard from since. Am I going to have to put out an all-points bulletin for my maid of honor?☺ When last seen, she was traveling in the company of her new best friend.☺

Although Lindsey had added in a couple of smiley faces to show she was teasing, I knew better. But her hurt feelings on top of Alex's defection last night was simply more than I could handle at the moment.

Especially since *she* still had a boyfriend.

And not only a boyfriend, a fiancé—someone who actually wanted to marry her and stick with her for the whole for-better-or-worse, in-sickness-and-in-health thing.

All I had were dashed hopes, lonely lips, and a job I didn't even think I wanted, now that I knew Alex wasn't coming back.

Maybe it was time to seriously consider Phil's job offer.

But is that what you want for me, God? I know I can probably do it, but I must confess I don't feel particularly called to do it . . .

I wrote Lins back a brief reply, trying not to stretch the truth too much.

To: LinsRuy
From: Movielovr
   Call off search party. Missing best friend is alive and well and still on the road in England.☺ Sorry this has to be so short, but no time to write—and it's not always easy to find an Internet connection. Miss you heaps and promise to send a *long* personal e-mail soon.☺ England's amazing. Love you, and love to Phillie too.

I thought about sharing my Alex disappointment with her, but I wasn't quite ready. Not yet. I just couldn't bear it if she responded with a quick word of sympathy, then three paragraphs about her wedding.

At breakfast the next morning, Mary Jo and I had oatmeal while Delia ate her Marmite. We watched in fascination as she spread the brown stuff onto a couple of pieces of bread.

"Mmm. Lovely," she said, taking a large bite and closing her eyes.

Feeling a bit reckless and remembering how adventurous Esther had been on her travels, I decided to give the uniquely British delicacy a try. But when I raised the brewer's-yeast concoction to my mouth, the smell almost knocked me out.

Going for the familiar, I made my eyes all big and Oliver Twistish and extended my oatmeal bowl toward Delia. "Please, suh, I want some more?"

"Sorry. All gone. But there's plenty of Marmite left," she said with a wicked gleam in her eye.

"Actually, you know what? I just realized I'm quite full after all." I gulped down my tea. "Shall we go?"

Delia spent the rest of the morning leading us on an insider's tour of her famed university and all its different colleges—Magdalen, Trinity, Christ Church, and more. I managed to snag a couple of Oxford sweatshirts for Jordy and Karen before she herded us to Blackwell's, one of the largest bookshops in the world.

"Whoa." MJ's eyes widened. "Books 'n' Brew is nothing like this."

"That's for sure." Enraptured, we wandered from floor to floor in the large multilevel store. Grateful that my paycheck had at last been straightened out, I used my ATM card to buy a gorgeous set of The Chronicles of Narnia for the kids, Lewis's *Surprised by Joy* for me, and the Lord of the Rings trilogy for Jordy before meeting back up with Delia in the coffee shop on the second level.

"Where's MJ?"

"In the loo," Delia said, absorbed in the sweets case. "She'll be back directly."

While she paid for some shortbread, I picked up a brochure from the counter and thumbed through it. "Wow, look at this cool class: 'Jane Austen in Film.' I'd love to take something like that."

"Why don't you?"

"Aside from the money issue, you mean? Hel-looo . . . not a student at Oxford, remember?"

Delia examined the brochure. "This isn't for regular students. It's with University Vacations, which means any adult can go." She looked at the date. "It starts in two weeks." Her eyes widened. "You should do it. That would be brilliant! And you could stay in my flat to save money. We'd have a blast. Plus," she shot me an innocent look, "that would give you more time with my idiot brother. I just know he'd come to his senses."

"True . . ." I chewed my lower lip.

The classroom lights brightened as the Emma *credits roll. And when discussion began, I quickly realized I could more than hold my own. Though my academic background can't match those of my classmates and professor (who looked remarkably like Michael Caine), there's no denying my extensive knowledge of all things film. Everyone is awed by my brilliant and well-expressed insights; it's a real* Educating Rita *moment. And afterward, as I jog down the stone college steps surrounded by an admiring throng of mostly male classmates, I see Alex waiting for me at the base of the stairs, a bunch of daffodils in his hand. "Darling . . ."*

I was definitely liking this idea. "I wonder if I could afford—"

Delia nudged me.

I blinked and saw MJ heading our way.

"Shh. Don't say anything. She'd have an absolute cow."

Back at the flat, Delia suddenly decided to get some takeaway for late lunch.

"How about curry?" MJ asked, plopping down on the blue squashy couch and flipping through a magazine.

"No," I said, my eyes watering at the very thought. "No curry."

"Right, then. I'll just pop down to the corner and get some Chinese." Delia raised her eyebrows and tilted her head in a tell-her-about-it gesture behind Mary Jo's back. "Back soon."

"Hey Thelma, I just found the most interesting thing at Blackwell's." I handed MJ the brochure with the Jane Austen class marked. "Doesn't that one sound brilliant?" Turning and heading for the kitchen, I added casually over my shoulder. "I'm thinking of staying over a few more weeks to take it. Wouldn't that be fantastic?"

"You're kidding, right?" Mary Jo's voice rose. "Please tell me you're kidding. Have you even prayed about this?"

"Yes . . . well, sort of." I fidgeted as I turned to face her. "I mean I'm going to. But surely it's not just coincidence that I happened to see that brochure for classes at Oxford . . . on film, no less—and Jane Austen. When one of my favorite movies of all time is *Sense and Sensibility*. I mean, what are the chances of that? This could be a total God thing."

"Uh-huh. And what about Alex?"

"What about him?" I put the kettle on. "This has nothing to do with him."

She shot me a penetrating look. "Doesn't it?"

"No! This is just an incredible opportunity. I mean, *Oxford University?* Come on. How cool is that? Who'd have ever thought that little Phoebe Grant from Barley would get the chance to go to *Oxford?*"

"But how could you even afford it?"

Go ahead, just pop my fantasy bubble with boring reality.

"It's really not all that expensive." *Yeah—in whose universe?* "And Delia said I could stay here with her for free." My mouth set in a mutinous line. "I'll bet Esther would be all for it."

"Maybe. Maybe not." MJ gave me a patient look. "Pheebs, I know you want to have a relationship with Alex, but he's already made it clear that you can't. Not at this time."

"But that's just on account of geography." I sank down next to her on the couch, eyes sparkling. "If I'm here, we don't have the whole long-distance thing to worry about, and we could just pick up right where we left off in Barley."

And I could still get that kiss.

Mary Jo gave me a curious look. "What's it like?"

"What?"

"To live where you do?"

"What are you talking about?" I looked at her, puzzled. "I live the same place as you."

"No, you don't, Peter Pan. You live in a dream world—your very own personal Neverland." She sighed. "Pheebs, life isn't like the movies. You can't just do things like this on a whim. Sure, it's great to be spontaneous, but—"

I filled in the rest for her. "But other people are involved . . . What about your job . . . your family? . . . Don't you have responsibilities?" My voice rose, and I began to pace. "I came to Barley because of family responsibilities. And I never really wanted to work at the *Bulletin* in the first place, but I took the job because of my family. And yes, because of Alex. But now that he's—"

"Darlings, I'm back." A musical voice interrupted us as the door opened to reveal Delia with the takeaway and a tall sandy-haired guy she introduced as her friend Ian.

Ian shook my hand while Mary Jo sprang up to help Delia with the food. "Lovely to meet you," he said, fixing me with gorgeous Paul Newman eyes.

"And you." I shook his hand and caught Delia's smile out of the corner of my eye.

I know what this is: it's a setup. Delia brought him round to help take my mind off Alex. How sweet of her. He is kind of cute . . .

Clueless Phoebe strikes again.

It was Ian and MJ who got along great, sharing a mutual interest in history, music, and horses. Having never been to the United States, he was fascinated to learn of her stable in California, and his electric blue eyes sparkled as she shared some funny kid riding mishaps with him.

That's all right, I told myself as I watched them laughing together. *It's about time somebody noticed all that Mary Jo has to offer.*

Besides, I added to myself only, *maybe there's still a chance for Alex and me.*

When it was about time for him to leave, Ian invited us all to breakfast the next day, and we gladly accepted. "But we can't linger too late," Delia warned, "if we're to drive up to the Cotswolds tomorrow."

"Delia's offered to give us a personal tour," I added helpfully. But I don't think he even heard me.

"Right, then," he said to Mary Jo. "Shall I knock you up in the morning, then?"

Her eyes grew huge. "I don't think so."

Delia threw back her head and laughed. "Careful, Ian. Mary Jo doesn't know all our slang yet. She most definitely doesn't want to wind up preggers."

His face flamed red. "What?! I never said . . ." Then a look of comprehension dawned. "Oh. Sorry. I take it there's a different meaning in the States?"

"Um"—MJ and I looked at each other—"you could say that."

I snorted with laughter, MJ joined me, and we were all still laughing like crazy when Ian left . . . and when the phone rang a few minutes later.

"Hello?" Delia said in her lovely, lilting British accent while Mary Jo and I continued to snort in the background. "Yes, just a moment, please. Phoebe, it's for you." She handed me the phone.

Still trying to control my giggles, I said, "Hello?"

"Sounds like you're having a party or something," the voice on the other end said.

"Lins! How are you? Sure wish you were here." I giggled again. "No party, just Delia, MJ, and I having a little girl time."

"MJ?"

"That's what I call Mary Jo."

"Oh. Well, if I'm interrupting, I can call back later," she said in a hurt tone.

"Don't be silly. You called all the way from Cleveland. It must be important. What's up?"

Lindsey sniffled across the miles. "Phil and I had a f-fight last night about the wedding, and I wanted to talk to you, but you're all the way over in England, and there's that stupid time difference, so I couldn't call and . . ." She began to cry.

"I'm sorry, Lins. What was the fight about?"

"He said he couldn't care less what colors I picked"—she blew her nose—"but there was no way he was going to wear a pink cummerbund."

"Pink?" I rolled my eyes. "I thought you were 'so over' pink."

"I was. But then I saw this beautiful bridesmaid dress in this great cotton-candy pink—it will look absolutely gorgeous on you—and this cake with baby pink roses all cascading down it, and changed my mind. I was telling Phil about it, and we ended up in this horrible fight, and he *yelled* and said he didn't care about party favors or center-pieces or flowers or food."

"Lins," I said gently, "*most* guys don't care about all the little details. They just want to get married. That's why you have your girlfriends to talk to."

"But I don't have my *best* friend," she wailed. "You're way over there in England." She sniffled again. "Besides, I've been waiting for this day my whole life. I want everything to be just perfect!"

"I know you do." I sighed. "But you have to remember, guys don't feel the same way. It's not as big a deal to them. They're a little more— a lot more—focused on the wedding night." I grinned into the phone. "Especially when they're good, upright Christian guys like Phil. He's been waiting a *long* time for that."

"So have I," Lindsey said. "But that doesn't give him an excuse to slam out of here like he did. He said he couldn't care less what col-ors I chose or whether we had salmon or chicken at the reception. There were just three things he refused to have: a pink cummerbund, cauliflower, and a plastic bride and groom on top of the cake. Just tell him where and when to show up . . ." She began to cry all over again. "What's *wrong* with cauliflower? It looks so pretty on a vegetable tray . . ."

"Lins—"

Delia gave a discreet cough, and I glanced over at her. She mouthed "sorry," then pointed to her watch.

"I'm sorry, Lins, but I'm afraid I have to go. We'll be late for Evensong if we don't hurry."

Her voice turned to frost. "Sorry. Didn't mean to bother you, Ms. Busy World Traveler." I jumped at the sound of the receiver slamming down on her end.

When we returned to the flat later that night, I sent Lindsey an apologetic e-mail and then checked my messages. There was a darling e-card from Lexie with a puppy on the front that wagged its tail while my niece's message appeared: "I love you and miss you, Aunt Phoebe. Please come home *soon*."

Her mom had sent an accompanying e-mail:

To: Movielovr
From: Kgrants7
  Hi, Pheebs. How's it going? Did you like Lexie's card? She picked it out, but I did the typing for her. Hey, guess what Ash and I did today in homage to you? Went to afternoon tea. One of my girlfriends told me about this elegant tearoom up in Sacramento, so I took Ashley there, and we had a fun girls-only day. It was great. Lots of china and lace and girly stuff to ooh and aah over. And the food! Little sandwiches and scones and sweets . . . I didn't think those things could fill me up, but we were stuffed afterward. It was nice to have the time together,

especially since we haven't been seeing eye-to-eye much lately. Ashley has a huge crush on this boy in her class—not a Christian—and is starting to behave like a typical teenager. Ah, the joys of motherhood. Hope you're still having a great time. Sure do miss you. See you soon.

Love, Karen

I hit reply.

To: Kgrants7
From: Movielovr
Hi, Karen. Loved Lexie's card! Please tell her I said so. Sure do miss that little munchkin. The rest of you too. Isn't teatime a kick? Don't worry about Ashley too much; I went through the same thing when I was her age and look at me—I turned out okay. Gotta dash. Love to all. —P.

But did I turn out okay? Or is Mary Jo right and I'm too much of a dreamer for my own good? No time to think about that right now; need to write my column. So much more fun than writing about emus and Christy Sharp's salt-and-pepper-shaker collection.

NOTES FROM ABROAD

For years, the Brits have gotten a bad rap for their food. And I have to admit that so far, it's been a bit hit-and-miss: The sausage is far too soft and squishy for my Jimmy Dean taste buds. The scrambled eggs are either too runny or powdery (one morning I'm sure we were served instant eggs from a box!). And don't even get me started on the curries (can you say incendiary?).

171

Ah, but those English cheeses—especially the Double Gloucester cheddar. Sheer bliss.

And the one aspect of England's culinary offerings that has never been a miss for me is the tea. I have been enjoying several "cuppas" a day, with milk and sugar, of course, and am enamored not only with the beverage, but with all the customs that attend its service.

I've also discovered, however—in a very inconvenient time and place—that tea is a diuretic.

I'm sure the other passengers in the Underground car with me that day wondered what strange American dance ritual I was practicing. They didn't have to wonder long. At the very next stop, I pushed my way out, my traveling pal Mary Jo hard on my heels—only to discover there were no loos to be found anywhere in the entire station!

Just what is it with this country and public restrooms—or the lack of them? I can understand Westminster Abbey's not having one, since it's so old and a national monument. But a subway station that thousands of people pass through daily? Seems like that would be a no-brainer.

In the end, I had to race up three flights of stairs and down an entire city block before finding a zero-star restaurant with loo accommodations that harkened back to the reign of Henry VIII. And don't even get me started on the toilet paper. I have only two words to say on that subject: *waxed paper.*

English bathtubs are another interesting phenomenon. Can you say narrow? I won't bore you with the details, but suffice it to say that one should be very careful to stand up before letting out all the water—to avoid winding up like that kid at the flagpole in *A Christmas Story.*

Don't get me wrong. I'm head over heels, totally in love with this land of kings and castles, churches and cathedrals, Shakespeare and sonnets. The great lexicographer Samuel Johnson once said, "When a man is tired of London, he is tired of life," and I couldn't agree more. I'm just going to go a little easy on the tea from here on out.

Either that, or skip the subway.

Cheerio!

Your Overseas Correspondent

chapter fifteen

Clueless in the Cotswolds

bright and early the next morning, Ian appeared to take us out to breakfast, but Delia and I might just as well have remained behind in the flat. The tall, young Englishman had eyes only for Mary Jo and hung on her every word.

The funny thing was: she couldn't see it.

"That Ian's sure a nice kid," she said as we headed west toward the Cotswolds in Delia's BMW.

"A nice kid with a crush," I said with a grin.

"On who?" she asked, turning to face Delia. "You?"

"Not hardly." Delia met my laughing eyes in the rearview mirror.

MJ swiveled around to look at me. "You, Pheebs? That's great! He's very smart. Knows loads about horses. Sweet, too."

"Yeah. Sweet on you, Ms. Hasn't Got a Clue."

"What?" She gave me an incredulous look. "You're crazy."

"And you're clueless, Alicia Silverstone. The guy is smitten."

She turned to Delia. "Will you please tell Phoebe that she's lost her mind?"

"Can't do that, MJ," Delia said. "I'm afraid you're the one whose mind isn't working properly. Once he met you, he hardly said a word to anyone else."

"You've both lost it." Mary Jo shook her head. "I think you inhaled too much of that Marmite goop and it's done something to your brains."

"Not true," Delia said. "I've known Ian a long time, and you had him mesmerized."

"Right." Mary Jo snorted. "With my stimulating conversation about oat mash, snaffle bits, and manure."

"Ian would eat all that up." Delia tore open a bag of salt-and-vinegar crisps. "He majored in business with me and did quite well, but he's decided what he really wants is to be a vet. He's researching veterinary schools at present."

"Well, that explains it. He's just interested in my horse tales."

"He was interested in a lot more than your horse tales," I said. "Trust me on that."

MJ pushed her maple-colored hair behind her ears. "But he's just a kid—must be at least ten years younger than me."

"How old are you?" Delia asked.

"Same as Phoebe—thirty-two."

"Hey," I protested from the backseat, "I still have a couple more months until I'm that old. I'm only thirty-one."

"And Ian's twenty-five." Delia slid a sideways smirk at Mary Jo. "Which makes him only *seven* years younger than you."

"Like I said. A kid." Mary Jo dismissed the subject and glanced out the window. "Ooh, look! Reminds me of a Thomas Kinkade painting."

"Only so much better because it's real." I drank in the pastoral tableau of honey-colored stone cottages nestled amid lush green hills. "Now I see why everyone insists this area of England is a must. It's like something out of a fairy tale."

The fairy tale continued as we visited the first stop on Delia's tour: Bourton-on-the-Water, pronounced "Burton" and nicknamed "the Venice of the Cotswolds" because the River Windrush flowed through the center of town.

"You call that a river?" Mary Jo looked down at the gentle meandering water and grinned. "Definitely no whitewater rafting here."

"Who cares?" I looked around in wonderment. "This reminds me of *Brigadoon*."

Delia and Mary Jo both gave me blank looks.

"The mystical Scottish village in the musical of the same name. The movie starred Gene Kelly and Cyd Charisse?"

More blank looks.

"With the gorgeous song, 'The Heather on the Hill'?"

Shrugged shoulders accompanied the blank looks now.

I sighed. Alex would have gotten the old-movie reference.

The only downside to the whole day was the weather—misty and in the high thirties, which MJ's thin California blood couldn't tolerate. Mine, although thickened by years in the Midwest, was also having a difficult time of it. We shivered through our first few stops, then at the Cotswold shopping paradise of Broadway, made a beeline to the Edinburgh Woolen Mill—with Delia laughing at us the whole way.

MJ had barely made it through the doors before she clapped a red knit hat over her icy ears. And try as I might, I couldn't talk MJ out of a sky-blue fleece jacket dotted with cutesy sheep on a green hill. (I picked up a Scottish plaid scarf that went well with my gray tweed blazer.)

Once outside again, I pulled my blazer tighter as the wind sliced through me. "Hang on a second." Two minutes later I returned with my own fleece jacket.

Minus the sheep.

Yes, the extra bulk made me look fat, but at this point, warmth was more important than my vanity. Besides, it was just us girls, so who cared?

Later that afternoon, we ended our Cotswolds minitour with a cuppa in the tranquil village of Lower Slaughter. MJ leaned back in her chair, looked out the tearoom window at the live sheep grazing on the hillside, and took a big gulp of fresh country air enhanced with the scents of tea, butter, and chocolate. "It doesn't get much better than this," she sighed. "Sure, London's exciting, and Oxford's fascinating, but at the end of the day, this is really what I like." She stretched. "The only thing that would make it complete is a good, long ride."

"You can have that tomorrow." Delia said, turning to me with an anxious look. "I talked to Mum, and she'd really like you to come for lunch and a ride. Is that all right?"

I looked at Delia, then Mary Jo, who was doing her best not to look too eager. "Sure. I'd love to see your mother again. But tomorrow's Monday. Don't you have to get back to the office?"

"Actually, I managed a bit of holiday." She crinkled her nose into a smile. "Sometimes being related to the boss can be an advantage. Especially when the boss's *wife* puts in a special word."

"Well, then, we accept with pleasure," I said, but added, "as long as I don't have to do the riding bit. Not really my thing."

Delia looked puzzled, then her face cleared. "Ah, I see. That was for George's benefit, right?"

"You got it."

"No worries." She slid a sly glance at me. "George won't be there tomorrow."

Thank you, Lord. Now I can wear my Manolos in peace.

"Look, MJ," I squealed, "It's Tiddles!"

"Who?"

"Tiddles the church cat," I explained. "Norm Anderson mentioned it when he was trying to get approval from the Barley Cemetery Board to let him erect a monument to his pet pig. Said when he was stationed in England, he saw a memorial to Tiddles the cat in a country churchyard. But I thought he just made it up to strengthen his case." I walked around the diminutive concrete cat-shaped memorial. "Guess he didn't. I mean, how many Tiddles the church cats can there be?" I dug around in my purse. "I've got to get a picture for him."

Mary Jo snapped a picture of me in front of the cement cat, whose tiny grave marker said he'd lived from 1963 to 1980. Then we wandered inside the church attached to the churchyard. The sign outside told us it was called St. Mary's. And according to our guidebook, St. Mary's in the village of Fairford contained England's only complete set of "medieval narrative glass."

The church was dim as we stepped inside. No surprise—it was cloudy outside. But when the sun peeked through a few minutes later, the windows—all twenty-eight of them—sprang to unbelievable, vivid life.

Every stained-glass scene depicted a chapter of the salvation story, beginning with Eve taking the apple in the Garden of Eden and going through Jesus' birth, crucifixion, and resurrection. And although every window was exquisite, the one that brought me to my knees and kept me there for some time was the one of Jesus sitting enthroned on a blue and gold rainbow with the earth as his footstool. And encircling Jesus were all the martyrs and heavenly host in a background of brilliant blood red.

Such a red as I'd never seen—even in Technicolor.

I stared at Jesus on the throne for a long time. And all the red around him. And wept. Gradually I felt a sense of peace steal deep into my being.

And for the first time in a long time, I didn't feel like a spiritual loser.

When Delia turned in the long, curving drive of the ancestral family home late that morning, I felt like I needed to go find the servant's entrance.

MJ gasped as the stately home hove into view. "It's a castle!" she said.

"It is a bit of a monstrosity, isn't it?" Delia said. "No castle though, just a manor house."

"*Just* a manor house?" I gulped. "It looks like something out of *Dynasty.*"

Behind me, I could hear Mary Jo gulp. "Uh, how old is your house, Delia?"

"About three hundred years, give or take." She grinned. "I never can keep track, but Father can tell you the exact figures if you really want to know—although I wouldn't ask if I were you. He'll run on for hours."

"That's older than our entire country." Mary Jo shook her head.

"And it shows in spots." Delia grimaced. "Thankfully, Mum had it all modernized when I was little. The loos were positively ancient, I'm told." She pulled her BMW up to the front door. "Right. Here we are then."

The massive oak door opened, and I steeled myself to see a starched English butler appear. Instead, I was relieved to see Grace hurry to welcome us, followed by her husband at a more sedate pace.

"Hello, darling." Grace gave her daughter a warm hug, and then turned to an awestruck Mary Jo and me and gave us each a quick embrace as well. "So lovely to see you both again. Please come in. I've got lunch all prepared."

She chuckled when she realized we were still staring wide-eyed at her home's imposing façade. "It is a bit overwhelming, isn't it? Imagine how I felt when I first came. I was used to cleaning grand houses like this, not living in them."

"Grace," her husband protested.

"It's true, David." She winked at us. "My husband doesn't like me to remember those days now that I'm the grand lady of the manor." She linked her arm with his as she ushered us inside a marble foyer lined with antiques, then led us through the house to a sunny, glass-enclosed room filled with plants at the back. "Since you're all going riding soon, I thought we'd just have a light lunch in the conservatory." (She pronounced it that lovely English way, of course: *conservatry.*) "It's a lot less stuffy than the formal dining room," she added. "Then after your ride, we'll have a more substantial tea."

We sat down at a round, glass-topped wicker table set with

beautiful, floral-patterned bone china and sparkling crystal. All except for Grace.

"Right," she said. "I'll just pop into the kitchen and get the food."

"I'll help, Mum." Delia started to get up.

"No need. I've got everything ready—just need to load it on the tea trolley and roll it in." Her eyes twinkled. "Besides, you need to stay and protect Phoebe and Mary Jo from your father."

David harrumphed. "Don't see why they need—"

"Only teasing, darling." Grace gave her husband a peck on the cheek. "Won't be a moment."

Mary Jo jumped into the breech. "Mr. Spencer, your house is wonderful. Has it always been in your family?"

"Please. Call me David." He gave her a warm smile and launched into a historical narrative of his ancestral manor home while Delia, behind him, grinned and rolled her eyes.

Grace returned with a tray of cold meats and cheeses on a platter, a basket of bread, a crock of butter, and some Ploughman's pickle relish. The latter looked a bit too much like Marmite, so MJ and I both passed on it, but we practically inhaled the thick, crusty bread and wonderful English cheddar.

Mary Jo was in her element during lunch, talking broodmares and foals with David and Delia while Grace asked me questions about my family and Barley and I chatted with her about living in England.

Finally, David pushed his chair back and stood. "Now, then. Are you girls all ready for your ride?" He glanced down at my Manolos. "Guess you left your gear in the car. You can change in the tack room."

Confession time, Pheebs. See what happens when you lie?

I took a deep breath. "Actually, I don't—"

Grace rode to the rescue with a gracious smile. "Darling, why don't you three go on ahead? I'd like Phoebe to keep me company."

I shot her a grateful look.

"But—"

Mary Jo pushed back her chair and stood up abruptly. "Mr.

Spencer, uh, David, I'm eager to see that new mare you were telling me about. Has she foaled yet this year?"

The three excused themselves and headed to the stables.

"Thank you, Grace." My cheeks flamed. "I wasn't trying to lie, I just—"

She held up her hand and smiled. "I know, dear. George can be a bit formidable, can't she? I've never taken to riding myself, much to David's chagrin." She began to clear the plates. "But he loves me anyway. And besides, everything else about living here in the country I adore. Especially my garden."

I helped her stack the dishes on the trolley. "Thank you again for the lovely flowers you sent to our hotel room. I've always loved daffodils."

Grace gave me a gentle look. "I know." She wheeled the trolley to the spacious kitchen with beautiful ancient slate floors. "Alex has told you of his plans to stay here and run the business for his father then?" she asked as we loaded the dishwasher.

My heart clutched, but only for a second. "Yes." I handed her a plate. "I'm sure you'll be glad to have your son so close again."

Her brow furrowed, and she said softly, almost to herself. "If he's staying for the right reasons." She smiled, and her adopted homeland's famous reserve fell back into place. "Alex has told me so much about Barley and the *Bulletin*. Will you continue to write for the paper?"

"I'm not sure." I gave her a crooked smile. "To be honest, I think I've written about all I can about pigeon racing, cemetery boards, and emu ranching."

Her laugh bubbled forth. "I can imagine." She wrinkled her nose. "Emus?"

"And cows. And goats. And sheep. And every other four-legged creature known to man—which is kind of funny since I'm about as far from an animal person as you can get." I handed her another plate. "When I lived in Cleveland, my pet was a plastic goldfish. No fuss and no mess, but bright and pretty to look at."

"A bit difficult to cuddle up to," Grace observed.

"True. But no shedding either."

"And now?"

"Now?"

"You said that in Cleveland your pet was the plastic goldfish. What about now?" Grace pulled out a chair and sat down at the scarred pine kitchen table, which also served as an island, and gestured for me to do the same.

"Now I have a cat named Herman. My five-year-old nephew gave him to me to keep me company *and* to help keep the mice at bay." I sat across from her and grinned. "Actually, Herman allows me the pleasure of his company only when he's feeling so inclined. Which isn't often. Except when he's hun—"

A deep howl behind me made me jump, knocking over my wooden chair in the process. I whirled around to see a dog that looked a little like Charlie Brown's Snoopy, only tricolored and much, much older. He stood with his graying muzzle thrown back, ready to howl again.

Grace's eyes twinkled. "I think you hurt Chester's feelings with your talk about not being an animal person." She patted her leg. "Here, boy. Come here. That's okay. Phoebe didn't mean it."

"Sorry." My ears burned as I set the chair to rights.

The beagle, uh, Chester, stretched in his doggy bed, which I hadn't even noticed, and padded over to his mistress, who stroked his head and scratched his ears. When he flopped on his back, stubby legs in the air, she slipped off her right loafer and began rubbing Chester's tummy with her foot. "So then what will you do?"

"Pardon?"

"If you leave the *Bulletin*?"

I sighed. "Actually, a friend of mine in Cleveland made me a really good job offer recently, but I've pretty much decided to turn him down. The money's great, and it would be wonderful to live in a big city again, but I'm afraid it would turn out to just be emus all over again . . ."

She looked a bit confused, so I took a deep breath and started over.

"Actually, I'm considering several options—including staying in England a bit longer."

Her eyes met mine, probing. Then she looked back at Chester and put her loafer back on. "Yes, Delia mentioned that."

I blushed. "Grace, do you mind if I ask you something?"

"Of course not."

"How difficult was it for you to adjust to life over here rather than in the States?"

She smiled. "It's quite lovely living here now, but it was a tremendous adjustment at first. Everything was completely different from what I was accustomed to." She stood up and moved to the sink while Chester padded back to his bed. "Not just the country, but the whole lifestyle I married into." She looked back at me, drying her hands on a tea towel. "I think Alex told you that when I met David, I was his parents' housekeeper?"

I nodded.

A shadow crossed her face. "My first husband was an alcoholic and had trouble keeping a job, so we never had much. When he died, we had nothing." The shadow disappeared. "But God provided me with a position as a housekeeper to the Spencer family, which in turn led to my meeting David, which in turn led to our falling in love and getting married and"—she made a sweeping motion with her hand— "my moving into all this. I still find it difficult to believe at times that I live here amid all this grandeur." She shook her head and gave me a rueful smile. "This Pittsburgh girl never expected to become the lady of the manor."

She glanced at me. "Would you like a tour of the house?"

"Would I?!"

Whoa! Dial it down a notch, California-girl.

Note to self: Remember new resolve to be less exuberant.

"Thank you," I said in a softer, better-modulated tone. "That would be lovely."

Although I tried not to gape and exclaim at room after grand room that Grace led me through, that proved impossible—especially when she showed me the library with floor-to-ceiling mahogany bookcases on all sides. "Omigosh! It's like the one in *Beauty and the Beast,* and there's even one of those attached rolling-ladder thingies."

Her eyes twinkled. "Would you like to try it?" Grace's voice took on a conspiratorial tone. "When Cordelia was little, I used to push her round and round on the nanny's day off."

Now I really gaped. Then shot a rueful look down at my thighs. "I'm not exactly little."

She waved off my objection. "You're fine."

"But what will your husband think?"

"He'll never know. They'll be out riding for ages." Grace giggled. "Don't worry, we've got the house to ourselves. Now climb on up and I'll push you."

And that she did. I flew past Shakespeare and Shelley and Grisham, Wordsworth and Coleridge and Clancy.

Then I pushed Grace. And she pushed me again.

And again. And again.

"Okay, hold on tight," I cautioned. "I'm going to go really fast this time."

Grace threw back her head, shut her eyes, and squealed with glee as she flew around the shelves.

"*Mother*—what in the world?"

I stopped in midpush, Grace's eyes flew open, and we both turned sheepish faces toward the door where Alex stood, his mouth hanging open.

Next to him were a tiny pair of Manolos I'd have recognized anywhere.

I cast an involuntary glance down at my own bare feet, having removed my boots and socks to improve my balance on the ladder. My heart lurched, and I felt my face flame.

Grace descended the ladder, smoothing her hair. "Hello, darling. What a nice surprise. We weren't expecting you today." She inclined her head toward the tiny Manolos. "Georgina." Then she linked her petite arm with my not-so-petite one. "I was just showing Phoebe the library, but I think it's nearly teatime. Your father and the others should be back soon."

The tea, complete with Grace's homemade scones and clotted cream, was scrumptious but stilted. MJ tried to dispel the awkwardness by regaling us with the story of Delia and David hoisting her up into an antique sidesaddle—in which she had elected not to ride. "I'm glad you weren't there with your camera, Pheebs," she said with a laugh. "I looked more than ridiculous."

"Oh, Phoebe, didn't you get a chance to ride?" George looked me up and down. "What a shame."

Before I could answer, Grace stepped in. "I asked Phoebe to keep me company. After all the wonderful things my son had told me about her, I wanted to get to know her better." She cast a warm smile my way. "I'm so glad I did."

Delia grinned, and George leaned in closer to Alex, who tugged at his collar. My heart did another little lurch as I took in his dear, familiar face. He really was a wonderful-looking man. But I kept my cool.

During our farewells, Alex hugged Mary Jo and said, "I'm glad I got the chance to see you both again before you leave." He frowned. "Just sorry we weren't able to spend much time together. So much going on, you know, and . . ." Then he turned to me with what seemed like a wistful look—I was probably just imagining it—and gave me a quick hug and a peck on the cheek. "Have a great flight home, and please tell your mom and everyone in Barley hello."

He lowered his voice. "Here's lookin' at you, Pheebs." But he couldn't seem to look me in the eye.

I was misinformed. Way misinformed.

When Grace hugged me good-bye, she lingered a little longer to whisper in my ear, "And this is my prayer, that your love may grow ever richer and richer in knowledge and insight of every kind, and may thus bring you the gift of true discrimination.'"

chapter sixteen

More Surprises

back at Delia's flat, an interesting message awaited us from Ian. Asking Mary Jo out. On a *date*. That same evening.

She was gobsmacked.

I was thrilled. So was Delia. We danced around the room and serenaded MJ with "Tonight" from *West Side Story.* (Turns out Delia had played one of the Jet girls in a school production, so she knew all the songs from the show.) Our serenade screeched to an abrupt halt, however, when MJ told us, "I'm not going."

"What? Why not?" I frowned. "You thought he was nice."

"And smart," Delia chimed in. "And sweet."

"*And* he loves history and horses," I reminded her.

"But it doesn't make sense." My practical friend ticked off the reasons on her fingers. "First, he's just a kid. Second, I don't even know whether he's a Christian or not. And third, we're going home in a few days. What's the point?"

"Oh, I don't know, let me think." Fist under my chin, I struck a "Thinker" pose. "To have a little *fun*, maybe?"

"Besides, Ian's no kid," Delia said. "He may be younger than you in years, but he's more together than most thirty-year-olds I know." She smiled. "And just for the record, MJ, he *is* a Christian. And loads of fun."

"Besides, it's just a date." I kicked off the spiffy-but-comfy Clarks clogs I'd snagged during one of our Cotswold shopping sprees, along with a replacement suitcase for the new clothes I'd bought. "It's not a proposal. It's not meeting the parents. It's just a fun evening. Go and have a good time." I shrugged. "Of course, if you'd rather stay here with us, we're planning some fun too. Delia, weren't you saying we could give one another facials tonight? And when we're finished with that, pedicures?"

"Don't forget the leg waxing, Phoebe. We have to do that before the pedicure."

Mary Jo shuddered and punched in Ian's number. "All right. I get the picture. But it's been so long since I've been on a date, I won't even know how to act."

Delia grinned. "Don't act. Just be your natural self. That's what he was drawn to in the first place."

Once she hung up, after agreeing to go to dinner with Ian, I pounced. "Makeup time!"

MJ shrank back. "But I don't usually wear makeup."

"You don't usually date either." I grinned and led her to a chair at the kitchen table, grabbing my cosmetics bag on the way. "This is a night of firsts."

"Do you need concealer?" Delia asked.

"Nope." I dotted my cover-up stick beneath the faint circles under MJ's eyes and rubbed it in. "But do you have any foundation? Mine's the wrong shade for her coloring."

Delia passed me a small bottle. "How about lipstick?"

"Got it. Blush too. But do you have any eye liner?"

Mary Jo put her fingers in her mouth and let loose with an ear-piercing whistle. "Now, just hold on a minute." She directed her attention to Delia. "Didn't you tell me a little while ago to just be my natural self?"

"Yes, but—"

She swiveled her head to me. "And aren't you the one who told me to just go and have a good time?"

"Yes . . ."

Mary Jo shoved herself away from the table and yelled, "Well, I can't be natural or have a good time with all that gunk on my face."

"Okay, okay. Settle down." My eyes widened. I'd never heard my laid-back friend yell before.

"Yes, MJ, don't get your knickers in a twist," Delia said.

"Sorry. I shouldn't have yelled." Her face reddened. "Look, I really appreciate what you're both trying to do here, but . . . it's just not me. I'm just not the girly-girl type." She lifted her shoulders. "He'll have to just take me as I am or not at all."

"He'd be lucky to get you," I said. The heat climbed up my neck. "I'm sorry too, MJ. Guess I got a little carried away."

"Me too," Delia said.

"Don't worry about it." Mary Jo pushed her hair behind her ears and slid a tentative smile our way. "I could use a little help figuring out what to wear, though."

Later that night, I was channel surfing and happened upon one of my favorite Julia Roberts comedies. Delia had already gone to bed—we'd skipped the whole facials-and-pedicure ritual, which had just been for Mary Jo's benefit—and MJ was still out kicking up her heels with Ian. So I settled in to enjoy the last half hour of *My Best Friend's Wedding*, disappointed that I'd missed the "Do You Know the Way to San Jose?" restaurant sing-along.

I did, however, catch the scene near the end where Julia is chasing after her best male friend, the seriously hot Dermot Mulroney, whom she thinks she's in love with, but who is engaged to Cameron Diaz. She's *literally* chasing him, in a delivery truck—while Dermot careens after Cameron Diaz in a regular car.

I've seen that chase dozens of times, and it's hilarious. But this time, watching Julia's frantic maneuvers, it suddenly hit me: *That's what I've been doing.*

No, I hadn't been tailing Alex through the streets of Chicago. But I'd been chasing him just the same, no matter how I tried to tell myself otherwise.

Then Rupert Everett, Julia's other male friend, says something to her on the cell phone as she screeches around a corner, barely missing traffic and parked cars.

What he says is this: "Who's chasing *you*, Jules?"

And when he said it, I had a full-blown epiphany: *That's it. That's how it should be.*

Like most of my friends, I'd always hated those platitudes about "don't chase guys" and "play hard to get." I mean, we're in the twenty-first century now; we don't need all that romantic game playing, right?

But now I saw the real problem with chasing after a man. It wasn't a matter of being unseemly or socially unacceptable or not playing the game right. It was just this: if I chase him, I'll never really know if he cares enough to chase *me*.

How nice to know beyond a doubt that you're really the one he wants—that he's not just letting you catch him because he's tired or doesn't have anything better to do. And I really don't know that about Alex. Or I didn't know it until recently.

Sigh. *So much for staying in England and attending Oxford.*

It was a night for surprises.

"Guess what, daughter? I've got a job!"

I spit out my tea when I read those words from my mother on Delia's laptop.

Mom wrote (using Karen and Jordy's e-mail) that Jeff and Amy from Barley Presbyterian, who also ran Books 'n' Brew, had left a couple of days earlier to move to Oregon. Jeff had been called to a full-time pastorate at a small church who needed him immediately.

I didn't even get to say good-bye, part of me wailed.

Never mind, the other part answered. *Just be happy for them. This is what they wanted.*

I continued reading. My mother was taking over Amy's place as resident baker for the bookstore and coffee bar. Karen was working there too, handling the book end of things with the help of a local boy named Redmond, who had worked for Jeff and Amy. "Everyone always likes my pies and pastries," Mom wrote. "So instead of giving them away, I'm going to earn a little money off them from now on. Best of all, this will mean a little extra money for Karen and Jordy, which we hope will relieve some of the stress on your brother. We've been really worried about him with all the extra work he's taken on. He's pushing himself way too hard. And I can't help thinking about your father."

My stomach clenched when I read that. I knew that Jordy was doing too much and that Mom and Karen were worried about him. I'd just conveniently forgotten about it while I was over here having fun.

And chasing after Alex.

Déjà vu flashback to my senior year in high school. My dad had taken on a part-time job in addition to his full-time teaching position in an effort to help make ends meet for our family.

Six months later, he'd died of a heart attack.

Chastened, I fell to my knees and whispered a fervent prayer for my brother. "Please Lord, watch over Jordy and keep him safe. We love him and need him."

I stayed there for a long time, alternately thinking of my family, praying for them, and sort of chatting with God about what was going on in my life. Then I reached under the table for my trusty carryall and unearthed my travel Bible.

Lord, show me what to do.

Opening to Philippians, I found the verse Grace had quoted in my ear: "So that you may be able to discern what is best . . . ." I continued reading. "Do nothing out of selfish ambition or vain conceit, but in humility consider others better than yourselves. Each of you should look not only to your own interests, but also to the interests of others."

I closed my Bible, lost in thought until the TV intruded. I started to hit the off button on the remote, but Mr. Spock caught my attention in one of the early Star Trek movies—*The Wrath of Khan*, I think. Spock was behind glass in a sealed chamber filled with some kind of toxins or radiation that, if released, would kill the entire crew. He was absorbing the poison into his own body instead and clearly dying, with his friend Captain Kirk on the other side of the glass, unable to prevent it.

Spock gasped the beginning of a Vulcan proverb, which the characters had earlier argued about: "The needs of the many—"

Kirk, almost in tears, finished his sentence, "outweigh the needs of the few."

"Or the one," Spock added and placed his hand on the glass, fingers spread in the Vulcan salute.

Before I knew it, I was having a major PMS meltdown over the onscreen death of the logical guy with the pointy ears. But I wasn't too hormonal not to realize there was a message there for me.

All right, God, I know I asked for some guidance. But Star Trek?

Wiping my streaming eyes with my fist, I got up and went in search of tissues . . . and chocolate. Then I went back to Delia's laptop and finished reading my e-mail.

> To: Movielovr
> From: GGreen
> Hi, Phoebe. Things at the *Bulletin* are running smoothly. Ryan, the intern, is doing a great job. And talking about jobs, I suppose your mother's told you her exciting news. Wait 'til you see her! She's having the time of her life—took to that job like a duck to water. Karen too.
> By the way, getting lots of good feedback on your col-

umn. Even Lou Jacobs has said nice things. I'm for-
warding an e-mail that recently came to the *Bulletin*
for you.

Dear Phoebe,

Hope you don't mind my being so familiar, but I feel
like I know you after reading your column. Girl, I
laughed myself silly when I read the story of you and
Mary Jo and your search for a potty in a tube station!
(The very same thing happened to my best friend
Sharlene and me. My name is Bobbi Lou Miller, and I
live in Lodi, but I'm originally from the great state of
Texas. I'm a little bit older than you. Okay, a lot. I turn
the big five-oh next month, so I guess that means I could
be your mama.☺) But for my fortieth birthday, Sharlene
and I spent ten days in England and had a ball. She still
lives in Dallas, but I've told her where to find your column on the Net, and we both love reading about all your
hilarious misadventures across the pond. You kind of
remind me of that travel guy who writes funny stuff
about going to Australia or just for a walk in the woods.☺
Keep up the good work!
Bobbi Lou

Wow. My first fan letter.

I read it again. Then I thought about my job, my family, and the
direction of my life.

Lord, what should I do with my career? I know you've given me
the gift and ability to write, but I also know there's not much money
in it—which is why most writers have a backup plan. Should Phil be
my back-up? Or do you have something completely different
in mind?

I reread both Mom's and Gordon's e-mails again, prayed some

more, then turned off the computer and went to bed, my mouth curving into a smile as a completely unforeseen plan began to unfurl in my mind.

"Tell all, MJ!" I demanded the next morning. "How was your date? We've been dying to hear." I wiggled my eyebrows, Groucho Marx–style. "Did you kiss?"

Hope so. That way at least one of us would be getting a little lip action.

"Did you have a good time? He wasn't too young then?" Delia asked innocently.

Mary Jo poured a cup of coffee and yawned. "I'm so tired. I haven't stayed up that late in a long time." She blew on her coffee before taking a sip.

"You're killin' me here," I said, putting my head in my hands. "Don't keep us in suspense. Where'd you go? What did you do? Come on—'fess up." I exchanged a glance with Delia. "You must have had a good time, or you wouldn't have gotten in so late."

Mary Jo buttered a piece of toast, then took another sip of coffee and smiled. "Yes, I had a good time. We went to dinner at this great Italian restaurant, then we walked around a little and Ian pointed out some really cool things about Oxford." She turned to me, eyes alight. "Did you know that Christopher *Wren* helped design the chapel at St. Mary's Church here? It looks completely different from the little St. Mary's in Fairford."

I groaned. "Skip the architecture lesson already and get back to the date."

"Well"—the corners of her mouth turned up—"then Ian took me to this club where they had karaoke . . ."

"I'll bet you blew him away!" I turned to Delia, eyes dancing. "MJ rocks! She's got pipes like Aretha. Our girl can sing."

Mary Jo blushed. "So can Ian. He's kind of a cross between Paul McCartney and Sting."

"Did you do any duets?" Delia asked with a sly grin.

She blushed again. "'Just My Imagination' and Smokey Robinson's 'Cruisin'. It was fun." She finished her toast and smiled at me. "Thanks for pushing me to go, Pheebs. You too, Delia. I had a good time. Made a nice end to our Oxford visit." She looked at her watch. "And now we'd better finish packing if we're going to catch that train."

I shook my head. Ever-practical Mary Jo. No romance in her soul.

Delia took us to the station, and we all hugged good-bye. "Thanks for everything," I said. "And come visit us in Barley anytime."

"Yeah," Mary Jo said to Delia. "Then I'll take *you* riding." She grinned. "Don't have a sidesaddle, though."

Just as we were boarding, we heard a shout.

"Wait!"

Ian came running down the platform, coat flapping, gangly legs flying, a bunch of freesia clutched in one hand and a small package in the other. He thrust them both at Mary Jo just as the train began to move.

I shrugged as the platform receded behind us, Ian and Delia waving good-bye.

Guess I got that romantic train-station send-off that I wanted after all. Wrong guy, of course, but that's all right.

To my amazement, I found that it almost was.

chapter seventeen

The Wild Moors

t hese English people sure have the gift of hospitality," Mary Jo said, sniffing her flowers as the train sped toward York. "First Alex's mom, then Delia, and now Ian."

"Ian's not being hospitable." I looked her straight in the eye. "He's *wooing* you."

She snorted. "I don't think so." Then she sighed. "Phoebe, I don't want to belabor the point or anything, but this isn't Hollywood. People don't fall in love that quickly."

"I'm not saying he's in *love* with you"—*yet*, I added to myself—"but that man has got a serious case of heavy-duty like going on."

"May I remind you that we just met? And that an ocean will soon be separating us?" Mary Jo shook her head. "He's simply doing the proper, polite English thing. They probably learn that stuff from the cradle."

"Uh-huh. Sure." I glanced at the still-wrapped package in her lap. "So why don't you open that and see what Mr. Proper and Polite gave you?"

"Probably just a little something to remind us of Oxford." The wrapping paper fell away to reveal a CD of *Motown's Greatest Hits*—including "Cruisin'" and "Just My Imagination." Mary Jo stared at the plastic case in her hand. And didn't notice a card flutter to the floor.

I snatched it up and read aloud:

Dear Mary Jo,

I had a wonderful time last night and am hoping it wasn't just my imagination that there was a connection between us. I've never met anyone like you before. You're so different from most of the English girls I meet! So open and natural.

I do hate that you're leaving so soon. I'd really like to spend more time with you exploring this connection. May I write you in California, please?

Hopefully, Ian

"Yep. I'd say that's the kind of stuff they teach 'em from the cradle." I passed the note to her.

As she reread the card, I replayed Mary Jo's comments in my head. *This isn't Hollywood. People don't fall in love that quickly.* I had a funny feeling that not too far down the Ian-road, she might find herself eating those very words.

But as far as Alex was concerned, though, had I really been in love? Had I known him well enough to be in love? Or (big embarrassed gulp) was I just in love with the whole idea of love?

Maybe a little bit of both?

Don't forget the lust factor, my puritan conscience reminded me.

All right already. So I went a little overboard on the kiss thing. What can I say? It's been a while.

I knew there were notable exceptions to the people-don't-fall-in-love-that-quickly rule—off the silver screen, I mean. Take my parents: One look at my mom on that Miss Udderly Delicious Dairy Pageant float, and my dad had been a goner.

Which is why I guess I'd expected the same.

But that's not the norm, my internal voice of reason reminded me gently. *And when it does happen, you both have to be on the same page.*

Alex obviously wasn't on the same page. I'm not sure he was even reading the same book.

197

"Look at the sheep." Mary Jo pressed her nose to the window and bleated, "Maaaa, maaaa."

I giggled. "You may not be able to get the plums in your mouth down, but you've sure got those animal accents licked."

"Brrr. Not quite California weather, is it?" Mary Jo pulled her fleece jacket close and power-walked to warm up as we walked the two miles of medieval walls that surround a portion of the ancient city of York and offer stunning views of the cathedral, which they call York Minster. "I'd kill for a hot cup of tea."

"Ditto."

Ten minutes later found us inside Little Betty's, a quaint tearoom with creaky, sloping floors and a wonderful cozy ambience. We ordered a standard full tea but also took our guidebook's recommendation and asked especially for a "Fat Rascal" scone, Betty's signature offering.

Fat indeed. That puppy was *huge* and bursting with currants and raisins.

Mary Jo slathered hers with jam and cream as Delia had taught us, took a bite, and swooned. I followed in her swooning lead. "This is the most amazing scone I've ever had in my life. We should get the recipe for Mom so she can serve them at Books 'n' Brew."

I took another sip and sighed. "I could really get used to this afternoon tea thing. So much more leisurely than gulping down a mocha in the car."

"I know." Mary Jo drained her tea. "I've got to say that I prefer this place to Brown's Hotel, though. It's cheaper, and I'm not expected to dress up. Plus, here I don't feel like I need to crook my little finger."

"Are you sure?" I shot a surreptitious glance around the tearoom and lowered my voice. "I think maybe they have etiquette police planted." I cut my eyes to a stout, well-dressed woman two tables over. "If you're not careful, they may stick your hands in some of those medieval stocks until you crook your finger properly."

Mary Jo snorted. The stout woman gave us a snooty look, which made my Thelma pal snort all the more.

Rolling our way out of the tearoom, we wandered through the Shambles, a crooked, traffic-free street crammed with ancient, narrow buildings, fabulous shops, and an Internet café where I could write my next column and send it to Gordon.

"How long do you think you'll be, Pheebs?"

"An hour or so," I said, looking up from the computer to my fidgeting friend. "Why?"

"I want to do a little more shopping and just wondered how much time I had."

My fingers stilled. "Did you really just say *want* and *shopping* in the same sentence?" I peered behind her and looked all around. "Where's my friend, and what have you done with her?"

She stuck out her tongue, waved, and set off—a woman on a mission. I pulled out my travel journal, typed up my column to Gordon, and then sent my mom an e-mail care of Karen and Jordy:

To: KGrants7
From: Movielovr
     Karen, this one is for Mom. Please tell her when it arrives. Thanks.
     Hey there, working mom. How's it feel to be back in the job ranks again after all this time? Congratulations! I'm thrilled for you, and I know everyone in town's equally thrilled with all your yummy goodies. Looking forward to seeing all of you again—miss you! Lots to talk about when I get home. Lots. We took scads of pictures—wait'll you see! Give the kids my love, especially that little namesake of ours. See you soon. Love, P.
     P.S. You've probably already heard from Gordon that Alex won't be returning to Barley. C'est la vie. Easy come, easy go. Right? (Don't worry. I'm fine.☺)

BTW, Alex's mom and sister are darlings. You'd love them.

Late that afternoon, Mary Jo and I attended Evensong at centuries-old York Minster, where young choirboys sang in Latin and the sinking sun blazed in through centuries-old stained glass.

Closing my eyes, I let the glorious music wash over me, and I thought of all the saints who had worshipped there throughout the centuries, listening to the same music, looking at the same stained glass, loving the same God. Then I opened my eyes and gazed at the vivid Technicolor windows, remembering the little church in Fairford. Once again, an uncanny sense of peace and reverence filled me. And suddenly that familiar line from *Casablanca* seemed to take on a whole new meaning.

"It doesn't take much to see that the problems of three [in our case, two] little people don't amount to a hill of beans in this crazy world . . ."

And the next phrase that flew through my imagination took me completely by surprise.

"Seek first the kingdom of God . . . and all these things shall be added to you."

Mary Jo and I walked back to our bed-and-breakfast in silence, each intent on our own thoughts. And once in our room, I sequestered myself in a Radox bath for a little more one-on-one time with God. I was surprised to find myself humming a hymn I'd learned as a child at our family church. That was odd. For years I'd been more of a gospel-chorus, praise-music sort of girl. But something felt like it was changing, shaking loose in me, and I was hearing God in completely new ways.

Okay, God, I'm all ears. What's next?

When I finally emerged from the bathroom an hour later, all wrinkled and pruney, my roommate handed me a small gift-wrapped box.

"What's this?"

"What's it look like?" She crossed her eyes. "It's a present. Open it."

Inside was a miniature replica of the Minster's stained-glass rose window. Carefully I removed the delicate glass circle and held it up to the light. "But we didn't even stop by the cathedral gift shop afterwards . . ."

"I know. I got it while you were at the Internet café earlier. Something, or someone"—she smiled—"compelled me to buy it for you."

That night I slept peacefully without one thought of Alex.

"How cute is that? It's the same car Charlize Theron drove in *The Italian Job.*"

MJ, who'd watched the heist caper with me on DVD, walked around the tiny Mini Cooper in the car rental parking lot, a skeptical expression on her face. "Except this one's a lot older."

"Don't be a spoilsport. Come on, get in. I'm a very good driver," I said in my best *Rain Man* voice as I slid behind the wheel.

On the right-hand side of the car, no less.

"This feels too weird; sitting on the driver's side without a steering wheel." Mary Jo buckled her seat belt in preparation for our day trip through the Yorkshire countryside.

"Uh-oh."

"Uh-oh what?" She shot me a wary look.

"This isn't an automatic." We glanced down at the stick shift between us. "And I'm not left-handed.

"But that's okay." I shrugged my carefree shoulders. "It will be one of our final Thelma-and-Louise adventures in England."

"Final?" Mary Jo dug her nails into the seat. "I'm glad this isn't a convertible."

I grabbed the gear stick and shifted into reverse. Grind. Grind. I tried again, but my little-used left hand refused to obey the signals my brain was giving it.

"Allow me," MJ said, shifting with her right hand while I pushed in the clutch.

"Right, then. By George"—*no, not George, anyone but George*—"I think we've got it."

Then we encountered my first roundabout—the Brits' answer to stop signs. The intersecting roads all feed into a little traffic circle—you just drive around the circle and take the road you need.

Except how exactly do you get in? Cars whizzed by from all directions, blaring their horns.

Holding my breath, I took the plunge.

But then I couldn't get out. It was like Chevy Chase in *National Lampoon's European Vacation*—only we didn't have to stay in the roundabout all night. But we did drive around in the same circle seven times until at last Mary Jo yelled, "Now! Go for it! To the right, to the right!"

Problem was, I always get my right and left confused. In air-force basic training, they'd had to tape a big *R* on my right shoe and an *L* on my left when they taught me how to march. Now here I was; sitting in the wrong side of the car, driving on the wrong side of the road, trying to shift with the wrong hand . . . and trying to remember which way was right.

In city traffic.

Can you say stressful?

At last we were out of the city and on a hedge-lined stretch of country road.

After trying in vain to pick up a decent radio signal with music we liked, we finally gave up. Instead, we sang Martina McBride's "This One's for the Girls" at the top of our lungs as we rode through the pastoral countryside, surrounded by thick hedges on either side.

"Wow, these country roads sure are narrow, huh, MJ?"

"Watch out!" All at once, a huge truck came barreling into view from around a curve—straight at us.

"It's just a one-lane road!" I shrieked. "What do I do?"

The truck slowed down.

So did I.

Then he idled a truck length away from us and gestured.

"Any idea what he's trying to tell me?" I glanced at Mary Jo.

"I think he wants you to move."

"To where?" I looked around wildly. "I'm boxed in on either side by these stupid hedges. And I read somewhere that beneath all this pretty greenery they've got thick stone walls. If I hit them, they'd crumple this baby like an accordion."

At last the truck driver gave an exasperated shake of his head. He revved his engine and backed all the way to the curve, pulling over to allow me just enough room to pass.

Which I did at a snail's pace.

"Sorry," Mary Jo yelled as we drove by.

He yelled something too. Something about Yanks and blood. And made another gesture.

We continued on our oblivious American way. After a couple more close calls, however, we finally realized that the unwritten law of the road was to pull over as close as possible to the lethal hedge when another vehicle approached. If there still wasn't enough room, then one of us would back up until we found a slightly wider spot.

So much for our idyllic day of driving through the English country-side. By the time we arrived in Thirsk and parked in the town square, we were both basket cases.

"I'm driving when we leave," Mary Jo said.

I didn't argue.

Thirsk was the hometown of Mary Jo's favorite author/vet, James Herriot. His house is now a museum, and I snapped a trembling-with-excitement Mary Jo's picture in front of the gleaming red door. Once inside, we made our way through a warren of rooms; my animal-loving friend clucking in delight at each one we passed.

All of a sudden she stopped short. "Phoebe," she said in awe. "This is the *dispensary*."

I peered into the small room and looked around. "What? It's a bunch of old bottles."

"But this is where the real James Herriot worked and dispensed medicines to his animal patients." Her voice caught. "I never thought I'd really be here."

Glancing at my traveling companion, I noticed tears in her eyes—a first for practical, no-nonsense Mary Jo. At least since I'd known her.

"I've got an idea," I told her as we exited the museum. "Let's stay here in Yorkshire an extra night instead of heading back to London."

Her eyes lit up momentarily. "But you wanted to see another show before we go home. You've got reservations."

"Which can be canceled." I looked at my friend's happy face and off into the distance.

"Besides," I added, "I like it here too. And I don't want to be this close and miss the moors."

"S'mores?" Mary Jo said with a mischievous gleam. "Not sure they have those here."

I rolled my eyes. "Very funny, Esther."

We headed west to the moors—Brontë country—where I found myself longing to follow in the footsteps of Jane Eyre and Heathcliff.

Minus all the torment, of course.

And not in my Manolos—or even my Clarks.

No, trudging across the wild moors called for some very specific British footwear: Wellingtons, affectionately known as Wellies. These strong, green rubber knee-high boots were perfect for mucking through rain and mud and traipsing through the countryside.

Not terribly attractive, but wonderfully functional and an English institution.

Fortunately, the hosts of our B&B outside of Haworth—home to the Brontë parsonage—kept a ready supply of Wellies for guests in their mud room. Mary Jo's fit like a glove, but mine were just a tad too big. It was sort of a Goldilocks encounter as I sat on the stone steps trying on pair after pair . . . too little, way too big, and finally, although not "just right," close enough.

Once we'd been properly equipped, we made our way up the grassy fell that swooped down just behind the B & B. Once over the crest we were out of sight of town—we might as well have been a million miles away. The wind whipped our hair and sliced into our faces, and mud kept sucking my right boot off my heel at regular intervals.

The funny thing was, I didn't even mind. It was the best not-so-quiet time I'd had in a while.

Tramping along behind Mary Jo, I replayed all that had happened on our trip—the sights we'd seen, things we'd done, people we'd met. And I found myself returning again and again to my friend's assertion that I lived in Neverland.

She wasn't, of course, the first person to make such an observation.

I know I tend to be a bit flighty, God, and walk around with my head in the clouds. And yes, I know I need to be responsible. I want to be responsible. But can't I be responsible and dream a little too? Does being mature have to mean being boring and predictable and living without imagination?

We topped another rise, looking back down over the town, and then down in a dished-out little valley. I kept on slipping and sliding in my slightly too-big boots. Then, part of the way down the next little valley, an answer floated lightly into my heart.

Unless you become like little children, you will not enter the kingdom of heaven.

At just that moment the heavens opened and a torrent of rain spilled forth. Slipping again, I grabbed at my traveling companion. "Hey, Mary Jo," I yelled over the wind, "time to become like little children."

We tumbled down the muddy hill, laughing all the way.

We arrived back at our cozy, warm B&B, sodden and soaked through—except for our feet. I gladly returned my ill-fitting Wellies.

But all the rest I'm taking with me—except for the blood-clot tomatoes, of course.

Back in London, Mary Jo indulged my need to check out the world-renowned Harrod's. We goggle-eyed our way through the immense food halls, wishing we could bring back one of the massive wheels of cheddar cheese or Stilton, but opting not to since we didn't want our clothes to smell.

My Thelma pal had to pull me out of the shoe department before I drooled on all the Italian leather. We did, however, nip down to the bargain basement that Grace and Delia had recommended, where I picked up several tins of tea and tea biscuits to take home to my family.

All my shopping at last accomplished, I turned to my traveling companion. "Well, Thelma, what else do you want to do in this marvelous city before we leave for home tomorrow?"

She didn't hesitate. "I'd like to go on the London Eye at dusk. That way we can watch the sun set and see the whole city light up."

It wasn't the most exciting Ferris wheel I've ever been on—can you say slow?—but it was definitely the biggest. All of London lay sparkling below us.

What a perfect way to say good-bye to this amazing city. And as dusk turned to night, I looked across at the illuminated Big Ben and thought of Esther. And how right she'd been about traveling.

You do discover who you are and what you're made of when you're on the road. Sometimes you even get a hint of where you're going.

"Second star to the right, my friend," I whispered as the big wheel started its slow descent, "and straight on 'til morning."

[chapter eighteen]

Sweet Home California

"Sure feels great to be back in warm California again." Mary Jo lifted her face to the sun as we stepped out of the air-conditioned coolness of Sacramento's airport.

"Enjoy it while you can." Gordon chuckled. "Supposed to get up to sixty-eight today, but weather man says we're due for a cold snap this weekend. Might get down to forty-five."

Mary Jo hooted. "You don't know the meaning of cold 'til you've spent a few days in the English countryside in what they call spring." She shivered in remembrance. "There was one day when it got down to thirty degrees."

We'd arrived in Washington, D.C., from London that morning as scheduled but discovered that our connecting flight to San Francisco had been canceled due to mechanical problems. That meant we'd have to spend the night in our nation's capital and continue on to San Francisco the following day. I'd called Mom, who was planning to pick us up, and told her to stay put.

But then we learned that, if we hurried, there was a flight to Sacramento we could catch, arriving late that same afternoon. Eager to get home and more than ready to sleep in our own beds again, we ran for it. As we were boarding, I called Gordon on my cell and asked him to make the one-hour drive from Barley to pick us up.

"Don't say anything to my family, though," I'd warned him. "I want to surprise them."

"Mum's the word."

Now at the airport, Gordon looked down at all our bags. "Did you buy out the whole country, or what, Phoebe?"

"Well, the airline lost my luggage, so I had to buy a new bag," I said with an injured air. "And then, just as we were about to fly out, we discovered they'd had my old one in a stray corner all along. So I have them both now. But," I sniffed, "I'll have you know that many of those bags belong to Mary Jo."

"Thought you weren't a shopper." He arched his eyebrows in surprise.

"I'm not." Mary Jo grimaced. "But shopaholic Louise there managed to pull me over to the dark side with her."

She held up a placating hand. "Not to worry, though. It was just a case of temporary insanity. Now that I'm back on American soil, I see no reason to repeat the offense."

Driving home, Gordon kept up a constant stream of chatter, wanting to hear all about our trip but never making direct eye contact with me.

Sensing his discomfort, I finally broached the subject he was doing his utmost to avoid. "You can mention his name. It's okay."

He fidgeted in his seat, then clenched the steering wheel tighter and stared straight ahead. "Phoebe, I owe you a big apology. I'm sorry I pushed you to go to England and see Alex and that things didn't work out between you two."

I laid a gentle hand on his arm. "Gordon, I'm glad you pushed me to go to England."

"You are?"

"Yep. Wouldn't have traded the experience for anything in the world."

Gordon stole a cautious glance my way. "But what about Alex?"

I twisted around and shot a wry grin at Mary Jo in the backseat. "Well, I must admit that wasn't my favorite part of the trip. Neither was meeting Gorgeous George, the family lawyer. But everything else was wonderful."

"Well, some of the food was kind of strange," Mary Jo interjected. "And that first grotty hotel—"

"Grotty?" He raised puzzled eyebrows.

"Tacky. Icky. Dirty. Apart from those couple of inconveniences, the trip was absolutely fabulous." I looked straight at him. "And if not for you, I'd never have gone and seen all those amazing things. So thank you."

"Yeah," Mary Jo piped up from the backseat. "Thanks, Gordon. And thank you too, Pheebs, for inviting me to tag along. It was quite an adventure." She giggled. "Phoebe and Mary Jo's excellent adventure."

Gordon cleared his throat. "I *am* sorry that things didn't work out with Alex though. I really thought there was something there—definitely saw some sparks."

"Me too." I sighed. "And if he'd stayed in Barley, who knows what would have happened? But things change and that's okay. Obviously it just wasn't meant to be." I gestured with my head toward the backseat. "But while we're on the subject of sparks . . . there's someone else in this car who set off a few over in Merrie Olde."

Gordon raised his eyebrows and looked in the rearview mirror at a blushing Mary Jo. "Is that so? Pray tell. I'd love to hear all about it." His mouth twitched. "And I'm sure our *Bulletin* readers would too."

"There's nothing to tell," she said, glaring at me. "Ian's just a friend."

"Uh-huh. A tall, blond, and gorgeous friend who saw her off at the train, bearing gifts."

"Ian, huh?" His eyebrows arched higher. "As in Ian Fleming and James Bond?" His eyes twinkled. "Careful, Mary Jo. You don't want to become just another Bond girl."

She glowered at him another minute, then switched her tone.

"So, Gordon, how *are* things going with you and Phoebe's mom these days?"

"Yeah." I switched teasing gears in no time flat. "Are you going to make an honest woman out of her one of these days?"

Gordon blushed to the roots of his thinning hair.

Mary Jo let out a relieved chuckle. "Will we be hearing wedding bells anytime—" She broke off as we neared the outskirts of Barley, where her attention was distracted by a horse grazing in a nearby field. "How are my babies doing?" She sighed. "I've sure missed them."

Gordon scratched his nicotine patch. "They're right as rain—don't you worry. Elizabeth, Gloria, and I have been feeding 'em and giving them their daily workouts. All right, here we are . . ."

He pulled up the long drive to Mary Jo's farmhouse, where she barely waited for him to stop the car before jumping out.

"Thanks, Thelma." I handed Mary Jo her backpack. "For everything. It was a blast."

She hugged me. "Thanks, Louise, for pushing me to go. And don't forget to mind the gap."

While Gordon helped Mary Jo carry all her bags inside, I rummaged around in the shopping bags in the trunk until I found what I was looking for.

Gordon slid back into the driver's seat and buckled his seat belt.

But before he could restart the car, I stopped him. "I brought you a present."

"What is it?" He slid me a wary look. "A stink bomb? Or maybe some plastic English dog cr—uh, excrement?"

"I seriously considered that, you old curmudgeon. But then I found something even better." I handed him a baseball-sized package.

Excited, he tore off the wrapping paper and opened the box. Slowly, eyebrows knitted in confusion, he extracted a small jar of Marmite. "You shouldn't have."

"Only the best for you, boss."

Gordon examined the jar and began to unscrew the lid.

I quickly rolled down my window. "You never want to open that puppy in a small, confined space."

One sniff, and he screwed the lid back on. "Guess I'll wait 'til I go duck hunting."

"You might scare away the ducks." I grinned and handed him another package. "Here's your real present."

He unwrapped it warily, holding it far away from his nose. Then he stared. First at the book in his hand, then at me.

"It's only a second edition, but I found it in a dusty antique stall in Portobello Market, and it still has the original book jacket, which I thought you'd like."

Gordon wiped his hands on his pants, then caressed the worn paper cover. "*For Whom the Bell Tolls* is my favorite Hemingway. How'd you know?"

I snorted. "You only talk about it all the time. And since it begins with the Donne poem that was one of my Dad's favorites, I just had to buy it."

I took a deep breath. "Okay, now that I've buttered you up, there's something I need to say." I looked him square in the eye. "I'm giving you my notice, Gordon. That's another thing I discovered in England. I don't want to write about emus anymore."

"You didn't want to write about 'em while you were still here." He chuckled and rewrapped his gift with infinite care.

"I know, but I let my thinking get clouded by the proximity of a certain good-looking English publisher."

"What—I'm not good-looking?" He backed up for the return trip down Mary Jo's driveway.

"I suppose you have your appeal, though you don't ring this particular Grant woman's bells." I gave him a sly look. "I can't speak for another member of my family, however."

Gordon smiled but refused to take the bait. "Whatever am I going to tell Christy Sharp?" He shook his head in regret. "She was really hoping you'd come do a follow-up piece on her salt-and-pepper–shaker collection. Says she's gotten some new ones since you were last there. She and Bob finally took that long road trip in their Winnebago and collected several from the Midwest."

"Gee, I hate to miss covering that breaking story." I released an exaggerated sigh. "Guess you'll have to assign it to your new intern."

"Ryan will love that. He's got big dreams of becoming an investigative reporter. He's even been sniffing around town trying to ferret out corruption in the local government somewhere." Gordon chortled. "Thought he had a hot story—that Betty Dixon on the cemetery board was taking kickbacks from Norm Anderson—but turns out the two of them are dating and were just trying to keep it quiet."

"Norm and Betty?" I gaped at him. "They can't stand each other."

"Well, you know what they say." He chuckled. "There's a thin line between love and hate."

I'll say.

Down girl, my moral compass reminded me. *You know you don't hate Alex. He's your friend and your brother in Christ. Just because he didn't live up to your romantic expectations—*

*And never even kissed you—*my libido interrupted.

Note to self: Strangle libido and remember to be content in all circumstances.

Gordon shifted in his seat. "So since you're not going to work for the *Bulletin* anymore, may I ask what you plan to do to earn a living, young lady?"

"Well, I'd like to keep doing my column, if that's okay, though I'll have to think of another angle. 'Notes from Abroad' won't work anymore. And I have some other things I'm looking into—nothing definite, so I can't talk about them yet."

He slapped his hand to his forehead. "Your column! I knew I forgot something. There's a few letters and e-mails come for you the past several days. I've got 'em over at the *Bulletin*."

"Letters?"

"Fan letters." He grinned. "You're becoming quite the celebrity."

Slipping into Karen and Jordy's, I tiptoed through the house to the back screen door. My family, taking advantage of the warm spring day, was eating dinner at the backyard picnic table.

I pushed open the door. "Hi, honey, I'm home."

Forks clattered to the table. "Aunt Phoebe!"

"An Beebee!" Lexie hurtled herself at me as I bounded down the steps, followed in quick succession by the rest of the Grant clan except for Jordy, who I presumed was at work.

Mom barreled her way through my nieces and nephew and enveloped me in a bear hug. "We thought you weren't coming 'til tomorrow. You should have told us you got an earlier flight; we'd have picked you up at the airport."

"What? And miss all this?" I hugged her back and nodded to the man behind me, "Gordon rode to our rescue." Glancing toward the table, my eyes lit on a welcome sight. "Is that fresh fruit?"

Karen slid over on the picnic bench. "Are you hungry? Sit down and dig in."

Mom piled a plate high with good old American bounty: hot dog, baked beans, potato salad, green salad, and fresh fruit salad. "Gordon, have you eaten? Would you like to join us?"

"No thanks. I've got some things to do over at the *Bulletin,* but, uh, I'll see you tomorrow?"

She gave him a warm smile. "Looking forward to it."

I inhaled chunks of juicy pineapple, oranges, bananas, kiwis, and grapes. "Boy, did I ever miss this." Then I grabbed a forkful of salad: a crisp mixture of spring greens and iceberg lettuce combined with hothouse tomatoes, cucumbers, carrots, celery, fresh mushrooms, green onions, sprouts, and sunflower seeds. "Now, that's what I call a salad." I mewled with pleasure.

"Don't they have salad in England?" Ashley asked with a puzzled frown.

"Yes, but it's not the same. Usually when you ask for salad, you get a piece of limp lettuce to go with your sandwich—at least the places where we ate. It might not be the same everywhere." I poured on more Ranch dressing. "And although I'm sure they have fresh mushrooms, the only ones I ever tasted were canned at breakfast." I gestured to the beans on my plate. "This they did have—at breakfast too. But they weren't baked. Just plain old pork and beans from the can."

"Beans for breakfast?" Karen asked.

I nodded, my mouth full.

The kids peppered me with questions. "Did you wide on dat big fewwis wheel, An Beebee?" Lexie asked.

"And go to castles and see swords and armor and everything?" Jacob chimed in. "Did you see Sherwood Forest where Robin Hood lived?"

"Hush, you two." Karen jiggled little Gloria on her knee. "Let Aunt Phoebe eat."

"That's all right. I don't mind." I snuggled Lexie up against me with one arm and Jacob with the other. "I've missed these little monkeys." I planted a kiss on Lexie's head. "Yes, sweetheart, I rode on the big Ferris wheel, but you wouldn't have liked it, because it moves really slowly. It was a great way to see the whole city though." I turned to Jacob. "And yes, I got to see a few castles with lots of swords and armor and other painful instruments of torture."

"Cool!"

Elizabeth gave me a curious look. "Did you really see the place where the king had all his wives' heads cut off?"

Her mother grimaced. "Uh, some of us are still eating here."

"Yes, Elizabeth." I took another bite of my hot dog, dripping nice thick ketchup as I did. "And he only had two of his six wives' heads cut off."

Ashley cut straight to the important stuff. "Did you see anyone famous? Like Gwyneth Paltrow or Madonna? They both live over there now, you know." Her eyes widened. "Or maybe Prince William?"

"No." I took a grateful gulp of Mom's iced sun tea. "But one day we saw the prime minister's car drive by, and another time we saw a limo near the Ritz with someone in the backseat who looked remarkably like Donatella Versace."

"Cool!" my fashion-conscious eldest niece said.

Unimpressed with prime ministers and fashionistas, Lexie had just one burning question. "Wheah's Awex?"

[chapter nineteen]

Phoebe's Great Idea

With only the tiniest of stomach flutters, I answered, "Alex lives in England now, Lexie. That's his home. Just like this is my home."

She pouted. "But Awex gonna mawwy you, An Beebee."

Ashley and Elizabeth gasped, Mom sucked in her breath, and Karen warned, "Lexie . . ."

"It's okay, Karen." I looked into my niece's confused brown eyes. "Sweetie, Alex is my friend—he's a friend of all of ours—but I'm not going to marry him. He's staying in England with his family, and I've come home to mine. You can't be married and live that far away from each other."

"Well, you can," Ashley said under her breath, "but it never works."

Changing the subject, I grinned at my nephew and nieces. "So . . . who wants presents?"

"I do, I do," the kids chorused.

"Okay. I have a few bags inside—"

En masse, they made a rush for the back door.

"Hey guys, hang on a sec."

Jacob collided into his older sisters.

"You need to be very, very careful with them 'cause there's breakable stuff in there. Okay?"

They nodded, eager to be off.

"In fact, Ash, why don't you take charge of the largest white bag?"

"Okay." They all scampered inside.

Once the kids were gone, I turned to my sister-in-law and saw traces of fine lines around her eyes I'd never noticed before. "So, I take it Jordy's still working most nights and weekends at that second job?"

"Yes." Karen expelled a tired sigh. "And it's really taking a toll. The kids never see him, and when they do, he's exhausted and irritable." She pushed her hair back from her face. "Even though I've started working part-time at Books 'n' Brew with Mom—which I love, by the way—it's only minimum wage, so it doesn't help all that much."

"Well, hold on to your hat—'cause I've got an idea that will—"

The kids' rambunctious return interrupted us. "Tell you later," I mouthed to Mom and Karen. "Okay, everyone. Let's open prezzies!"

"Prezzies?" Jacob looked at me.

"Actually, that's what they call presents over in England."

Mom raised her eyebrows at my "ack-shwally." "Looks like someone picked up an accent."

"Yeah." Ashley stared at me. "You sound like Madonna since she moved over there."

"It's really easy to develop an accent when you're surrounded by it all the time." I reached for the largest bag and rummaged around inside. "Although there's no way I'd ever say 'shed-yool' or 'al-loo-minium.'" Finally I found the box I was searching for. "Ah, here it is." I handed the package to my youngest niece. "Lexie, you go first."

She struggled with the wrapping paper until her eager brother stepped in to help.

"Oooohhhh." Her big brown eyes grew even bigger as she gazed at her sparkling treasure, which I placed atop her golden curls.

"Princess Diana wore a tiara just like that, Lexie." I knelt down beside her and said solemnly. "Only very special princesses are allowed to wear this tiara."

She flung her chubby little arms around me and laid her head on

217

my shoulder, careful not to displace her new rhinestone crown in the process. "I wuv you foweveh, An Beebee."

I hugged her tight. "And I love you forever too, sweetheart."

In the next moment she was off, scampering to show her mother her gift.

"Now it's Jacob's turn." I lifted a bulky, unwieldy box.

After tearing off the paper, my nephew reached in and pulled out something silver and shiny too. "It's a knight's helmet," he said in awe.

"Yep." I helped him put it over his head. "And see, it's got a real visor that opens and closes." I flashed him an apologetic smile. "I wanted to bring you home a sword, buddy, but I was worried about getting it past security."

Ashley loved her Notting Hill T-shirt and the cool toe rings I'd picked up from a stall in Portobello Market, while Elizabeth was entranced with her traditional English horse brass.

Finally, I presented the kids with the Chronicles of Narnia set from Blackwell's, which resulted in a chorus of oohs and aahs from everyone except Lexie, who didn't quite understand all the fuss.

"It's a really neat story about kids who travel through a magic wardrobe to a special land with all kinds of magical creatures," Elizabeth explained.

"Wike de Wizard ob Oz?" Lexie clapped her hands. "Wanna wead. Wanna wead."

"Ashley, would you take the kids inside and read the first chapter to them, please?" Karen asked.

She pouted. "But I want to stay and hear all about England. And I want to tell—"

Lexie started to wail. "Wanna heaw stowy."

"Ashley . . ."

"Oh, all right." She flounced away, muttering, "Always get treated like one of the kids."

"Hey Ash," I called after her. "Why don't you come over to my apartment for a girl's night soon—just you and me—and I'll give you the whole scoop, okay?"

A dazzling smile replaced her pout. "Okay, Aunt Phoebe." Then she took Lexie's hand in hers and we heard her say, as they all walked toward the house, "Just wait until you meet Aslan . . ."

Karen shook her head and sighed. "That's my quick-mood-change daughter."

"How well I remember those days." Mom glanced at me and chuckled.

"What?" I flipped my growing-out hair and stuck out my lower lip. "I was never like that."

No, you were worse, my guilty conscience reminded me. *You were a brat to your mother up 'til six months ago.*

That's 'cause I was under the mistaken assumption that she'd held my dad back from his dreams. How was I supposed to know she had dreams of her own?

You could have asked.

All right, already. Ancient history. Mom and I are good to go now, so give it a rest.

"Okay, Miss English and Drama Major," I said to Karen. "Your turn."

My sister-in-law was thrilled with her Oxford sweatshirt and the CD from the London production of *Les Miz.* (I'd also bought her a beautiful bone-china teacup, but I was saving that for Mother's Day.)

"And now for the *pièce de résistance* . . ." I reached into a separate bag—the big white one—and pulled out a large, heavily padded box, which I presented to my mother. "I had them wrap it really well so it wouldn't break."

It took a while, but she finally cut through all the tape and wrapping and opened the lid to reveal . . . more wrapping. Around a bulky round object.

"Told you I didn't want it to break." I grinned at her. "Careful now."

She gasped at what she could see beneath the final flimsy layer of tissue paper. "Oh my." Gingerly she removed the antique Blue Willow teapot.

"That's to replace the one I broke years ago when I was a bratty teen."

Her eyes glistened.

"I found it in this great little shop in the Cotswolds that you'd have loved. The only thing—it's over a hundred and fifty years old, so you probably don't want to use it when you play tea party with Lexie."

Mom carefully set the teapot down on the table, gently tracing the ancient blue-and-white pattern. "It's absolutely beautiful, daughter. Thank you so much. I can't believe you brought this all the way from England." She leaned over and hugged me. "I'll treasure it always."

"It's the least I could do after all the grief I've given you over the years," I said quietly. "But now," I added with a Monty Python flourish, "for something completely different."

Glancing around to make sure all the kids were still inside, I outlined my idea to Mom and Karen.

The next morning, Karen and I researched small-business loans on the Net while Mom held down the fort at Books 'n' Brew and Ashley babysat.

And that night when Jordy got home from his second job, we filled him in on our plan.

"You want to do what?" he said, his head swiveling from one of us to another in disbelief.

"We want to buy Books 'n' Brew from Mr. Webster and run it ourselves," I said calmly.

He gave me an incredulous look. "But you can't afford that—*we* can't afford it. None of us has that kind of capital to invest."

"Not alone, we don't, brother dear." I stuck out my chin. "But it's very easy these days for small, women-owned businesses to get loans, so that's what we're going to do."

Jordy started to interrupt, but I didn't give him a chance. "Mom and Karen are already working there and loving it, and Books 'n' Brew does a good business, so why watch all the profits from their hard work go to someone else?" I folded my arms across my chest. "A San Francisco businessman who doesn't even live here, no less. Let's keep Barley money in Barley."

My brother looked at his wife, then his mother, and finally back to me, "Pheebert, I hate to remind you, but you've never been so good with numbers," he said gently.

"I know." I gave him a triumphant smile. "But *you* are. Which is why we want you to be our bookkeeper and financial adviser." I hurried on before he could interrupt. "With Mom's baking skills, Karen's educational and organizational skills, my understanding of the retail market, and your financial acumen, we can't lose."

"But what about your job at the *Bulletin*?"

"I've already given my notice to Gordon." I shuddered. "If I had to write about one more goat or emu, I'd tear my hair out."

Jordy gave me a knowing look. "But you love to write. Won't you miss it?"

Mom and Karen had raised the same concern, but I had a ready answer.

"That's the good part." I flashed my brother another triumphant smile. "I'll still keep writing the column I started while I was in England—*and* I can write about whatever I want! How great is that?" I rushed on before he could raise another objection. "The thing is, it will only be a monthly column. Not enough work to keep me busy, and definitely not enough money to pay the rent, so I need another job—and I love the idea of working in the family business. At the very least, I could play janitor."

He sighed. "Do you know how many mom-and-pop businesses fail every day? Especially with all the giant megastores and chains to compete with? It's not easy getting a business off the ground. Most don't see a profit for at least two years."

Mom stuck in her two cents. "Jordy, the Books 'n' Brew has been going strong for nearly four years now. It's not going to go belly up all of a sudden because three women have taken it over. Right now, it's the only bookstore and coffee bar in town, and business has been booming—especially with the influx of all these Bay Area folks moving to the area lately. People *like* a good cappuccino and pastry"—two spots of color appeared on her cheeks—"and if there's one thing I know how to do well, that's bake pastry!"

Karen tackled her husband next. "*And* thanks to Phoebe's new awareness of all things English, once a month we're going to offer an afternoon tea—a literary tea." She clapped her hands in delight. "Women will love it! My friends and I have been saying we wish we had a tearoom closer than the one in Sacramento. Please, honey," she implored her husband. "This is something I can do to contribute financially to our household again, so you won't have to work so hard. This would be great for us."

Her voice grew stronger. "The kids miss you, I miss you, and we're all worried about you. Besides, this can be a whole-family venture; something we can take pride in and have fun with at the same time." She shot him a sly grin. "*And* it will give Ashley a positive outlet for all that teenaged hormonal energy."

"She's right about that, son." Mom chimed in.

Jordy glanced from his wife to his mother, taking in their shining eyes and hopeful looks. Then he looked at me. "And you thought this up, little sister?"

"Yes-s."

He hugged me, his eyes bright. "Sounds like a great idea. Where do we start?"

Checking e-mail before I went to bed that night, I was delighted to find messages from both Cordelia and Grace.

To: Movielovr
From: Learschild

Hello, Phoebe. How was your flight home? Hope it wasn't too bumpy. Did Mary Jo have to take another Xanax? Too bad Ian wasn't along; he'd have calmed her nerves.☺ The man is absolutely besotted! It's really quite sweet, actually. He talks about her incessantly. (She'll probably have several e-mails in her inbox from him.) I'm glad to see that at least one man in my life isn't a great idiot when it comes to women. My brother can be so thick at times. But I won't go there.☺

I have a bit of good news: Dad's actually asked me to take more responsibility in the company—he's even talking about a promotion. I think he's finally beginning to realize that my being young doesn't mean I'm stupid. (The conservative clothes and hair color help, and I keep my little tattoo under wraps.☺)

Must run. Give my love to Mary Jo and write soon.

Cheers, Delia

I decided to hold off on answering Delia's e-mail until I'd had a chance to read her mom's as well.

To: Movielovr
From: Gspencer

Dear Phoebe, I wanted to drop you a brief note to say again just how lovely it was to meet you when you were here in England. I'm delighted you had the time to visit us, and I hope your journey home was smooth. Do know that you're welcome here anytime. (I don't know anyone else who will give me a push on the library ladder.) I think you're a warm and lovely young woman, and I wish

you only God's best in your writing and in your life.
Warmly, Grace Spencer (Jeremiah 29:11)

I sent thank-yous to both Delia and Grace and told them of our new family business idea. Then, as I snuggled beneath the covers, I repeated the familiar words from Jeremiah that Grace had referred to in her note:

"'For I know the plans I have for you,' declares the LORD. 'Plans to prosper you and not to harm you, plans to give you hope and a future.'"

Interestingly enough, that same verse was part of the sermon at church the next morning. Usually I find myself zoning out during the services at Holy Communion Lutheran, counting the minutes until I can zip over to Sunday school at Barley Pres. But when I returned to Holy Communion with my family that first Sunday home, something felt different.

It was still the same traditional Lutheran service I'd grown up with—the same hymns, the same plastic gladiolus arrangement on the altar, the same elderly Mr. Soames snoring in the back pew. Only this time, for the first time, as we sang the familiar hymns, I recognized the beauty and the reverential, contemplative attitude of the service.

I closed my eyes and was back at Evensong in Oxford, back in the stained-glass light of St. Mary's and York Minster.

When the minister began to preach, I actually paid attention.

And it wasn't the church that was different. It was me.

Another thing that was different was Sunday school at Barley Pres. Things simply weren't the same since Jeff and Amy had moved to Oregon. Since their departure, I learned, different church members had taken turns leading the class in teaching and worship. And today, one of the elders, a man in his late sixties who'd been married since he came out of the womb, had decided he'd do best with an antisex message. (After all, he was teaching singles, whose minds are filled with nothing but lustful thoughts twenty-four/seven.)

"Remain pure!" he thundered at us from the lectern. "And if you can't, remember what Paul says in Corinthians: 'It is better to marry than to burn with passion.'"

I glanced around the estrogen-heavy class, then leaned over and whispered to Mary Jo. "And who exactly are we supposed to marry? Seventeen-year-old Ryan or Hubert the Horrible?"

"I've got dibs on Ryan," she whispered back. "I like 'em young, remember?" She grinned. "So you go for the H-man—although you'll have to fight Sylvia Ann for him. But I'm not worried; I think you can take her."

We ended the class singing "Create in Me a Clean Heart."

Afterward, Sylvia Ann, clad in leopard print from head to toe, made a beeline for me. "Phoebe, I was *so* sorry to hear about Alex."

"What—has something happened to him?"

She fluttered her false eyelashes and pasted on what I think was supposed to be a solicitous look. Instead, it made her look as if she'd eaten one too many prunes. "No, I mean that you're not together anymore." She patted my arm. "I'm sure that must be so hard for you."

"It's fine, Sylvia. We were just casually dating," I said. "No strings."

She tut-tutted. "You young girls today—so independent and thinking you've got all the time in the world." Sylvia leaned in closer and lowered her voice. "Let me give you a little advice from someone who's been around a little longer than you, sweetie. Strings are essential if you want to hold on to your man. You just need to make sure he doesn't see them—"

"Sylvia? I hate to interrupt, but I think Bruce could use your help." Mary Jo nodded her head in the direction of the far corner. "He's over there talking to that new waitress who just started at the Barley Twist."

Sylvia peered over the top of her leopard-print bifocals at the curvy thirty-seven-year-old divorcee who'd just moved to town—and who was currently engaged in an animated conversation with Sylvia's one-and-only.

"Excuse me, girls," she murmured lethally. "As one of the leaders of the singles hospitality team, I *must* go make our visitor feel welcome." She sprinted toward the couple; her leopard-print slingbacks click-clacking furiously the entire way.

"I have a feeling Bruce will be feeling that unseen string around his neck pretty soon." I grinned at Mary Jo. "Thanks for getting my back, Thelma."

"Anytime, Louise." She stretched her arms and wriggled her fingers. "And now I think I'll go home and e-mail my friend Ian. With great purity, of course."

"I'm really sorry about Alex, daughter."

Mom carried a stack of dirty plates into the kitchen, and I followed with silverware and glasses. It was late in the afternoon, and everyone else had gone home after enjoying one of her famous Sunday dinner pot roasts.

Her forehead wrinkled and she threw me a concerned look as she began rinsing the plates. "I know how much you cared for him and how difficult it must be for you knowing he's staying in England."

"It's okay, Mom. Really." I began loading the glasses into the dishwasher. "I mean, I miss him, and all. But clearly, Alex and I getting together wasn't what God wanted for us, so who am I to argue with that?"

She stopped in midrinse to turn and stare at me. "Well, my goodness, Phoebe Lynn, you've come home all wise and spiritual." She handed me a plate. "This trip was a good thing for you."

"I found myself in Paris," I said in a dreamy tone.

"Huh?" Her brow furrowed. "I thought you and Mary Jo didn't have enough time to go to Paris."

"We didn't. Julia Ormond said that to Harrison Ford in the *Sabrina* remake. Remember? She'd gone to Paris to get over her obsession with

Greg Kinnear, who played Harrison's younger brother—the part William Holden played in the original . . ."

I realized Mom was looking at me with an amused smile. I took the plate from her hand and sighed. "Anyway, that's how I felt about England. I found myself there."

"I didn't know you were lost." Mom smiled and handed me another plate. "I am glad to see that you haven't lost your movie madness, though. Otherwise I'm not sure I'd recognize my only daughter."

"Not to worry. Just listen for a pair of thighs that whisper when they walk." I grinned. "And speaking of not recognizing someone . . . you look a little different yourself, Mother dear. What put that rosy glow in your cheeks? Or should I say who?" I put my hands on my hips. "Anything you'd like to tell me?"

Her hands fluttered, but she morphed the flutter into a fanning motion in front of her face. "Nope. Just my hot flashes, dear." She snapped the dish towel at my hips. "But I want to talk about our new business venture some more. I don't know when I've been so excited!"

chapter twenty

Family Business

arriving ten minutes early at Barley High on Tuesday afternoon for the one-on-one girl time I'd promised Ashley, I slid into an empty space near the school end of the parking lot, rather than the far end as I'd told her. And while I waited for my niece, I checked out the kids getting out of my old high school.

Some things never change, I sighed. *There's still the jocks and the cheerleaders, the nerds and the bad boys, the goody two-shoes, and—*

All at once I saw my niece. My sweet, innocent freshman niece with her thick Julia Roberts mane . . . wearing a *very* short skirt that I doubted her mom or dad had even seen. Ashley was talking to one of the bad boys, who sported a large dragon tattoo on one arm and what looked like a bunch of snakes twisting down his leg beneath the bottom of his baggy gangsta shorts.

This kid was no freshman. Sophomore, either. Probably a senior. And even from this distance, I could sense my niece's excitement that an older boy had deigned to talk to her. An older, cool boy. She giggled and looked up at him like he was all that. Then she looked at her watch, gave him a little wave good-bye, and headed toward the parking lot. He stared after her with a look I didn't like and said something to his buddies, who all laughed.

Shading her eyes while she looked for my car at the far end of the parking lot, Ashley didn't notice me almost right in front of her. As she drew near, she glanced again at the other end of the lot. Then her hands snaked beneath her new Notting Hill T-shirt, and she unrolled the waistband of her skirt. Twice.

I honked the horn. She jumped and looked up at me with that deer-in-the-headlights look.

You are so busted, sweetie.

Ashley approached the car sullenly, a scowl marring her pretty features. Yanking the door open and sliding into the passenger seat, she said, "I guess you're going to tell mom—"

"Ash, if you're going to do the skirt trick, you should at least be a little more discreet." I pointed to the old storage shed at the edge of the parking lot. "I always unrolled my skirts behind there where no one could see."

She looked up at me and grinned. I was still cool Aunt Phoebe.

Careful. Proceed with caution. "But what I want to know is, how do you hide the short skirt from your dad, seeing as how he's one of your teachers?"

Ashley buckled her seat belt. "I just roll it back down before his class." The scowl returned. "Besides, Dad's been so busy these days, he wouldn't even notice."

I backed out of the parking lot, keeping my voice light. "So, was that the guy you like?"

Her face lit up. "Yeah. That's Jesse. Isn't he cool?"

"I couldn't really tell from this distance. You should bring him over sometime."

The light went out of her face. "Uh, he doesn't really do the family scene."

"Does he do the church scene?" I asked gently. "Is he in your youth group?"

"Not *even*." My niece stuck out her chin in a mutinous pout. "All the guys in youth group are geeks—all four of them. Especially this one guy, Caleb, that Mom and Dad really like; Mom's always pushing me to do things with him, invite him over and stuff. But he's a total dork. I mean, yeah, he can quote the whole Bible backwards and forwards, but he picks his nose!" She shuddered. "Gross."

I shuddered too.

"And he's been homeschooled his whole life, so he has no idea how to act around cool kids," Ashley continued. "He never watches TV—except for G-rated videos. And he only listens to Christian music and thinks I'm sinning 'cause I listen to regular radio and have read *Harry Potter*."

"Sweetie, lots of kids are homeschooled today," I said. "There's nothing wrong with that. In fact, studies have shown that many homeschooled teens score higher on SATs and get into better colleges."

She rolled her eyes. "I know, Aunt Phoebe. I'm not saying *homeschooling's* bad. My friend Kari's homeschooled too, but she's cool. I mean, her parents don't keep her in this tight little Christian cocoon and isolate her from everything else, like Caleb's do." She sighed. "He doesn't know what music is hot, how to dress, or *any*thing about movies, other than G-rated ones. And his favorite TV show is *Little House on the Prairie*—his family has all the videos." She tossed her hair. "He's such a geek."

I can remember a time not too long ago that it was your favorite TV show too. "So aren't there any other boys in youth group?"

"At Holy Communion?" Ashley rolled her eyes. "No way. Well, there's a few, but they all have girlfriends." She slouched in her seat, the mutinous frown reappearing. "I don't see why I have to hang out with only Christian guys anyway. I mean, they're not perfect either." She stole a glance my way. "Look what happened to you." Ashley rushed on. "I'm not trying to be mean or anything, Aunt Phoebe. But you met Alex at church, and he's a Christian and everything. And I thought he really liked you, that eventually you guys would get married." Her face flushed with anger. "But then he left, and now you're all alone again. I don't want to wind up all alone."

"Yeah. Like that's going to happen, Ms. Over the Hill. Ash, you're only fourteen," I said gently as we pulled up to my apartment. "I think it's a little early to be worrying about that." I grinned. "Besides, I'm *not* alone. I've got you guys. And Grandma. And God. What more does a girl need?"

"A guy."

"Actually, that's not really a *need*, except when it comes time to program the VCR." I sighed. "I'm not going to lie and tell you it didn't hurt when things with Alex didn't work out. It did. I liked him a *lot*." I thought back to all the fun Alex and I had together and the special movie connection we'd shared. Then I thought back to my trip. "But Ash, I learned—actually, I'm still learning—that the only One who will never leave me or disappoint me is God."

She rolled her eyes again. "I know, I know. I hear that all the time at Sunday school and from Mom and Dad." But she gave me a thoughtful look as we walked up the outdoor staircase.

Unlocking the door, I turned to her. "No more preaching, I promise." I grinned. "But I do want to know what happened to the girl who not even six months ago told me she didn't want to get married until she was at least thirty because she was determined to see the world first."

Ashley looked wistful. "Jesse says there's no need to ever leave the United States." She stuck out her chin. "Or even California. Everything cool is right here."

Including Jesse.

"So what did he think of your new Notting Hill shirt then?"

She flushed and dropped her backpack on the living room floor. "He liked it."

"Even though it's from another country?" I raised my eyebrows and then said gently, "Honey, visiting other places opens our eyes to so many things—amazing things, beautiful things." I smiled and paraphrased Esther. "Genesis says God created the heavens and the earth, not God created California."

Thought you said no more preaching? I pulled out the photos from my trip. "Would you like to see my pictures? I just picked them up from the drugstore."

She hesitated, conflicting emotions warring across her face.

I opened the first envelope and started flipping through prints. "Oh, there's Buckingham Palace." I laughed. "Mary Jo and I thought, wouldn't it be cool if we were this close to Prince William and Harry?"

"Ooh, I wanna see." Ashley sat down beside me, and we spent the next hour oohing and aahing over the English sights together. She especially liked the one of me making goofy faces at a red-coated guard in an effort to make him smile. (I didn't succeed, although I thought I detected the barest twitch of his stiff upper lip.)

At last I lay down the sheaf of photos with a wistful sigh. "I can't wait to go on another trip . . . hey! We should do a girls-only trip to Paris—you, Grandma, and me! Your mom too. Whaddya think?" I expelled a sigh of regret. "There wasn't time to go to Paris this trip, and I've always wanted to see the Eiffel Tower and stroll alongside the Seine munching a croissant."

"And have espresso in a sidewalk café on the Champs Élysées and check out some high-end fashion shows." Ashley got a dreamy look in her eyes. "And practice my French on some hot French guy."

My eyebrows did some serious arching.

"French *language*, Aunt Phoebe." She giggled. "I wasn't even thinking about kissing!"

Me either.

But before I went to sleep that night, that's all I could think about—that, and the stand-in Sunday-school teacher's exhortations on purity.

After throwing up a quick prayer, I pounded out a column on lust, lips, and brotherly love. My theme? That if we singles got a little more of the latter within the church, we might find it a little easier to deal with the former.

The next six weeks or so were a blur of activity as we got our business loan through Karen and Jordy's credit union, finalized the sale and transfer of ownership, and started putting our own personal stamp on *our* bookstore.

We debated long and hard about the name. Armed with notepads, pencils, and caffeine around Mom's kitchen table one evening, we all offered suggestions.

I liked the idea of A Cozy Cuppa, and so did Karen, but Mom and Jordy pointed out that it would appeal mostly to women. "Besides, that name makes it sound like it's just a tearoom," Jordy said. "And since we don't want to lose our male customers, our coffee drinkers, or our bookstore customers, I think we need something a little less cute. Why not just keep it Books 'n' Brew?"

"I've never liked that name." Mom doodled on the notepad in front of her. "I always thought it sounded like one of those microbreweries with all different kinds of beer. Besides, we don't want to confuse people. We want them to know that it's coffee that's brewing."

"How about A Cup of Joe, then?" Jordy drained his own coffee.

Squeezing my new addiction, a PG Tips tea bag, against the inside of my cup, I deposited it on the china tea-bag holder I'd brought Mom back from England. "No, 'cause then you're leaving out the tea."

"Books too, honey." Karen smiled at her husband.

"What about Coffee, Tea, and a Good Book?" Mom suggested.

"Too long." Jordy refilled his cup.

"That's fun, but I'm afraid not everyone would get the sixties reference." I tossed my mother an apologetic glance. After reading *Coffee, Tea, or Me* as a young woman, my mother had dreamed of being a stewardess, a dream she later set aside in favor of marriage and motherhood.

"Would they even need to get the reference?" she asked, and I shrugged.

Ashley sidled into the kitchen. "How about Read a Lot, only spelled L-a-t-t-e?"

We all turned and stared at her.

"Read a Latte," I said slowly, savoring the sound of the name on my tongue. I looked over at my three partners and beamed. "I love it! What do you think?"

"Me too," Mom and Karen chorused.

"Ash, that's brilliant!" Jordy hugged his eldest. "I think we need to put you in charge of marketing and publicity."

Ashley turned pink with pleasure and remained in her father's arms a moment longer than her teenage coolness had allowed of late.

Mom held up her coffee mug. "A toast."

We all raised our assorted mugs and cups.

"To Read a Latte, and"—she cast a warm smile at Ashley—"my very clever granddaughter."

"To Read a Latte," we agreed in unison, clinking our cups. "And to Ashley."

"This calls for bikkies," I said, reaching for a tin and setting it on the table.

"'Bikkies?'" Jordy looked at me over the rim of his mug.

"Short for biscuits, which is what the English call their cookies." I helped myself to a couple. "I picked these up in the bargain basement of Harrod's. They're great for dunking in tea. Or even coffee."

Karen tried one. "Yum. These are delish. We need to serve some at our monthly teas."

"Already way ahead of you." I grinned and turned to my brother, who was brushing the crumbs off his mouth. "So, Mr. Financial Adviser, what do you think of our selling some English tea and bikkie products at the store?"

Financially cautious and non-tea-drinking Jordy frowned. "Let's try a few just as a test, and we'll see how it goes."

While Karen and I were stating our case for having more than just a few, a knock at the back door admitted Gordon, who, upon Mom's invitation, pulled up a chair and helped himself to coffee.

"Shall we talk about furniture?" Mom asked.

"Well, we already have the bookshelves and the table and chairs in the coffee area. But I always like curling up in a nice wingback chair when I'm reading," Karen said. "And we don't have nearly enough tables for the monthly tea events."

"I love wingback chairs too." I sighed. "But have you checked the furniture-store ads lately? Chairs are pretty expensive."

"We'll go the garage-sale route then," Mom said. "I can make new slipcovers that will hide a variety of sins." She gave Jordy a teasing smile.

Karen and I snorted in unison and glanced his way. "That's for sure."

"What? I thought my old couch was fine for your apartment just the way it was."

"Only if you like brown, gold, orange, and puke-green polyester plaid, Dad." Ashley rolled her eyes.

"That's why the women will handle the decorating, big brother."

Gordon cleared his throat. "I know where you can get a couple of nice wingback chairs in good condition for free. I've got a couple in my spare room that belonged to Esther."

"I thought you had some estate-sale people pack up all her things to sell at their showroom." Mom gave him a quizzical look.

"I, uh, planned to." Gordon fidgeted. "But I just didn't feel right about selling off her possessions to a bunch of strangers. I'll bet she'd be glad to have them put to good use in your bookstore, though."

"Are you talking about those great tapestry-covered chairs she had in her living room? Those are gorgeous." I smiled at the memory. "That's where she and I sat together talking about her trip to Europe right before she left."

"Then that settles it." Gordon gave me a warm smile. "I can't think of any better home for them. Plus, there's a nice old bookcase with glass doors you might like too."

Now it was Mom's turn to stare. "That beautiful lawyer's bookcase with the leaded glass? That's an antique!"

"Maybe so." Gordon grinned at her. "But right now it's just a dust catcher in my spare room, holding some odds and ends from Esther's trips."

Esther's words about broadening my horizons filled my head. I snapped my fingers. "We could fill the bookcase with travel books—all except the middle shelf, which we'd use to display some of her travel souvenirs."

Former schoolteacher Karen caught the vision. "And we could hang a world map on the wall, and put a globe on the top shelf, along with a pretty framed picture of her. We could call it Esther's Travel Corner," she said softly.

The room went quiet until Gordon punctured the stillness by blowing his nose.

Jordy grabbed his wife and kissed her. "Did I ever tell you how glad I am that I married you?"

We scoured garage sales and flea markets for inexpensive castoff furniture and were thrilled the day we found two cushy love seats in a hideous mock-patchwork velour. Mom whipped up some pretty slipcovers and bingo, we had comfy, homey-looking reading couches.

And Gordon learned of a soda fountain in Modesto that was going out of business and selling off all their furniture and equipment for a song, so he and Jordy took the truck and the checkbook and proudly came back with six square gleaming chrome-and-laminate tables for four, three round tables for two, and thirty chrome-and-vinyl chairs.

"Thirty chairs?" I squealed. "Where are we going to put thirty chairs?"

Gordon's face fell. So did my brother's.

"You don't have to put them all out," Jordy said defensively. "Some can go in the back storeroom. When we saw them, we figured they'd be perfect for your monthly tea thing."

Chrome and vinyl for tea? I was thinking more rich wood and upholstery like Brown's Hotel . . . And they don't look anything like the tables we already have.

"They're perfect, honey," Karen said, kissing her husband. "Exactly what we need."

Mom hugged Gordon. "Thank you so much. You guys did great."
Pleased, they swaggered off.

My head swiveled from Karen to Mom. "Okay, now I know why
I'm still single." I looked at the laminate tabletops again. "But I still
don't see this as looking very English and tealike."

They exchanged a smile. "You will."

We spray-painted the shiny chrome white, and Mom and Karen
sewed floor-length chintz tablecloths, along with delicate cotton and
lace skirts for each chair that could be removed when not being used
for tea.

Finally, everything was finished and we were ready for the grand
opening.

We'd agreed we would inaugurate the store with its first literary tea.
And in a nod to my recent travels, we had decided to go with an
English-author theme.

Having fallen in love with *Jane Eyre* on my trip, I really wanted to
do the Brontë sisters, but since we were a new business trying to establish ourselves, Karen thought—and Mom and Jordy agreed—that we
needed to go for a little more mass appeal. We settled on Jane Austen.

The tea was a smashing success.

Karen used her drama-teacher and community-theater connec-
tions to find period-style costumes, and Mom, Ashley, Elizabeth,
Lexie, and I all dressed up to look like characters from *Sense and
Sensibility*.

We tried in vain to talk Jordy—who ran the bookstore side with a
little help from Redmond that day—into wearing a Hugh Grant pair
of breeches, coat, and cravat. But quiet Redmond surprised us all by
showing up in full costume, looking for all the world like romantic
Willoughby from *Sense and Sensibility*.

"My mom sews pretty well," he told us bashfully, "and I'm kind of
interested in that period in literature."

All the rest of that afternoon, I noticed Ashley sneaking looks at him. *Maybe Jesse has a little competition.*

We served dainty cucumber sandwiches, chicken-and-almond salad on miniature croissants, and small wedges of my mother's homemade Quiche Lorraine on the bottom level of the three-tiered silver racks at each table.

On the middle tiers we arranged slices of assorted tea breads alongside our best re-creation of the plump Fat Rascal scones from the Yorkshire Betty's, with cut-glass bowls of mock Devonshire cream and strawberry jam on the side.

And the top tiers proudly boasted lemon squares, Amy's famous shortbread, and plump strawberries dipped in chocolate, all nestled on snowy paper doilies.

"Mmm, this is scrumptious." Mary Jo, who had donned her Brown's tea outfit for the occasion, leaned back at the table she was sharing with Gordon and sighed as she finished her scone. "You've all done yourselves proud. I feel like I'm back in England again."

"Yeah, the only thing missing is Ian," I whispered as I refilled her cup.

"Shh," she hissed, cheeks flaming.

Mom and I had talked a reluctant Gordon into attending our tearoom debut. "But tea's not a guy thing," the crusty newspaper editor had protested.

"It is in England." I'd batted my eyelashes at him.

We'd assured him that he wouldn't be the only man.

And he wasn't. Our pastor from Holy Communion also showed up with his wife, and Sylvia Ann had also coerced Bruce into escorting her.

At the end of the day, when we closed the doors and propped up our aching feet, my brother counted out the day's take—nearly double that of Books 'n' Brew's normal daily receipts.

Jordy grabbed me and whirled me around the store. "Pheebert, you rock!"

chapter twenty-one

Life in the Man-Free Zone

i still can't believe you're running a coffeehouse!"

"It's a bookstore, Lins." I corrected her. "Read a Latte."

"Right. Sorry. But who'd have ever thought that *you'd* be a business owner! Little Miss Math-Impaired. In your wildest dreams, did you ever imagine it?"

"No, not really." I chuckled. "But things are going great. Jordy's handling all the financial stuff. And Karen and Jordy are loving the fact that they get to spend more time together—as are the kids. And of course Mom's totally in her baking element."

"But what about you, Pheebs?"

"I'm great. Hey, I'm thirty-two years old—well, almost—and my own boss, a partner in my own thriving business. Doesn't get much better than that."

"You don't have to sell me—I'm hoping to do the same thing someday with my beaded jewelry." She paused. "But what about your writing?"

"I'm still writing. I'm doing my monthly online column, which I absolutely love." Opening the fridge, I pulled out the last can of Diet A&W cream soda and popped it open. "In fact, I just turned one in yesterday about the joys of getting weighed in a doctor's office. In *Cheers* everybody may have known your name, but in the doctor's office, everybody knows your weight."

Lindsey guffawed. "I hear ya on that. I just love your column—so do all the Lone Ranger girls, especially since you started writing about single women's issues. It's hilarious. In fact, I think it's the best thing you've ever done."

"What about my movie reviews?" I bristled.

"Now, don't go getting all mad. I loved your movie reviews, but I love this new stuff even more." She paused, and I could hear her swallowing—her favorite, Diet Dr Pepper, probably. "Not everyone's into old movies, you know. But every unmarried twenty-, thirty-, even forty-something woman can relate to your column—especially that last one on kissing and lust. Even Susan loved it."

"You're kidding!" I nearly dropped the phone. "Super-WOG Susan? The same Susan who started up Lone Rangers and operates on a higher spiritual plane than the rest of us?"

"The one and only." Lindsey giggled. "She told me to tell you that the next time we talked. In fact, I think she's planning to e-mail you herself. She said, and I quote, 'It's real, it's funny, and it's honest. And it's nice to have someone telling it like it is for women whose lives haven't turned out the way they told us it would in Sunday school—the whole happily-ever-after, white-knight bit.'"

"Except for yours, Lins," I said dryly.

"Well, yeah, but until Phil came along, I was in that same single place—as you more than anyone knows. And even though I'm getting married, I can still relate." She sighed. "Been there, done that. I only wish your column came out more often."

"Not me." I took another swig of soda. "I wouldn't have the time to write it. The bookstore, the column, and these teas pretty much keep me hopping."

"Do you ever miss being a reporter?" Lins asked. "I'm sure those emus really miss *you*."

"Uh-huh. And the goats and the pigs and the cows. And don't forget the Miss Udderly Delicious pageant contestants."

"They're pretty hard to forget." We giggled together. "But seriously,

Pheebs," Lindsey said, "what about the writing? Don't you miss doing it full-time?"

Do I? I'd been so busy with the store, I hadn't even had time to think about that.

"Um, well . . . a little, I guess."

"You could have had a full-time writing job, but you turned it down." She sighed. "And with it, untold riches and glory. But never mind. Who am I to say anything? Just your best friend, that's all," she murmured sotto voce. "And what do I care if you spit in my husband-to-be's face? Just shaming him in front of all his employees?" More sotto voce.

"Have you been watching reruns of *Everybody Loves Raymond* again?" I stretched out on the couch. "You've got the martyr-mother thing down cold."

"That's 'cause I just got off the phone with *my* mother."

"So, how's she doing with your decision to scale back the wedding and move up the date?"

"You mean after she threatened to throw herself off the balcony?" Lindsey sighed. "She's disappointed, of course, but she'll live. And speaking of my mother, I apologize for turning into her and trying to guilt you into taking the PR job. I'm glad you didn't listen to me. You'd have been miserable writing about stocks and bonds and investment portfolios."

"And Phillie would have been miserable when I put a decimal point in the wrong place and cost him hundreds of thousands of dollars."

We laughed in happy agreement, and I felt almost like dancing. It felt so good to have my best friend back—and not either manic or mad at me.

Shouldn't have been surprised. Lindsey and I always manage to sort things out. It's a little weird, though, doing it long-distance.

"Pheebs, I have a confession to make," Lindsey said, growing serious. "I was really jealous of your going to Europe, and then the whole time you were gone, I was kicking myself for not jumping at the chance when you offered it to me. That's why I was such a total . . . well, you know."

"I'll say."

"You're not supposed to agree with me. Couldn't you protest even just a little?"

"Not in this lifetime." I stretched out on the couch.

"Okay. I get the message." She laughed. "So give me the whole 411 now. Was England unbelievably wonderful? And did you absolutely love it?"

"Quite," I said in my poshest, plummiest accent—definitely *not* Hyacinth Bucket. "The theater, the galleries, the stores, the country-side, the churches . . . all brilliant." I paused and went back to my normal voice. "It wasn't just the country, though, it was the whole experience." I thought again of St. Paul's and Westminster Abbey and St. Mary's in Fairford with the glorious stained glass . . .

". . . are you feeling about Alex these days?" Lindsey's voice brought me back. "Because if it will make you uncomfortable, Phil and I agreed that we wouldn't have him in the wedding. You're our nearest and dearest friend in the whole world, and even though he's Phil's buddy, he's not at the same level on the friends-meter. We don't have a problem telling him that if it would be too hard for you to see him in the wedding party," she continued.

"No, don't do that." I shifted on the couch. "I'm actually fine about the whole Alex thing now."

I tested my words. Were they really true? Or was I just saying them for Phil and Lindsey's sake?

Repeating them in my mind, I waited to see what happened. *Nothing. I really meant them.* Emboldened, I continued. "Really, Lins. It just wasn't meant to be. And God taught me a lot through the experience—showed me how I have a tendency to get too romantic too quickly and live in my fantasies a lot of the time."

I waited. She didn't contradict me. So I chuckled. "Of course, you caught me on a good day. Don't know how I'll feel tomorrow."

"Just keep me posted, okay?"

"Will do."

"And Pheebs?"

"Yeah?"

"We're cool now. Right?"

"We're cool. Except for one little thing."

"What's that?"

"If you're not going to nix the bouquet-throwing torture, then I at least get a sit-out waiver."

Hanging up from Lins, I decided to check my e-mail and found the most wonderful surprise. Jeff and Amy wrote to say they loved Oregon and their new church, but what had them most delighted was that they were expecting a child.

In a baby frame of mind after that exciting news, I decided to pop by Karen and Jordy's and spend a little time with my namesake niece, Gloria Phoebe. I knocked on the back door, but nobody answered, so I poked my head into the kitchen. "Hello, where is everybody?"

An answering roar met my ears, and my nephew came rushing at me full-tilt in his knight's helmet, brandishing a red plastic baseball bat as his sword. "You bad witch, you can't have the princess and lock her away in a tower. I'll protect her 'cause I'm Sir Jacob."

Before I had a chance to react, Lexie came scampering in behind her brother, wearing a pink nightgown and her Princess Di tiara. "My hewo. You saveded me fwom da wicked witch." She offered a grubby fist of sticky M&M's to Jacob. "Heaw's youw tweazhur."

"Where's the princess Lexie and her trusty Sir Jacob?" Jordy came charging in, a tinfoil crown askew on his messy head and a stuffed lion under his arm. "King Aslan says it's time for a nap." He led my compliant niece and nephew away as his wife entered the kitchen, baby on her hip.

"Well, that's a nice sight, I must say—seeing Jordy playing with the kids again."

"I know. They're in heaven having him around more, and so am I."
She gave me a quizzical look. "So what brings you by?"

I stretched out my arms for little Gloria. "Just needed a little baby
fix. Gimme, gimme." Sitting down at the table with the chubby bundle
in my arms, I nestled my face into my sweet niece's cheeks. "Mmm,
there's nothing like that sweet baby smell."

And nothing like that not-so-sweet baby smell. I stood and held her at
arm's length.

"Sorry. I just fed her a little while ago, and she always has really
stinky diapers after that." Karen scooped her up just as Jordy returned.
"I'll go change her."

My brother sat down across from me at the table and reached for
the bowl of salted-in-the-shell peanuts. "Hey Pheebert, I'm glad you
stopped by," he said, cracking one of the nuts in his hand. "Been wanting to talk to you about something."

The "something" turned out to be a guy—a guy he wanted to set
me up with. Tim was a jock friend of his from Lodi whom I'd met and
talked to a couple times.

"Nice guy," I said. "And kind of cute too. But he doesn't even know
who Spencer Tracy was."

"So?" Jordy said. "I'll bet you don't know who Roberto Clemente was."

"What movie was he in?"

My brother groaned. "He wasn't in a movie. That's the point. He
was the greatest right fielder ever to play the game of baseball. The guy
won four National League batting titles!" He sighed and shook his
head. "Pheebert, you don't have to have *everything* in common to date
someone. Haven't you ever heard of opposites attracting?" He gave
Karen, who'd just rejoined us, a sexy smile.

"Sure," I said, "but there's got to be at least a spark of chemistry."

Like you had with Alex? Look how well that turned out.

It was my turn to sigh. "Actually, I've decided that dating is highly
overrated," I said with a sniff. "So I'm now entering a date-free phase
of my life. From here on out my focus is going to be on God, work,

family, and friends." I stood up to leave. "And getting in shape for a certain upcoming wedding. I think I'll go take my walk now."

The sun was just setting behind Therman Munson's stock pond as I headed out from Karen and Jordy's. Since returning home from England, I'd discovered that usually I managed my best times of quiet reflection just before or after sunset, and walking really helped. The cares of the day slipped away, and the rhythm of walking generated a lovely peacefulness that helped me sort my muddled thoughts, which were especially muddled tonight.

As I walked and prayed, I replayed my earlier conversation with Lins and realized I really did miss writing on a regular basis.

Leave it to my best friend to call me on it.

Running the bookstore and everything was cool, and I had thought I'd really like the tea part since I'd loved the tea ritual so much in England. But enjoying a relaxing cuppa in the afternoon was one thing, and putting on a full-fledged tea complete with atmosphere and all those little finger sandwiches, scones, and stuff was another. Plus a lot of hard work. And if I was completely honest with myself, I had to face the fact that I wasn't all that good at it.

I certainly hadn't inherited my mother's culinary abilities. Or desires. All the time I was chopping celery, slicing cucumbers, or dicing chicken, my fingers were itching to be flying over the keyboard instead, crafting just the right phrase or sentence.

So what exactly am I supposed to do about that now? Kind of late in the day to realize this, Ms. New Business Owner.

I looked at my watch. Time to head in. I had an important date.

And no, it's not what you think.

Showering quickly, I put on my jeans and headed over to Mary Jo's, where I helped her rearrange her couch, love seat, and *Frasier* recliner. Afterward, we kicked back with a bowl of popcorn and some M&M's and watched *Bridget Jones's Diary*.

"Now, this is the life," I said, purring with man-free contentment. Hey, even Thelma and Louise need a little downtime.

A week or so later, I got two phone calls that rocked my contented—well, mostly contented—little corner of the world.

It had been a slow day at Read a Latte. Well, slow for me. As usual. Mom was busy baking, Karen was busy waiting on customers, and Jordy was still at school. (He did the bookkeeping for the store in the evenings.) Redmond was busy stocking shelves—with Ashley's help.

And I was busy doing absolutely nothing, as I so often did these days at the store. One can only wipe down the same counter so many times. And refill the hot water carafes. And adjust the window display.

I know! Maybe the restrooms need cleaning.

I had gotten pretty darned handy with a toilet brush and pumice stone after a brief stint—very brief—at Happy Holly Housecleaning in Cleveland last year. So humming under my breath, I pulled on my yellow rubber gloves and gathered up cleaning supplies to attack the loos.

Only someone had already beaten me to it. Both the men's room and the women's room were pristine and sparkling. I sighed and went home early, feeling restless and out of sorts.

And I wasn't the only one.

When I opened my apartment door, Herman streaked down the stairs to rejoin his siblings in Karen and Jordy's backyard. If I'd had an alley, he'd have spent all his time there. I watched him disappear around the corner of the house.

"Domesticated much?"

Hungry, but wanting to be healthy, I grabbed the lone yogurt in the fridge and spooned up a mouthful. Bleeech! I spit the sour clots into the sink, then checked the expiration date: three month ago. Major ick. I grabbed my mouthwash, but the lonely drops at the bottom took too long to make their way to my curdled taste buds.

In a frenzy, I yanked my crumpled toothpaste from the medicine cabinet and squirted it into my tongue, then grabbed my toothbrush and furiously scrubbed, trying not to gag in the process.

That's when the phone rang.

I spat and answered, coughing a little as I did. "Hello? . . . Yes, this is Phoebe Grant . . . Uh-huh. Yes, that's right." I nodded my head, then gripped the receiver tight. "Say what?!"

Ten minutes later, I hung up the phone in a daze.

An editor friend of Gordon's was calling from San Diego. Seems she liked my online columns. Liked them a lot. So much that she was offering me a full-time writing position at her major daily newspaper— with a once-a-week column geared toward women.

At more money than I'd ever made from my writing.

A full-time writing job with a weekly column? And in sunny Southern California, no less, with nary an emu in sight.

Why couldn't she have called just a couple of months earlier, Lord— before I went in with everyone on Read a Latte? Now what am I supposed to do?

I told her I had a major commitment coming up—I did, Lindsey's wedding—and asked her for a couple of weeks to consider.

While I was still staring at the phone in my hand, it rang again.

"Pheebs," Lindsey's voice on the other end sounded strained. "I have something to tell you . . ."

"You're pregnant?"

"No!" She sucked in her breath and got all huffy. "You know we're waiting 'til we get married."

"I'm only kidding, Lins. Sheesh. Guilty much?"

She laughed. "As charged. It's getting harder and harder to wait. Now I know why so many Christian couples have short engagements. Or even elope. There's a lot to be said for that." Lindsey sounded wistful.

"Excuse me. Let me just get the wax out of my ears. I don't think I heard you right, Ms. Star Jones has got nothin' on you, wedding planner."

"I know. I know. But who knew planning a wedding would be so stressful?" She giggled. "And we don't even get the benefit of sex as a stress releaser, like the rest of the world."

"Hang on, Lins. Only a little while longer." I studied my thighs in the mirror and sucked in my stomach. "I'm going to have to step up my exercise plan if I want to look good in that slinky pink brides-maid's dress." I drained my Diet A&W. "But back to what you need to tell me. If you're not pregnant, then what is it?"

She hesitated.

"Lins," I put on my best stern voice. "You're not going back on your promise to give me a waiver from the bouquet toss, are you?"

"Never. I want to live to make it to my honeymoon." She gave a shaky laugh, then sighed. "There's no easy way to tell you this, Pheebs, but Alex and that lady lawyer—and I use the term *lady* loosely—well, they're dating."

Full body slam to the solar plexus.

Breathe, Phoebe, breathe. Relax. *I don't know why I'm reacting this way. I thought I was so over Alex.*

"So George finally got her claws into him, huh? I knew it was just a matter of time." I gave a wry half laugh. "His dad should be happy."

"Yeah, but is Alex? I wonder," Lindsey said, growing thoughtful. "Phil said he's a changed man—all stressed and everything. Not fun and easygoing like when we knew him."

"It's that stiff upper lip she requires him to maintain. Plus, she's so skinny she probably cuts him with her cheekbones when he hugs her. That's gotta hurt."

"Pheebs, you are evil, and you must be destroyed."

"Aw, I bet you say that to all your best friends."

There goes the last nail in the Alex coffin, I thought as I hung up. I called Mary Jo to tell her the news, but she already knew. I suspected a little birdie from across the Atlantic had been singing.

"Are you okay, Pheebs?" she asked.

"I'm fine. If he's with George now, then he was *so* not the right man for me. Oh well. Just wasn't supposed to be. Besides, they have that whole shared-neighbor-history thing. Kind of hard to fight that." I glanced out my window at the grassy field behind Jordy and Karen's. Just two months ago, that field had been dotted with clumps of golden daffodils.

Your history was so much shorter . . . "Wonder if they'll send their kids off to boarding school too?" I mused. "And Oxford. Keep that Spencer family tradition going."

Spencer. Wonder how Grace feels about all this? And Delia?

It had been a while since I'd written Alex's sister. We'd kept in touch pretty regularly since my return to the States, but I hadn't heard from her lately.

Now I knew why.

> To: Learschild
> From: Movielovr
>
> Hey Delia, you can come out of hiding now. My friend Lindsey just let the lawyer out of the bag; I know Alex and George are a couple. And I hope they'll be very happy. Just like Cameron Diaz and Dermot Mulroney in *My Best Friend's Wedding*. Anyway, thanks for keeping your promise not to tell me.☺ But it's okay. Really. I've moved on.
>
> I know you're really busy with work these days (any word about your promotion?). But Mary Jo and I really hope you'll find time to come out for a visit soon so we can play tour guide. We're already fighting over whose place you'll stay at. Hers is bigger, but mine is cuter. Decorating's really not her thing.☺ Maybe we'll take turns.
>
> How's Ian? Does he talk about Mary Jo all the time? She plays it cool, but I know she's enjoying their e-mail connection. Say hi to your family—yes, even Alex, if you

think it's appropriate. And ask your mom if she's done any ladder rolling lately.☺ (BTW, you don't need to pass on my regards to George.) All the best. —P.

Logging off, I flopped down in my toile-covered easy chair and mulled over my new job offer. Definitely head and shoulders above the last one I'd received, the one from Phil. Instead of finances and boring numbers stuff, I'd be writing about what I knew. *All too well.* And every writer since Jo March in *Little Women* has had that drummed into her: Write what you know.

Although, on that whole knowing front, I don't know a soul in San Diego.

You didn't know anyone in Cleveland when you first moved there either, my logical self reminded me, *and look how that turned out.*

But I'm a business owner now. I have responsibilities. I can't just go and leave my family in the lurch.

Would you really be leaving them in the lurch? Think about it. They seem to be doing pretty well without a lot of help from you.

There was a knock at the door.

Lexie, her chubby face wreathed in smiles, thrust a grubby handful of golden dandelions at me. "An Beebee, I pickded dese jus' for you."

And how could I ever leave my little Lexie?

chapter twenty-two

Going for It

i'm sorry I was such a Bridezilla."

"You weren't a total Bridezilla, Lins," I said, picking flower petals from her hair.

"Yes I was. I was the Queen of Bridezilla, the T-Rex bride, the Eva Peron of Bridezilla," she said, her voice rising. "I put every other obsessed, controlling, dictator bride-to-be to shame."

"Okay." I looked in the mirror of the cluttered dressing room at the church reception hall and touched up my lip gloss. "Yes, you did have kind of a wedding lobotomy."

"Pheebs, we've been over this," she said, flouncing her satin and lace. "You're not supposed to agree with me."

"Oh. Sorry. Can I have a do-over?" I went into full, reassuring, best-friend, maid-of-honor mode. "Lins, from my limited experience with all things wedding and white, this was pretty standard bride behavior—especially for someone with your Type-A personality." I smiled. "Actually, I'm thinking it might even have been a God thing."

"What?"

"Maybe he's preparing you for a whole new career—as a wedding planner."

"Very funny." She stuck her tongue out at me as she tried to remove her veil. It wasn't as easy as it looked. It was long and flowing, and she kept stepping on it.

I smiled and stood up to help her. Even tangled in her veil, my best friend made a beautiful bride.

And she'd had a beautiful wedding. Small, intimate, and understated.

I couldn't decide what the best part was—the look on Phil's face when he first saw her come walking down the aisle, or the way they both looked at each other as they said their vows.

"So your mom seems to be holding up pretty well, considering you moved up the date on her and ditched the megawedding-of-the-century plan." I shoved a plastic dress bag and a couple of bouquet and boutonniere boxes off a chair so I could sit down and remove my strappy high-heeled sandals. Since my trip to England, my tolerance for stilettos has dropped considerably.

Lindsey snorted as I sighed in relief. "That's her public face. You haven't seen her—or heard her—behind closed doors. She started to hyperventilate when I told her I wasn't going to have all my second and third cousins as bridesmaids—that I only wanted you, and Phil only wanted Scotty. Well, and little Teddy as ring bearer and Amanda as flower girl." She looked down and gingerly extracted a few petals from her cleavage. "And the way it turned out, maybe I should have reconsidered Amanda."

"Oh come on. She was adorable, even if she did go a little wild with the flower petals. And little Teddy—I can't believe how much he's grown. Stood right there throwing Amanda superior looks. And he never dropped the ring."

"You're right." Lindsey looked down at the gleaming wedding ring on her finger, a soft smile curving her lips. "And cutting back on the wedding was absolutely the right thing to do. Phil's my husband. I had to do what was best for him and me."

"You go, wifey!" I jumped up to high-five her. "Ow!"

Lins whirled around, a concerned frown puckering her bridal forehead. "What'd you do?"

"Stepped on a pin." I sank back into the chair, nursing my throbbing foot.

"If I'd known my wedding would be so fraught with danger for you, Pheebs, I'd have had caution signs posted. I mean, first your ribs, then your ankle, and now your foot."

I kicked my stiletto sandals out of the way with my uninjured foot. "That's what I get for trying to do the noble, sacrificial thing and actually participate in the dreaded bouquet toss." I rubbed my sore ankle. "That new Lone Rangers gal is sure desperate to tie the knot with someone; she was trying to take me out! What is she, anyway—twelve?"

"Nineteen."

"Well, she needs to get those skinny elbows registered as lethal weapons."

"Jake didn't seem to mind," Lindsey said. "He was following her and her bouquet around like a puppy dog."

"That's just wrong." I grimaced. "He's old enough to be her father!"

"Don't worry. It won't go anywhere. Jake is the original commitment-phobe. He'll be single 'til his dying day."

"Hey, don't knock it. Maybe I will too."

"I doubt it very much. But even if that happens, you'll still have me."

"Actually, Lins, I've been thinking about that. You know how we always said we'd never let a man come between us?"

She grinned at me. "Hey, we never said any such thing."

"Well, someone did."

Where had I heard those words before? They had such a familiar ring.

Then I remembered. It was in *White Christmas* when Vera Ellen was telling Rosemary Clooney that she was engaged to Danny Kaye and had to break up their sister act—even though the engagement was just a ruse to try and push Rosemary into Bing's arms.

Back from my tangent. "Well, anyway, I've been thinking it wasn't very practical to say something like that."

"I didn't say it."

"Well, maybe I thought it. But what I've been thinking is that when you get married, things change," I said. "They have to. They're *supposed* to. It's even scriptural." I went into full-on philosophical mode. "Life is not static. Nothing stays the same. We'll still be best girlfriends, but now I realize that I'm not the first one you're going to call with exciting news. Or sad news. Or scary news. You'll go to Phil, which is as it should be."

"I can't imagine Phil wanting to know about my latest pair of shoes," Lindsey said dryly.

"Me either." I snickered. "Okay, for things like that, feel free to still call me first." I got serious again. "You know you can call me anytime, though. About the hard things too." I bit my lip. "Lins, I'm so sorry I wasn't there for you when you called me in Oxford after your fight with Phil. I feel really bad about that."

"Don't, Pheebs." She sighed. "I admit I was really hurt and angry at the time—even called you some awful names . . ."

"So that's why my ears were ringing. And here I thought it was just the church bells over there."

"I'll church-bell you. Would you let me finish? I really need to say this."

"Sorry. Go on."

"Anyway, after I hung up on you, I railed and ranted for a while. At you. At Phil. Even at God." She chuckled. "Even though you and Phil weren't there—which was probably a good thing."

"I'll say."

"But God was there. And He showed me what a self-absorbed, wedding-obsessed brat I'd been." She chuckled. "I'm surprised Phil didn't run screaming for the hills—I know he wanted to sometimes."

"Nah . . ." I started to protest.

"Oh yes, he did, Pheebs. And that's when he put his foot down. Which of course made me mad, which is why I called you over in England. But when you didn't agree with me and then didn't have the time to listen to me, it made me all the madder." She took a deep breath. "That's when God and I had some serious one-on-one time. I realized that even though all the wedding planners and florists and caterers and everyone says 'it's *your* day, it's all about *you*, the bride'—

which of course, I glommed onto and ran with full-tilt—it's really not that." She sniffled. "It's about God joining Phil and me together as one in holy matrimony. Emphasis on *holy*."

Lindsey continued. "It wasn't just my wedding; it was Phil's wedding too. And it's not just a wedding; it's the start of our *marriage*. I didn't want our life beginning with us all fighting and stressed. So that's when I called Phil and cried and asked his forgiveness and told him I'd scale way back and that we wouldn't have pink cummerbunds or cauliflower at the reception. I'd never intended to have a plastic bride and groom anyway."

"Good girl. Way to get started on that whole submission bit."

"And good thing there's that scripture that says 'submit to one another.'" She chuckled. "Otherwise, I can't see how it would ever work. Certainly not on my part."

"I hear ya on that. Glad they took that obey thing out of the vows too."

I took a deep breath. "Okay, my turn. I'm sorry too. For being jealous, even though I was—*am*—happy for you. But I have to confess that I was jealous of your getting married and worried I would lose our friendship." I sighed. "But I had to realize that Phil comes first now. Not me. That whole 'a man shall leave his mother, a woman leave her home' thing. Although it doesn't actually say anything about leaving *friends* . . ."

"Phoebe, you know perfectly well—"

But that thought had led me quickly to another. "So, was Alex hurt when Phil told him he'd decided to only have his brother stand up for him?"

Lindsey shook her head. "Not at all. He completely understood. In fact, when we changed the date, it wasn't going to work for him anyway. He had some longstanding family commitment he couldn't miss." She gave me a sharp look. "Which I'm guessing you didn't mind?"

"You got that right. I have a feeling Gorgeous George would have found a way to wriggle her Manolos over here with him." I cut a wry glance at Lindsey's beautiful gown. "And since blood spatters, I'd have hated for your wedding dress to get caught in the crossfire. Besides, murder tends to cast such a pall on a wedding."

"And the wedding night." Lins giggled. "And speaking of that, help me out of this dress already so I can grab my man and get the honeymoon started!"

Back in Barley a week or so later, I sank deep into a tub of Radox—that was another thing I'd brought back with me to the States, boxes and boxes of these amazing bath salts—and thought about Phil and Lindsey, now on their honeymoon in the Caribbean.

I could picture them there on the beautiful beaches, the sand warm under their toes, the sea breeze tossing their hair, their eyes only on each other as they leaned in for yet another deep, passionate ki—

Uh, maybe better not to think about honeymoons.

Instead I weighed the newspaper job offer yet again. I needed to give the San Diego editor an answer soon. But what would my answer be? I'd gone over the pros and cons a million times.

To work on a major daily at long last. And as a columnist, no less! Talk about dream job . . .

But there's no way I can. How could I even consider it what with just starting up Read a Latte and everything?

But they don't really need you. They've got it handled. And to work on a major daily at long last . . .

The arguments kept running through my mind in circles like the English roundabouts, and I couldn't seem to find a way to break free of the dilemma.

But maybe that's just it. I pictured MJ and me in that little Mini Cooper, driving round and round the circle while the traffic whizzed by us and horns honked, until finally MJ yelled, "Now! Go for it!"

And I had. And everything had been all right.

Is that what I need to do, God—just make a decision and floor it? But what if . . .

The answer I heard then seemed to come from deeper within me . . . and completely outside myself.

No matter what, no matter where you go, I'll be there. I can take care of the what-ifs.

I sat in the bath a long time, the soothing water going cold around me, thinking about everything that had happened the past six months. All the changes. The disappointments. The discoveries.

The possibilities.

And then, just as my skin turned pruney, I did it.

I went for it.

I made my decision.

And hoped everything would be all right.

chapter twenty-three

It's My Party

i had just come back from my walk the next day and was changing my shoes when I noticed my toenail polish was chipped. So I decided to give myself a pedicure before washing the dishes. Just as I was polishing my last toe, my phone rang. Careful not to smudge the wet polish, I splayed out my toes and waddled to the phone.

"Pheebs?" The voice on the other end was muffled.

"Who is this?"

"M-Mary Jo." An indistinct sound, almost like a sob, escaped my friend.

"Mary Jo? What's wrong?! Are you all right?" I gripped the receiver.

"Uh, physically, yes. But, I, um, can you come over? I really need to talk to someone." More indistinct sounds muffled her words. "I-I'm really struggling with something, and I need your help. I don't know what to do."

Mary Jo needing my help? That's a first. Maybe I'm more of a spiritual giant than I think.

"I'll be right there." I threw on a pair of jeans and a T-shirt and sped off into the night.

Seven minutes later I knocked on her back door. "Mary Jo?"

She opened it, her head hanging, a wadded-up tissue clutched in her hand. I'd never seen her so down in the mouth. Actually, I couldn't even see her mouth, since most of her face was obscured by her curtain of hair.

"Mary Jo, have you been crying? What is it? What's wrong? Is it one of your horses? Your sister? Something with Ian?"

She shook her head and didn't answer, just turned her back to me and headed toward the living room.

I caught up to her and put my arm around her shaking shoulders. "Good idea," I said in my most soothing tone. "You go and sit down. Just let me put the kettle on . . ."

Her shoulders shook even harder.

"Okay, never mind the kettle right now. We can do that later. Let's just get you into the other room where we can be comfy and talk." I pushed open the door and steered her through.

A chorus of shouts assailed my eardrums. "Happy Birthday!"

My mouth dropped open at the sight of wall-to-wall people. I swiveled around to look at Mary Jo, whose head was no longer down and whose shoulders were shaking with laughter. She no longer needed the tissue to cover the grin she'd been hiding.

"An Beebee, An Beebee!" I felt a tugging on my jeans. Looking down, I saw Lexie sporting her Princess Di tiara and a dazzling smile. "Did we supwise you?"

I scooped her up in my arms and nuzzled her cheek. "You sure did, you little pumpkin. You really got me good."

She clapped her hands in delight. "We got An Beebee good, Daddy, an I din spoil de supwise."

Jordy relieved me of his daughter and gave her a big kiss. "That's my good girl."

The rest of my family crowded round for hugs and birthday greetings. It seemed like the whole town of Barley was in Mary Jo's living room.

Thank goodness I helped her rearrange the furniture.

"Happy birthday, Phoebe." Norm Anderson, holding Betty Martin's hand, enveloped me in a crushing bear hug. "And thanks for that picture of Tiddles the cat. Sure brought back some fond memories."

Betty giggled. "See, honey. I knew you liked cats."

All the people I'd worked with on the Save the Bijou campaign were there, as well as Bruce and Sylvia Ann, who gave me a sparkly bag filled with shampoo and nail polish and a coupon for a free haircut. "You could use a little trim, honey," Sylvia whispered.

Christy and Bob Sharp proudly presented me with a pair of Big Ben salt-and-pepper shakers, and everyone crowded around, munching on hors d'oeuvres and chattering.

I shook my head, unable to take it all in.

Mom came up to me and squeezed my waist. "Having a nice birthday, daughter?"

"I'll say. You guys really went to town. And it's not even a milestone one either. Not like the big three-oh or forty or anything." I chuckled. "Actually, thirty-two seems like kind of a nebbish age to me."

"Nebbish-schmebbish," Gordon said, appearing at Mom's side. "There's nothing about you that will ever be nebbish, Phoebe." His eyes sparkled as he squeezed my mother's shoulder. "I'd like to give you my present now. Okay?"

I nodded.

He reached down to pull off a silky cloth that was covering a bulky object on Mary Jo's coffee table. Beneath the cloth stood a gleaming black, ancient Royal typewriter. "I thought you might like this," he said. "It was Esther's when she first started working at the paper." He shook his head in fond remembrance. "Even though we had electric typewriters by then, she preferred this old thing. Said it kept her from getting lazy."

Esther, old girl, are you giving me a sign?

"I couldn't have asked for a better present, Gordon." I hugged him tight. "Thank you so much."

"I have a surprise for you too, daughter," Mom said. "But you have to close your eyes. And no peeking!"

Dutifully, I shut my eyes. I heard a door opening and then sounds of rustling and whispering around me.

"Okay, you can open them now."

Ashley and Elizabeth stood in front of me, grinning from ear to ear as they held up a big white sheet. "What?" I gave my mother a sideways look. "Is this turning into a toga party now?"

At a nod from their grandma, the girls giggled and dropped the sheet, saying, "Ta-da!"

"Lindsey!" Tears sprang to my eyes, and I hugged my best friend. "What are you doing here, you silly girl? You're supposed to be on your honeymoon!"

"We got back from St. Thomas last night—and had a *wonderful* time." She gave me a wicked grin. "But there was no way I was going to miss my best friend's birthday." She frowned. "Unfortunately, my *husband*—I love saying that!—returned to a work fire he had to put out, so he couldn't come." She smiled. "But he did send you this." She pulled a silver framed photo from her purse—a goofy shot of the two of them behind prison bars at Alcatraz.

I giggled, remembering our day with Alex in San Francisco and all the fun we'd had. Lindsey pulled me to one side and whispered, "I have another little surprise too." Her eyes sparkled. "Guess who's not dating you-know-who anymore?"

The tiniest of flutters started to kick up in my stomach, but I squashed them down. "That's nice, Lins. But he's there and I'm here, and we both have totally—"

"Hey Louise! Think fast." Mary Jo tossed me an orange-and-yellow foil-wrapped package that looked and felt remarkably like a can.

It was a can.

Of neon-green English mushy peas. I threw back my head and roared. "Nice one, Thelma."

Lindsey raised her eyebrows.

"Louise, I mean Phoebe, hates peas—the whole texture thing," Mary Jo explained.

"I know." Lindsey turned to me. "I take it this is MJ, your traveling companion?"

"Oh, sorry. I thought you two had met." I inclined my head. "Cleveland best-friend Lindsey, meet Barley best-friend MJ—I mean Mary Jo."

They nodded at each other. Then Mary Jo got a good look at Lindsey's frosty face. And proclaimed, "I think it's time for a little karaoke." She crossed over to the corner of the room, where a rented karaoke machine stood proudly. She started with a little Aretha just to warm things up, belting out "Chain of Fools."

Then she handed me the mike. And I'm no Aretha—or Mary Jo, for that matter—but who could resist? I called up *both* of my best friends for backup on "It's My Party (And I'll Cry If I Want To)." Lindsey still looked a little miffed, but she didn't protest. And with both her and Mary Jo doing their sixties girl-group thing, we brought down the house.

Ashley and the girls quickly got into the act, and we all jammed on "I Will Survive" followed by "YMCA," with a thawed-out Lindsey teaching the hand motions to Mary Jo.

In the midst of forming the *M* over my head, I caught sight of a familiar face at the door. And completely forgot about the song.

"Delia!" I squealed and made my way through the crowd, MJ close on my heels. As we drew nearer, I saw that Delia wasn't alone.

"*Grace!*" I moved to enfold her in an exuberant hug but stopped myself just in time. I stretched out my hand to Delia and Alex's elegant mother and dialed it down a notch. "How lovely to see you again."

She laughed and grabbed me in an all-American bear hug. "Happy birthday, Phoebe! I'm so glad we could be here to celebrate it with you." She released me and embraced Mary Jo next while Delia and I swapped hugs.

I looked from mother to daughter. "Just what does bring you here? I know you didn't come all the way from England just for my birthday party."

"No, but we would have," Delia said. "Right, Mum?"

Grace smiled and nodded.

"Actually, I had to come over on business. And now that Dad's been given a clean bill of health," Delia said, "Mother decided to come along too and visit some family and friends. Of which you are one."

"Fantastic!" I turned to Mary Jo. "Isn't this a great surprise, MJ?"

"Uh-huh. For *you*." She shook her head at me. "Someone had to give them directions."

I punched her on the arm just as Lindsey, my mom, and the rest of the family joined us. Introductions were made all around, and Mom and Grace immediately started chattering away.

I pulled Delia aside. "So what's really up? You're absolutely beaming." My eyes gleamed. "Is it a guy?"

"No. Well, in a manner of speaking, I suppose it is. Dad, with a little help from Mother, has finally seen the light and come through with my promotion." She shot me a triumphant look. "He's made me chief financial officer of the firm. Alex is going to be CEO, and Dad's going to take it just a wee bit easier and just chair the board."

"That's great!" I hugged her again. "I'm so happy for you. No one deserves it more." I narrowed my eyes. "How'd Alex take the news?"

"He was thrilled. Both for me and him." She lowered her voice. "Although George was a little less so." Her voice rose again in excitement. "So anyway, in my new role, Dad thought it would be good for me to visit some of our stateside papers. Which is why I'm here. I thought I'd start with the *Bulletin* and get to see you and Mary Jo at the same time."

She looked around for Mary Jo, who was laughing at something Lindsey had said. "Speaking of which, I have a little gift for her that my mate Ian asked me to hand-deliver . . ."

Seeing Delia so excited about her new job gave me fresh resolve. I'd made my decision about the new job. But I needed to tell my family.

Okay, God. I can do this. But I'm going to need You to hold my hand.

I rejoined my mother, who was deep in conversation with Grace. "Well, you two look like long-lost friends."

"I was just telling your mother what a fool my son was to let you get away," Grace said.

"And I was agreeing with her," Mom added.

I waved my hand. "Ancient history. Besides, my life is a man-free zone right now. Time for me to figure out some things on my own, without any romantic distractions." I tilted my head. "Or Hollywood fantasies."

Grace smiled. "Sounds like a good place to be." She sighed. "Although I still hope that someday . . ."

"You never know what God will do. And speaking of what God's doing, do you mind if I steal my mother away for a few minutes?" I linked arms with Mom and shepherded her toward the kitchen, whispering, "I need to tell you something."

"Why, that's fine, daughter. Actually I have something to tell you too."

Looking around for Jordy and Karen, I signaled them with my eyes to join us. Gordon, too. When the kitchen door shut behind us all, I cleared my throat and gave a nervous laugh. "You're probably wondering why I called you all here. I, uh . . ."

And I caved. I couldn't get it out. "Mom, didn't you say you had something to tell us?"

Mom's hands fluttered to her throat. "Well, yes," she said with an apologetic smile and a glance at Gordon, who patted her arm and gave her an encouraging smile.

"You see, Gordon and I have been spending a lot of time together lately, and we've decided to, um . . ."

Was she really saying what I thought she was saying? I looked over at Karen and Jordy, and they looked as gobsmacked as I felt.

"You've decided to do what, Mom?"

Mom's face flamed. "That is, we think, um . . ." She lifted her chin. "The thing is, I just want you to know that Gordon and I, we . . ." Another encouraging nod from Gordon. "What I'm trying to say is we've decided to go steady. In other words, I guess I'm saying that Gordon is my . . . boyfriend!"

She didn't say it with quite the same intensity as Cloris Leachman's

Frau Bleucher in *Young Frankenstein*, but I'm sure I heard horses whinny in the background.

Jordy, Karen, and I exchanged glances, then burst out laughing. "Gee, Mom. We hadn't figured that out," my brother said. "Guess we'll have to alert the media."

Gordon reached for Mom's hand and held it to his chest. Mom blushed but laid her head on his shoulder. "But Phoebe, didn't you say you had an announcement too?"

This was it. My practical self and my moral voice-of-reason self and all my other selves, even the silly, selfish ones, were all yelling, *Go for it!*

I cleared my throat again. "Well, my news isn't as romantic as Mom's, but equally exciting, I think." I took a deep breath and rushed on. "I—I've been offered the most amazing writing job in Southern California . . . and I've decided to take it."

I ducked my head and held my breath, waiting for the protests.

Instead, the room erupted in applause.

"Gee, if I'd known you didn't want me around, I'd have left a lot sooner."

"Phoebe, the editor's a friend of mine," Gordon said. "She called and told me she was going to offer you the columnist job—a job that's tailor-made for you, by the way. And ever since she did, I've been waiting—we've all been waiting—for you to tell us about it."

Mom took my hands between hers and smiled. "Daughter, you came back and helped when I broke my arms. You've stayed and helped ever since. And I appreciate it. I appreciate *you*." Her thumbs stroked the backs of my hands. "But God has something for you beyond Barley. He's calling you to use the gifts He's given you. You don't need to tie yourself down here—not when God has a big, wide world out there just waiting for you. I want you to go and follow your dreams. We all do."

"But what about Read a Latte? Don't you want me at the bookstore?"

Jordy and Karen double-hugged me. "Of course we want you

there." My brother winked. "As long as you stay away from the cash register."

"You'll still be a partner, Pheebs," Karen said.

"Just a silent one." Jordy grinned at me. "As if you could ever be silent."

A thought suddenly hit me. "But what about my apartment? I've already said yes to the paper, and they want me to start in two weeks." I bit my lip. "I'm not giving you much time to find a new tenant." My voice trailed off.

"Not to worry, Pheebert. God will provide. He always does."

Just then the kitchen door flung open and an excited Mary Jo burst through, waving a letter. "Pheebs, guess what? Ian's applied to the veterinary program at UC–Davis! He's coming to California in a week or two for interviews!"

I gotta give You Your props, God. Once You decide to move, You really do it fast.

[chapter twenty-four]

On the Road Again

t he next week, Mary Jo and Ashley were helping me pack while Mom and Karen held down the bookstore. I was in serious purge mode, wanting to start my new life without too much to weigh me down.

Ashley held up a stuffed giraffe I'd won at a carnival in Cleveland. "Keep or toss, Aunt Phoebe?"

"Toss."

She smiled and put it in the box marked "Ashley."

Mary Jo held up a baggy, stretched-out, rainbow-striped sweater. "Keep or toss?"

"Toss."

She put it in the box marked "Mary Jo."

Ashley held up something green and glittery. "Uh, what is this, Aunt Phoebe?"

Mary Jo turned and stared at the strange item. "Yeah, what exactly is it?"

I snatched it from Ashley's hand, stretched it across the front of my T-shirt, and adopted the John Travolta *Saturday Night Fever* dance pose. "It's a tube top from the days when disco was king. I found it at a little thrift store in Cleveland and wore it to disco night at Lone Rangers a few years ago. Isn't it cool?"

Mary Jo looked at Ashley. Ashley looked at Mary Jo. "Toss," they chorused.

"You'll be sorry, Ash. Vintage clothes are really hot, and I hear disco's going to make a comeback. You'd probably be the only girl on your block to have one."

"That's okay. But thanks for thinking of me." She shot me a sweet smile. "I think we should send it to someone who really needs it."

"Yeah. Like Cher," Mary Jo said, and they both dissolved into giggles. I took the top from them and chunked it into the "toss" box.

Now came the hard part. Shoe time. What to keep and what to get rid of? My new place didn't have a built-in shoe hive like the one my sweet brother built for me here, so I had to be ruthless.

My low-heeled Kenneth Coles?

Definitely keep.

My Jimmy Choo wannabes?

Get rid of.

My classic black pumps?

Keep. Same for the practical Clarks clogs.

My Manolos?

I picked them up and drank in the rich leather smell, remembering how I'd walked all around London in them—and gotten the blisters to show for it. Then I glanced over at my fashion-conscious niece, whose head was bent over a box. "Ash, what size shoe do you wear now?"

"Eight."

"Here's something you might want to add to your box." I tossed her the boots.

She looked and screamed. "Your Manolos?! Aunt Phoebe, those are so expensive!"

"I know. Which is why you'd probably better not wear them to school. Save them for special occasions, okay?"

"More than okay." She body-slammed me, and we fell to the floor together, laughing, while Mary Jo gave me a thumbs-up.

There was a loud knock at the door.

"I hope that's Jordy with more boxes." I got up to answer it, still giggling, while a beaming Ashley pulled on her new boots.

A mass of daffodils filled the doorway, obscuring the person holding them. But this time when the flowers were lowered, it wasn't a teenage delivery person.

Alex Spencer stood there with a sheepish grin and said, "Frankly my dear, I've been an idiot." He thrust the daffs at me, and those gorgeous lips curved into an apologetic smile.

"I'm sorry I missed your birthday party, Phoebe. I really wanted to be here, but I had to tie up some loose ends back in Britain. Once I did, I flew all night from London and drove here straight from the airport." He gave me a pleading smile. "I was hoping we could start again."

Behind me I heard Ashley gasp.

Mary Jo, too.

This was what I'd longed for.

And dreamed of.

And prayed for.

And spent countless hours thinking about.

And three months ago, this moment would have been a dream come true.

Except I wasn't living in a dream world these days. The new Phoebe was beginning a new job, a new life, and a new adventure rife with possibilities. Real possibilities, not fantasies. Sure, she planned to take frequent vacations to Neverland, but she wasn't going to live there anymore.

"I'm sorry, Alex, but you're a little late." I turned and gestured to the box-strewn room. "As you can see, I'm moving on."

He glanced behind me and noticed Ashley wearing the boots he'd given me. Alex's eyebrows raised. "You gave away your Manolos?"

"I outgrew them."

Two days later, my Bug was packed and ready to go. My family and friends clustered around to say good-bye.

"I still can't believe you got a dog," Mary Jo said, shaking her head.

"Well, I just decided Herman would be happier staying here with his cat family. And you're the one who told me dogs are good company to snuggle up to." I cuddled Sam, the three-year-old terrier I'd found at the pound. I thought he looked a lot like Dorothy's Toto.

"But you're not an animal person."

"And you're not a dating woman—or at least hadn't had a date in four years." I cut a glance at Ian, who had arrived the day before and was playing with Jacob. "Things change."

Moments later, I drove off into the sunset to my new adventure, humming my old air-force anthem: *"Off we go into the wild blue yonder . . ."*

Then I cranked up my stereo. I'd stocked my car CD holder with a lot of strong-women CDs: Bette Midler, Martina McBride, Shania Twain, and even a little Aretha, in homage to Mary Jo. But for now, on my way to sunny San Diego, this California girl turned on the Beach Boys full blast and flew along the coastal highway with the sunroof open and the wind in my hair, singing along at the top of my lungs.

In the backseat, strapped into his Toto basket, woman's best friend howled along. "Want me to play it again, Sam?"

I was Melanie Griffith in *Working Girl,* beginning an exciting new career.

Minus Harrison Ford.

Just You and me, God. And Sam too.

Note to Self: Who needs a man anyhow? It's great to be male-free.

Pulling into a gas station a couple of hours later, I filled my tank. And at the pump next to me, I noticed a man. A tall, attractive man, in that rumpled-professor sort of way. He was helping an old woman into her car. After his Good Samaritan bit, he jogged back to his Bug—cherry red, with a golden retriever in the front seat—and drove away, flashing a brilliant smile at me as he did.

Mmm. Nice lips.

Amended note to self: Or not . . .

Acknowledgments

Sincere thanks to:

Dr. Henrietta Blackmore, for answering endless e-mails and for your eyes-and-ears insights on Oxford, the church, and being a twenty-something single in England.

Davis and Isabella Bunn, for introducing me to Henri.

Patricia Smith, my dear Dorset friend, for her explanation of Christmas pudding, fox hunts, British slang, and other things English.

Brian Morris, for his London insights.

Sue and Roger Garlick of Grey Gables for the "wau-tuh, not wa-derr" lesson.

Kari Jameson, who helped refresh my memory on important details from our England trip. We'll always have *Les Miz*. (Ditto to her mom, Sheri.)

The Martinusen family, for letting me stay at their wonderful dream home. Cindy, thanks for reading an early draft and for your gentle suggestions to "introduce more conflict" without causing a conflict between us. You're the best!

Annette and Randy Smith, for my Texas writing getaway. And for catfish, homegrown steaks, and Ruby Faye. But most of all, for your friendship, Annette.

Pat and Ken McLatchey, longtime friends and fellow Anglophiles, who graciously let me stay in their beautiful and quiet room with a view during another much-needed getaway.

Anne Peterson, for the witty, sarcastic, single-woman's perspective. You rock!

My writing pals, Jan Coleman and Judi Braddy, as well as our Monday night Acts2U group and my Westside family for praying me through this one.

Chip MacGregor, my friend and agent, for making it possible to use those two words in the same sentence. And, as a former visiting professor at Oxford, for jogging my memory about Evensong, Blackwell's, and the Eagle and Child pub.

I thank God on a regular basis for my brilliant editor, Ami McConnell, who makes the book-birthing process such a joy even through the editing pain and my descents into neurosis. Your encouragement, gentle guidance, and belief in me mean the world.

Anne Christian Buchanan, fellow movie lover and excellent line editor. If God is in the details—well, you're not God, but He's certainly working through you. Thanks, wonder woman!

Allen Arnold, Amanda Bostic, Rebecca Seitz, and the rest of the gang at WestBow Press, for the prayers and the partnership.

Mom, for always cheering me on.

And as always, Michael, my beloved, who puts up with an absent, neurotic wife and acts as the guardian at the deadline gate, turning away distractions. Thanks for the PG Tips in the morning and the sustenance in the evening, honey. Without you, I couldn't do this. Thank you for your sacrificial love and for your artist's heart and soul. Je t'adore.

To contact Laura,
visit her Web site at
www.laurajensenwalker.com

Also available from
LAURA JENSEN WALKER

Not your typical size two chick-lit heroine, Phoebe Grant aspires
to the madcap life of a forties-style career gal—she lives in a
cool apartment (even if it does need a little work), works at the city
newspaper (ok, she writes obits—but she's sure she'll get her
dream job reviewing movies), and has a best girlfriend (that would
be Lindsey) to play straight-woman to her life's witty script. But
when she loses her job and her mother breaks both arms, Phoebe finds
her carefully constructed screenplay being re-written in ways she hadn't
planned. And when Lindsey secretly signs her up for an online personals
service, the script suddenly becomes a slapstick.

dreaming in black & white

[a phoebe grant novel]

laura
jensen
walker

WestBow
PRESS
A Division of Thomas Nelson Publishers
Since 1798
visit us at www.westbowpress.com

Discover More Great Novels at WestBowPress.com

And coming
September 2006
from Laura Jensen Walker

Reconstructing Natalie